HYPNOTIC

SHERRY HOSTLER

for the fabulous
Kath + Flash

Happy Reading!
♡ Sherry x

WAGGLING
WOO

For my husband Jon, who really wants this book to be a huge success so that he can retire to the South of France. I'm not actually sure if I'm invited…

1

TOM

"Be nice," Gemma said as she headed to the front door to greet their new neighbours. Tom rolled his eyes and swigged back the last of his beer. He followed his wife's lead in greeting the couple stood on the front step, who were proffering a bouquet of flowers and a bottle of wine.

Bloody Pinot Noir, thought Tom as he took the bottle, letting his wife deal with the flowers and idle chatter. What was the point of something with such a low alcohol content? Might as well be drinking Ribena. He clutched it nevertheless and thanked their neighbours, ushering them through to the dining room.

Jane and Richard had seemed decent enough from the safety of their side of the garden fence. In fact, Richard probably had the potential of being someone Tom could sink a few jars with down at the pub if he gave him half a chance. He wasn't sure Gemma would feel the same about Jane whose conversation, from what Tom had garnered so far, was somewhat limited to an encyclopedic knowledge of handbag brands. Gemma had never been a girly girl, but Tom knew she'd suffer the boredom as long as she could as she so desperately wanted some local friends. They'd drink through it tonight, and Gemma could make her own mind up.

If Tom were honest, he'd rather have watched TV tonight with a few pints to help him nod off, but Gemma had been insistent. They'd kept themselves to themselves since they'd moved to the area, not wanting to stand out too much. Neither of them wanted to be the focal point of any local gossip, especially bearing in mind what had happened before they came here.

He took the Pinot to the kitchen where he opened it, along with something a little more full-bodied, making sure to fill his own glass with that one and taking a quick furtive sip.

"Ooh, something smells good." Tom turned to find Jane standing behind him. "Anything I can do to help?"

Bloody hell, the woman was like a stealth bomber. "No, you're fine thanks, Jane." Tom dashed out a smile. "Actually, you can take yours and Richard's drinks through if you don't mind? I'll be right behind you."

"Of course." Jane took the offered glasses. "We've been looking forward to this. It's so nice to get along with your neighbours, isn't it?"

"It certainly is." Tom toasted her retreating form before knocking back the rich red liquid, darker in comparison to that in the other glasses. The taste was wasted on him, but it had the desired effect, softening the hard edges of his armour a little. It was all Tom was worried about, and he refilled his glass before joining the others.

"Where did you live before you came here?" Richard's very ordinary question caught Tom like a jab to the chin, and they were only at the small talk and starters phase of the evening so far. His eyes flickered across to Gemma who looked up from admiring Jane's gaudy pink nail gel. 'It's ok,' her gaze told him. 'We're ready for this.'

Tom took a breath. "Nottingham. A small village you wouldn't have heard of."

The rehearsed lie hid the nightmare that had so firmly put their hometown on the map. Those of a darker nature had even used that map to find the exact spot where Tom and Gemma had lived, making their lives just that bit more unbearable.

Richard nodded, turning his attention to the plate of asparagus wrapped in Parma ham that Gemma had slid in front of him. He seemed more than happy with Tom's answer, and probably wasn't even that interested in it.

"We're from Bristol, originally," Jane chimed in with blatant disregard for anyone who didn't wish to see her masticating her food as she spoke.

Even though slightly repulsed, Tom was glad for the distraction as she chatted on, leading them on a virtual tour through her hometown. Tom could imagine her holding up an umbrella and counting heads to make sure no one had snuck off for a sneaky fag. He snorted to himself, drawing a sharp look from his wife.

With the starters and both bottles of wine finished, along with Jane's monologue, Gemma got up to clear the table and Richard excused himself to go to the toilet. Before Jane could turn her attention to the only other occupant left in the room, Tom jumped to his feet with the excuse that he needed to help his wife in the kitchen. It wasn't that he disliked his guest, but he didn't really like her either.

"You're doing great," Gemma whispered as she pulled the casserole from the oven. "Just try and relax, ok? They haven't got a clue who we are."

"Easy for you to say," Tom shot back, biting his thumbnail.

"Just remember what Ash tells me." Gemma started dishing up the food, not appearing to notice the sneer on Tom's face at the mention of the name he'd heard far too often of late. "It's all in the breath. Deep breaths whenever you feel like you can't handle the moment. In through the nose, out through the mouth."

Ash the omnipresent, never showing his face but always whispering advice in Gemma's ear like an unwelcome guru. Twat. Tom mimicked the words she spoke silently behind her back, before swearing under his breath.

"Pardon?" Gemma seemed oblivious, which was for the best.

"Nothing." Tom opened some more wine. "I'll top up the glasses, shall I?"

Gemma turned to look at him, a spoonful of rice poised in the air, her gaze flicking to the bottle in his hand. "Please take it easy, Tom."

"Yeah, yeah."

He headed back to the dining room. He hated it when Gemma nagged him about drinking. It wasn't like it was an issue, he just had one now and then to take the edge off, to help him sleep. Anyway, it was a dinner party, wasn't it? Gemma needed to loosen up a bit.

The main course went down a storm with their guests and Tom watched Gemma's face glow with pride as Jane raved about it, insisting she must hand over the recipe. He liked to see his wife happy and relaxed for a change.

The conversation ebbed and flowed pretty well, and Gemma was really on point in distracting Jane from meandering down any unlit paths of discussion. They'd covered the weather, touched on holidays, and skirted around what they all watched on Netflix before starting to delve into their working lives.

Tom had known that subject was going to rear its ugly head at some point, and he excused himself to fetch more wine, hoping that Gemma would be able to change the topic by the time he got back. She hadn't, and in fact, she was still describing some funny nursing anecdote to their guests as he sat back down at the table. He guessed it must be nice for her to be able to talk about work with someone who wanted to hear about it for a change. Jealousy nudged at him, like a stick poking an angry dog.

"Anyone for a top-up?" Tom interrupted, catching the despairing look from Gemma and deciding to ignore it. "No? Just me then." He filled his own glass, and put the bottle down, close to hand.

Gemma's story tailed off and Jane swivelled in her seat to face Tom, her eyes pinning him like an insect in a display cabinet. "What about you, Tom? Gemma says you work in retail."

That had been kind of her, and he momentarily felt like a prick yet again. "Yeah, retail."

"What kind? Cars? Clothing? Department store?" Jane was treating it like some kind of quiz show. "Any chance of a discount for friends?" She laughed at her own joke and Tom felt himself tensing at her exasperating humour. "So?" Jane obviously didn't want to let the chance of a good deal on handbags pass her by.

"Actually, I'm an inventory replenishment specialist for a leading supermarket chain."

"Ooh, that sounds fancy." Jane fanned herself, shooting him a coy look.

"Yeah, well, I don't get paid the big bucks for nothing." Tom was warming to his theme now, ignoring the looks Gemma was shooting at him to shut up. "Not everyone can do what I do y'know, Jane."

"I'm sure." She fingered the bracelet on her wrist.

"Tom, could you come and help me with the dessert please?" Gemma stood and Tom saluted her before stage whispering across the table to Jane.

"She's still the boss at home though, eh Jane?" He tailed Gemma to the other room, calling behind him, "Do top your glasses up!"

"Pack it in!" Anger tinted the whispered words that Gemma fired at him.

"What?" Tom backed away from her against the kitchen cupboards, holding his hands up in mock surrender.

"You know what. We're trying to be friends with these people, so don't take the piss. It's not fair."

"No, Gemma. We aren't trying to be friends with them. *You* are. And to be honest I don't know why. She's a pain in the arse."

"Maybe so, but—"

"Can I help with anything?" Jane's voice filtered from the other room, her timing impeccable.

"No, thanks Jane," Gemma called out. "You just sit there and relax. Won't be a mo." She turned back to Tom. "Maybe she is a pain, and maybe it is just me that wants to make friends, but—"

"What?" Tom challenged.

Gemma paused, breathing in slowly through the nose before releasing it from her mouth. "Now isn't the time."

Tom sat sullenly quiet throughout the rest of the meal. From the glances that Gemma kept throwing in his direction, he knew that she desperately wanted him to join in but, to be honest, he just couldn't be arsed. Jane was doing a perfectly good job of boring everyone rigid with stories about people they didn't know or care about. She wouldn't notice if he slipped into a coma.

Richard excused himself to go to the loo yet again, making Tom wonder if he had a bladder infection, or whether he was banging his head against the wall, having to listen to his wife droning on. As he left the room, Jane plucked her phone from her bag and started showing Gem photos of her sister's baby. Tom could see the effect it was having on his wife as her cheeks started to flush.

"Ever thought about having kids yourselves?" came the question from Jane before long.

It always arose at some point, especially once people found out they hadn't been married long. Why the hell did anyone think that it was an appropriate question to ask? For all Jane knew, they couldn't have kids. Then how would she feel? Maybe it would be fun to find out. Tom swallowed the rest of his drink, which hit the creme brûlée already restless in his stomach with an unwelcome clash. "No, Jane. We can't have children." He saw Gemma's face register total shock as the lie launched itself out of his mouth. In fact, it was almost funny to see her jaw drop open like a cartoon character. He half expected to hear a boiyoingyoing noise as it fell.

"What are you doing?" she mouthed.

Jane, too tipsy to notice, continued to focus on Tom and proffered a sympathetic head tilt. "I'm so sorry." She reached over the table and placed a hand on his arm.

"Yes." Tom topped up his glass. "Unfortunately, I had a terrible STD back in my youth. Chlamydia, I think. Anyway, long story short is that it made me infertile."

Jane snatched her hand away as though scared Tom may still be infected. "I…oh…I'm sorry. I should never have asked."

"That's right Jane." Tom took another gulp from his drink, enjoying the fun he was having at her discomfort. "You shouldn't have asked. But never mind, eh? We're all friends here. We can share these things." He winked.

As Richard walked back into the dining room, none the wiser about what had happened in his absence, Jane leapt up from the table, her chair crashing down against the wooden floor.

"Everything ok, love?" Richard asked, bending to pick it back up.

"Oh yes, yes. Fine. It's just getting on a bit and we should really head off before we overstay our welcome."

Gemma stood then too, chair legs scraping against the floor, reminding Tom he never had got round to sticking those cushioned protectors on. Hey ho. He necked the rest of his drink.

"Please don't feel you have to leave," Gemma practically implored boring old fart Jane who was packing her expensive shiny handbag with her phone and her rude questions. "I'm so sorry about Tom. He's had a bit to drink."

"What are you on about?" he asked. "I'm just having a laugh. Jane knows that, don't you Jane?"

As the front door closed behind them amid false promises of "You'll have to come to us next time," Tom slumped back into his chair and poured himself a brandy to prepare for a verbal attack from Gemma. Instead, she came into the room, sat in her seat, and took his glass away. "I think you've had enough."

Pissed off with her audacity of treating him like a child, he spat back that he'd certainly had enough of her. He was too far gone to notice how she was feeling now. And he *had* had enough of her. He'd had enough of everything, full stop.

Gemma's eyes glistened. Crocodile tears, thought Tom meanly as he screwed up his napkin in his hands, and tossed it on the table. "You make out you're on my side Gemma, but you're not really, are you? You never stood by me, not properly."

"What do you mean?" she asked. "I gave up everything for you. Our home, our friends, maybe even my chance to have children."

"But not your precious job. Your 'career'." The final word was deformed by the curling of his lip, his hands raised in inverted commas. Even as he spoke the words, he knew he was being unreasonable. He knew damn well she'd given up all she could for him, but he wanted more. After all, misery liked company.

"It's not my fault, Tom." Gemma stood up and headed for the door. Her calmness was infuriating.

"So, you're saying it's mine, are you?" Tom followed her, his hands clenching into fists. "My fault? Just like the fucking newspaper headlines said it was my fault and every prick that spray-painted our house or hurled abuse at me?"

"I'm not saying that." Gemma backed away.

"Bullshit," Tom sneered, his words jaundiced with resentment.

"You need help." Gemma broke eye contact with him and took hold of the door handle. As she did so, Tom felt as though a small synapse in his brain suddenly exploded, there was a hazy fury, and everything went black.

EVERYTHING FELT loud as the dawn chorus of birds clamoured for attention and light filtered around the edges of the curtains making Tom want to vomit. The sudden rainfall that followed muffled the birds a little but pounded like drums against the windowpane.

Tom could hear Gemma moving about downstairs in the kitchen and he traced her movements around the room by sound. A boiling kettle, the clink of a mug on the worktop, her calling the cat in from the garden for his breakfast. He was filled with a familiar feeling of guilt, but as usual, he didn't know why.

Forcing his aching body out of bed, he wrapped his dressing gown around himself, blanketing the acidic smell of stale alcohol that emanated from his pores. He struggled to tie the cord as the sore knuckles of his right hand protested against the movement and his brain tried to reach for the memory of why. It came back empty-handed.

Moving slowly, he eventually joined Gemma who was standing at the window in the lounge, both hands clasped around a mug of tea. As he entered the room, she turned to face him with words he had dreaded for the longest time.

"I just can't take this anymore, Tom." She crossed the room and her body seemed to collapse in on itself under the weight of her words as she lowered herself onto the sofa. As was her habit, she curled her legs up underneath herself, the stiff denim of her jeans chafing against the worn leather.

Tom gritted his teeth. If he was honest with himself, he was surprised it had taken her so long to come out with it. After all, their lives hadn't exactly panned out how they were supposed to. Only six months married and instead of building a proper future they were here, uprooted from everything they'd once known. New lives in a place where no one knew them, and tiptoeing around each other like polite but distant relatives. Well, Gemma was polite anyway. Tom knew far too well his shortcomings.

"I'm sorry, Gem," he mumbled, unable to meet her eyes. He perched himself at the other end of the sofa and put his head in his hands, immediately regretting it as a rush of nausea met him.

"I know you are, Tom, but it's not enough anymore."

"I don't know what to do, Gem. I just…" He looked across at the dining-room door, taking in the smashed wooden veneer. The size of a fist. Shit, that was why his knuckles were so swollen. He flexed them, watching the bone move behind the thin, grazed skin.

Christ, what was wrong with him? Another night of arguing, then drinking too much to blot out the pain. Another blackout. Try as he might to keep on top of things, it was the night terrors that ripped into him, trying to prise his soul from his body. And then, the screaming passage into wakefulness which would last until the early hours. The restless pacing, the dark, lonely passing of time. Insomnia for the faithless.

The only thing that helped was the booze. It helped him get to sleep and blot out the memories of that God-awful night. It also helped to drown out Gemma when she kept going on and on about wanting to start a family. Tom would do anything for his wife. But a child? Not a hope in hell. Not after what had happened.

As if sensing his defeat, Gemma's cat, Baloo wound his way between Tom's legs, the soft fur of his tail providing a small comfort. Then he leapt up onto an empty armchair, curling into his favourite spot where the sun normally came through the window to warm the leather.

"Can you even remember what happened last night?" Gemma asked.

He could feel her looking at him and Tom forced his eyes up from the floor, just briefly, scared of what he might see. He knew his number was almost up. Almost, but not quite. There was still a glimmer of love in her eyes and Tom looked back to the floor in shame.

"I didn't think so," she said.

They were at a stalemate. Gemma had placed an ultimatum on the table, and he had placed a hole in the dining-room door.

2

BETHANY

I t was the first time that I'd been left on my own inside Leigh's office. I'd arrived just as her mobile had rung, eliciting the first few lines from a song that I wouldn't have pictured her listening to in a million years, let alone choosing for a ringtone.

"Take a seat, Bethany." She'd signalled to one of the three armchairs in the room. "I've just got to take this, then I'll be right back." She'd closed the door behind her, the lyrics from 'Blinded by Your Grace' cutting off as she must have answered her phone.

I couldn't help the grin spreading across my face. The muscles, unused to working in an upward direction, felt strange and I rectified things immediately by bringing them back to my usual look of cool indifference. I thought it was cool, anyway. Most would probably say it was my resting bitch face. Whatever.

I mean, come on, a woman who had to be in her late thirties wearing tailored trousers and a silk blouse did not listen to Stormzy, for God's sake. She was undeniably trying to be trendy. Probably an exercise in getting her patients to feel like she was on their level.

I supposed it might work with some of the younger ones. The fifteen-year-old runaways who were into gang culture and Love

Island, but not me. It'd take a lot more than a grime artist's ringtone to make me open up in one of these sessions that were forced on me every week.

At least while she was out of the room, I could take the opportunity to have a bit of a look around. Keeping one eye on the door, I wandered over to the desk. Behind it on the far wall were some certificates boasting about Leigh's qualifications. I guessed they were just the tip of the iceberg though, and somewhere handy would be a folder full to bursting with multiple awards all in date order with tabs for easy reference.

I turned a framed photograph on the desk round to face me, expecting to see a photo of her significant other. Just a picture of a ginger tom, though. Not that surprising really, although I *had* had her down as more of a dog person.

The door to the office swung open and Leigh came back in with a waft of expensive perfume. "I'm sorry to have kept you waiting," she said with one eyebrow slightly lifted. Obviously choosing not to acknowledge the fact that I was looking at her personal effects, she placed her phone on her desk and walked over to the armchairs which were arranged invitingly around a small low table. She pulled her scarf from her neck, letting it pool in a puddle of silk on the table by the customary box of tissues. Standard fare in any counsellor's domain. They pissed me off. "Come and take a seat." She did all but pat the seat of the chair next to her.

I went over and sat, not in the chair next to hers, but the one opposite. Contrary, my mother had always called me. Maybe she had a point.

"How's it going this week?" Leigh asked, completely un-phased, and removed her watch, placing it face-up on top of her scarf. I knew she did it so she could subtly keep an eye on the time without making it blatantly obvious by looking at her wrist. I liked her watch. Nice little pale grey strap and white polka dots to match the face. It was a Radley, with a little silver Scottish Terrier charm dangling from it, which was probably why I'd thought she liked dogs.

"Yeah, pretty good."

"Do you think you've settled into your university now?"

Oh dear, I thought to myself. Not a great start for Leigh on the question front today. It's Psychology 101 not to ask closed questions to a patient. Otherwise, I could just answer with—

"Yes."

It must be a nightmare having a psychology student for a patient.

Leigh smiled, crossed her legs, and leaned in towards me, elbows resting on her thighs. Her fingers reached for the locket that hung on a slender chain around her neck and she twirled it distractedly. Maybe I *was* getting to her. "I imagine it was quite a wrench having to leave your old one so suddenly and to start afresh?"

"Hmm." I decided not to reward her with eye contact.

"Tell me about it," Leigh prompted.

I ran my fingers along the book spines in the small Ikea cabinet next to my chair. No light reading to be found there, just textbook after textbook about therapy and various mental-health disorders.

"I'm here to help you, Bethany. This is a safe place to talk about whatever you want."

"I've read a couple of these." I ignored her prompt and pulled out a copy of 'Counting Sheep' giving myself a mental pat on the back. Next to it, a small, dog-eared copy of 'The Killing of Robert F Kennedy' fell into the space created against 'The Nocturnal Brain'.

Reaching for the volume, I put it on the table on top of the last book. "This looks interesting."

Distraction number one: get her talking about something other than me.

"Yes, it's about the assassination of JFK's brother. The story isn't as well-known, but it's probably even more intriguing."

Bingo.

"How come?" I asked.

"Well, it was a massive conspiracy theory in its time. It was alleged that the assassin was actually hypnotised by the CIA to carry out the murder."

"Oh my God, really? Is it true?"

"No idea I'm afraid." Leigh straightened the two books in front of her so that their spines lined up. "Apparently, to this day, the assassin claims it's the truth. Unsurprisingly, the CIA claim otherwise."

I picked the book back up and flicked through it, a small idea forming in the back of my mind. "Would you mind if I borrowed this?" I asked.

"Be my guest," she replied, tucking her dark bobbed hair behind her ear. "It's an interesting read. Now, what I'd really like to know is how you've been getting on since I last saw you. Have you made any new friends at uni?"

"Hmm, I suppose so." I pulled my gaze away from her light roots, which could do with a touch-up. Unusual for someone to dye their hair so dark when they were obviously a natural blonde. I guessed she wanted people to take her more seriously bearing in mind her work. "There's Jordan. You know, my lab partner. But it's only been a few months and I'm not that bothered about making too many friends as I'll be going back home again once I've finished my degree anyway."

"I see."

She didn't see though, really. She thought she knew me because she'd read my case file, but that isn't actually knowing a person, is it? That's just knowing about my actions, not what led me to carry them out.

"Do you miss home, Bethany?"

"Sometimes."

"What exactly do you miss?"

Ah, the crux of the matter. I knew it wouldn't take long before she started asking that again. There's only so long you can put these tenacious counsellors off for. I sighed and stopped flicking through the book, placing it on the arm of the chair. "I don't really want to talk about home if that's ok? I'm sorry. I know it's what you want me to talk about but I...I just don't think I can yet." I eyed the box of tissues poignantly. "It's just too upsetting."

"It's ok, Bethany." She smiled. "We don't have to talk about home. We can talk about whatever you feel comfortable with."

That was the problem. I wasn't that comfortable talking about anything. I never had been. Another reason why I'd always struggled to make friends, no doubt. Those I chose to open up to were few and far between. My sister had got the talkative gene in our family, but she wasn't around anymore to be my voice. I missed her, in my own way.

"Why don't you tell me some more about Jordan?" prompted Leigh, pulling me out of the trip that I was about to embark on down memory lane. That was a near miss.

This was much safer ground, and I didn't mind talking about Jordan. He was one of life's good guys. 'Salt of the earth' as my father used to say about anyone jovial who came from a working-class background. I was never sure if that was meant as a compliment or not, but it seemed to fit Jordan really well.

"He's decent," I explained. "And kind." I left out the fact that ever since we'd met in our first lecture he'd pretty much done nothing but moon about after me like a love-struck teenager. He might be decent and kind, but subtlety wasn't his strong point.

"And you're lab partners, you said?"

"Yes, but friends too, I guess."

"Well, that's good. Do you feel as though he could be someone you can confide in?" Leigh probed further.

My tongue poked around at the back of my lip piercing, moving it in a circular motion as I thought about how best to answer my counsellor's question. It was a bad habit, but I did it almost without thinking. My mother hated it. Before I got the piercing, she used to tell me I looked a bit like Rene Zellweger when she was younger. Kind of cute and quirky. I didn't want to look cute and quirky. I wanted to look edgy. Perhaps that's why I got my lip pierced. Perhaps I just did it to piss off my mother. "Maybe one day. I don't know."

I caught Leigh glancing down at her lovely Radley watch, probably hoping she could tell me my time was up for this session. That would be one thing we had in common, then.

I felt a bit sorry for her, actually. I doubted very much that I was one of her more forthcoming patients, but she always kept her cool and never pushed me too much about the past. I liked it like that. What good was the past anyway when you couldn't go back even if you wanted to? Not that I didn't want to, but I couldn't really argue with the restraining order, could I?

3

TOM

Tom had always hated being on his own when Gemma was on a night shift, and even more so these days, as it gave him too much time to think.

It had been nearly a week since that bloody awful dinner party and since then, he and Gemma had been skirting around each other like flatmates who had nothing in common. They probably *didn't* have that much in common anymore, to be fair, other than their shitty, horrible past. They'd always have that, unfortunately.

He had been trying to sit through an old episode of *Grand Designs*, something they used to watch together religiously back when they were making plans for their shared future. Before they got married and it all went tits up.

"They say marriage ruins everything, don't they?" Tom asked Baloo, who was snoozing in his usual position on the armchair.

Putting his beer down – the third one of the evening so far but who was counting? – Tom reached for the iPad which lay next to him on the sofa. Even when they weren't talking, it was lonely without Gemma around and Facebook seemed to be the only logical way he could feel close to her.

Scrolling through his timeline had become a lot quicker these days. He had a fraction of the friends on there that he used to have. Funny how some people ditched you at the first sign of trouble, wasn't it? Of course, there were still a few hangers-on, keen for gossip, and intrigued to know whether he was going to get the punishment that was so eagerly awaited. They were like rubberneckers at a roadside crash. Bastards.

Well, they weren't going to get any news from him. He'd become a social media ghost, especially when the abusive messages had started flooding in. They weren't just from strangers either, but so-called friends, also. They were deleted and blocked but they still hit their mark. Mission accomplished.

So, now, a low profile. No updates posted and no comments made. It was purely a tool for entertainment, lurking behind virtual corners, and now and then to see what Gemma was doing, because she sure as hell didn't tell him anymore.

"Shall we see what Gem's been up to?" he asked Baloo, who'd woken up to start his grooming regime, uninterested in Tom's suggestion.

———

Scrolling past a sponsored post for walking boots and a stupid meme about glitter and unicorns or some such crap, he found Gemma's last post. She'd always been a fan of inspirational quotes and often sandwiched them in between pictures of her cuddling Baloo at various spots around the house and funny memes about being an over-worked nurse in the NHS. It felt like forever to Tom since he had been there with her.

Before they were married, her posts were all about the two of them. A tidal wave of loved-up selfies of them together at the beach, in restaurants, on the sofa. Images of Tom, generally unaware that a lens had been trained on him until he came across it later on Facebook with the sub-heading, *the love of my life*.

Christ, they'd been happy. Sickeningly happy. He supposed it was only to be expected that the one place to go from that great height was down.

There was nothing about him on Gemma's timeline anymore, though. And why would there be? No one wanted to post the ugly truth about their lives on social media, did they?

The first post he came across showed an arty image of a dark sky and a rainbow. *Sometimes you have to walk away from what you want to find what you deserve*, read the text that ran across it.

Tom's heart dropped and he scrolled down to the next one.

I miss you. The old you. The one that used to care about me. This one was imposed over a black and white image of a woman sitting alone and crying.

Like a crack addict, he kept going.

Sometimes, the things that hurt you the most teach you the most important things in life.

These weren't inspirational, these were about a loss of hope. He kept scrolling down. There was one about stars not shining without darkness, another about pain making you stronger. And, finally, there was a photo of Baloo on his favourite spotty cushion by the fireplace. Tom had never been so glad to see him.

Scrolling back up, Tom was tempted for the first time in ages to comment on one of Gemma's social media posts. He had the overwhelming urge to try and take some of her pain away, but just as he was about to do it, he noticed there were several comments there already. Expanding the view, he found a conversation, albeit a short one, between Gemma and Ash.

Stay strong x Ash had written.

I'm trying, but it's just so hard xx From Gemma.

You know I'm always here if you need me x

xxxx

Tom clicked on another post.

Don't let it get to you, you are amazing and don't ever forget that x

Ash again.

I don't know what I'd do without you x

DM me and we can talk more x

So, this was the guy whose name lingered so often on his wife's lips. Now on a mission, Tom started scrolling through as many of Gemma's posts as he could. Without fail, there would always be a comment or a bloody love heart underneath all of them from Ash. No matter what the post was, even if it was some utter shite about descaling a kettle, there would be good old Ash liking it, laughing at it, or loving it.

Jesus, this sounded like more than just friendship. Tom wished he'd paid a bit more attention when Gemma had told him about how she'd met this dickhead. He had a vague recollection that she'd met him on some kind of online forum, but he couldn't quite remember. He'd dismissed him as unimportant. What *was* clear though was that for someone who hadn't been around for more than a couple of months, he seemed pretty damn close to his wife. Maybe it was time Tom stopped just shrugging it off and found out a little bit more about Gemma's new online soulmate.

Gulping his beer, he clicked on the little image next to one of Ash's comments to bring up his profile.

All there was, was a profile photo of a cat with a cover picture behind it of a seaside view which looked like it could be anywhere in the country. And that was all he could get access to. No friends could be seen, no personal information, not even that bloody ridiculous 'interested in men or women' question. Just a bloody stupid tortoiseshell cat and a beach. Damn security settings.

"Fuck it!"

Tom drained his glass. He knew exactly what he was going to do next, but he wanted to give himself the benefit of the doubt before he went ahead and did it anyway.

The chance was there to not be a dickhead and to speak to Gemma rationally about things. To ask her what exactly this Ash meant to her and to take things forward like two grown-ups. Unfortunately, Tom was now three beers down and being rational was no longer high on his agenda.

He logged out of Facebook and then typed in Gemma's email and password. If the mountain wouldn't come to Mohammed, then Mohammed was going to get into the mountain through the back door. He pressed enter.

The screen refreshed and told him he'd entered the wrong password.

"Shit!"

He tried again. Obviously, he'd mistyped it.

Once again, the refresh and the message claiming he'd used the wrong password.

"Fuck it!"

Three strikes and Gemma was going to be locked out of her own account. As it was, he wasn't sure if she'd get a notification saying someone else had tried to log in as her. Thank God he'd used their joint iPad instead of his phone.

Anyway, it could all just be completely innocent, he tried to convince himself. Just a friend checking she's ok. It was good that she had someone to lean on, as God knows he'd been bloody useless.

Tom knew something had to give, and he knew deep down it had to be him. Gemma was right, the drinking was getting to be too much. He knew that. But he only did it so he could get some sleep. It wasn't as though he was an alcoholic. He was completely in control.

If only she could understand that all this was temporary. The night terrors would pass soon enough and then he'd be able to sleep again and everything would be ok. She just needed to give him a bit more time. And, in turn, if she needed to lean on her friends in the meantime, that was fine with him.

But that comment, though – *I don't know what I'd do without you.*

And why would she change her password unless she had something she wanted to hide? It had been the same one ever since they'd known each other, so why change it now? What was going on? Yes, life was pretty shit, but she was still his wife.

Suddenly aware he was going round and round in circles, Tom slammed his palm down on the arm of the sofa, his already bruised knuckles wincing their discomfort.

"What the hell am I going to do?" he asked the cat.

Baloo looked at him with what appeared to be contempt, then stretched and hopped from the chair, undoubtedly off to do his night-time patrol around the neighbourhood.

Tom was really on his own now.

4

BETHANY

All I could think about was the idea that had started manifesting in Leigh's office the other day. I'd managed to make it through Experimental Psychology and now I was seated in my second lecture of the day, not listening to a word my tutor was banging on about. Instead, I was busy scribbling notes on the pad in front of me. I'd forgotten to charge my laptop last night, so an old school pad would have to do.

"Bethany?"

Was that my name being called?

"Bethany? Are you with us?"

Crap. Busted.

Mr Jenkins, or Mike as he liked to be called by his students, was looking straight at me, along with the first few rows in the auditorium.

"Sorry." I felt my face heat up.

"And she's back in the room." Mr Jenkins turned away and headed towards the whiteboard, displaying the bald patch on the back of his head. What a prick, I thought, mentally flicking my middle finger at him.

Jordan, who was sitting next to me as per normal, gave me a grin and crossed his eyes behind the smudged windows of his glasses.

"As most of you know," Mr Jenkins continued, "hypnotherapy is a form of alternative medicine in which practitioners use relaxation, imagination, direct hypnotic suggestion and post-hypnotic suggestion techniques to treat patients suffering from psychological or physical illnesses."

Blah, blah, blah. Jenkins managed to make even this subject sound boring. Jordan mimed putting a gun into his mouth and pulling the trigger before collapsing back on his seat. I followed suit by pretending to stick a samurai sword into my stomach and falling back, also.

It wasn't just us, either, by the looks of things. The whole room had settled into a kind of coma as our tutor droned on about its uses in practice. Even Seb was uncharacteristically quiet, which amazed me, as normally he'd be the one person who'd ask if you could hypnotise someone to eat an onion.

"All practitioners must be absolutely committed to the sincerity of helping their patients. If this is the path you want to follow with your careers, you will be studying this as your specialism and ultimately be licensed to use it in your practice. None of this 'look into my eyes' Derren Brown mind-control nonsense."

"But what if you want to get someone to eat an onion like it's an apple? Like, just for a laugh?"

There it was.

"Then you will lose your licence, Seb."

There were sniggers around the room and, as they were silencing again, I found my hand sneaking up in the air. As usual, I made sure to securely hold my sleeve to my palm with my fingers first, to make sure it didn't slip down to show any skin.

"Yes, Bethany?"

"Could you hypnotise someone to do something they didn't want to do?"

"How do you mean?"

I lowered my arm again, crossing it over my chest. "I mean, could you make someone fall in love with you, for example?"

"That's actually a very good question. And it all depends on your conscious critical faculty, which is the internal filter we use to interpret how the world works based on what we've learnt since we were born. Such as water being wet, and the sun only coming out during the daytime, and four-leafed clover being lucky. It's how we interpret the world around us. The way hypnotherapy works is by bypassing the conscious critical faculty to remove beliefs from the subconscious mind so the patient can see the world from a completely new angle and be open to possibilities."

"Mike?"

Mr Jenkins turned to Seb, resignation clear on his face.

"If I wanted to hook up with a girl but didn't have the guts to ask her out coz my conscious critical faculty says I can't, you could override that too, couldn't you?"

"Technically, yes. It would be possible to give you the confidence to approach things in a new way. Not that I'm sure you need any help with your confidence, Seb."

"Just asking for a friend," said Seb, winking at Jordan who laughed it off, pushing his glasses up his nose.

Poor old Jordan. Not for the first time, I thought it was a good job his skin colour saved him the embarrassment of blushing.

"Ok, ok," Mr Jenkins interjected among the sniggering room. "Well, we're going to carry on with this topic for a few sessions, so by then, I imagine we'll all have our love lives sorted out in one way or another. Just bear in mind that for all the showmen out there who use hypnosis for monetary gain, hypnotherapy is a tool that can and should be used to help change people's lives for the better."

It was like the group sensed he was making a closing statement as, before he'd even finished speaking, books started to be shoved into bags and arms angled into coat sleeves. I finished scribbling my notes, aware of Jordan packing up his bag then standing, waiting for me, rubbing the bridge of his nose with his forefinger and thumb where his glasses rested.

The remainder of the group jostled their way out of the room like a stampede of wild animals all heading to the nearest watering hole. In a sense, they were. If you could classify the canteen as a watering hole.

BY THE TIME we reached the canteen for lunch, the best of the food was already gone, the rest of the herd having picked the carcass dry. Bloody Serengeti analogies. Where the hell had that come from? Although, looking around the room, it was easy to compare some of them to wild animals.

Seb was obviously some kind of crazed chimp, always showing off and making a lot of noise about nothing. Then there were Hayley and her friends, the Kardashian wannabes. All competing for the best pout and glossiest image they could portray on Instagram. They reminded me of a flock of flamingoes. All style and no substance. I smirked to myself as I didn't even have a clue which animals came from the Serengeti. Good job I was studying psychology and not geography.

"Do you fancy going to see a movie this weekend?" Jordan asked me as we joined the dwindling queue for lunch.

"Ah, Jordan, I'd love to, but I've got to head back home." The lie tripped off my tongue as I reached for a sad-looking cheese sandwich. My sleeve rose a little, giving a hint of a raised mark on my wrist and I pulled the fabric back down quickly before edging my tray along in front of the half-hearted display of food.

I'd got the impression Jordan had clocked the scars on my arms

a few times before, not that he'd ever in a million years say anything
about them. Unlike some people. There were plenty who would
seize upon those marks as a sign of weakness or a good story to latch
onto. Something to show fake pity over and then whisper about
when my back was turned. Not for the first time, I was glad I'd
chosen Jordan to be my friend and not some other vacuous idiot.

"Yeah, I guessed you might be." I could tell Jordan was trying to
hide his disappointment. "Just thought I'd ask in case you wanted to
hang out."

"You know I always go home at weekends, Jordan. It takes a lot
of effort to make a long-distance relationship work."

"Yeah, I'm sure it does. Maybe he could come and visit you here
one weekend, then I could meet him."

"Are you mad? Why would he want to come and hang out with
a bunch of kids?"

"So, he's older than us then?"

"Er, yeah. He's older."

I had to shut this conversation down before it went any further.
I should never have mentioned Daniel in the first place, but it had
seemed easier to say I had a boyfriend back at home than to go into
any details. I paid for my crappy sandwich, most of which was likely
to end up in the bin anyway.

Finding an empty table, we sat down and I took a bite of bread
which had probably surpassed its sell-by date the day before. Jordan
looked crestfallen as his gaze fell to contemplate his macaroni
cheese. God, he looked like an infant who'd been told off by his
mother for being too needy. It really wound me up.

"Listen," I told him, pushing away the remains of my sandwich
that I'd opened up like a body on an autopsy table so I could remove
the insides. "I wanted to talk to you about something much more
important than going to watch a stupid film, anyway."

He looked up with barely concealed hope in his eyes. Oh my
God. Why did he have to catch the feels for me? Surely, he must

know how firmly he was in the friend zone by now. I'd be more likely to ask him to plait my hair then go on a date.

"I've been throwing some ideas around for a project."

He looked at me quizzically while shovelling a forkful of glutinous pasta in his mouth.

"What do you think about Kennedy?" I sat back triumphantly.

Jordan continued to chew his food before swallowing and taking a glug of his drink. "Kennedy?"

"Yes," I told him. "You know about the Kennedy assassination, right?"

"Well, yeah. JFK, the killer on the mount. What's that got to do with psychology?"

"Nothing, you numpty. I'm talking about his brother, Robert's assassination."

Jordan stared at me blankly, his jaw still moving, a cog in the wheel of food to stomach. I should have known better than to talk to him while he was eating. "I'm still not clear," he said.

The irritation started raising its ugly head again and I sighed emphatically, rolling my eyes to let him know he was doing my head in. "The guy who supposedly killed Robert Kennedy was allegedly hypnotised by the CIA to do it."

"Why on earth would they do that?" he asked, lowering his fork. I had his attention now.

"To stop him becoming president."

"Bloody hell. Was it ever proved?"

"Nope." I twirled my lip ring around with my tongue and watched his gaze fall towards it.

"Jesus. Is it even possible to do that to someone? To hypnotise them like that?"

"That's what I was wondering."

Jordan pushed himself backwards on the rear legs of his chair. They wobbled rather worryingly and he let it rock back onto all fours before he embarrassed himself completely by falling off.

"Hang on a minute, so you're suggesting we should try it for a project?"

"Just wondering if it's possible."

"It could be really interesting," he said.

"I know, right?"

"But what about the fact that neither of us are qualified in hypnotherapy? Don't you think that might be an important factor?"

"Not really. We've covered the basics in our course already, and I'm pretty sure we'll be able to get the rest of it from YouTube. If it works, we could focus on the psychology behind it all for a write-up."

"I'm not sure."

"Come on, Jordan. We know what we're doing, and you had all that hypnotherapy practice when you did your apprenticeship in the holidays. No one else is going to come up with anything even remotely as interesting or challenging as this. We could really nail it. What do you think?"

"What I think is that we'd never get it approved in a million years. The university would say it wasn't ethically sound to use human subjects." Jordan resumed the repetitive motion of raising and lowering his fork between his plate and his mouth.

I'd had a feeling his sensibilities would kick in, but I was ready for that. "So, we don't tell them."

The fork paused. "We can't do that."

"Of course we can. We carry out the study off-campus and, if anyone finds out, we just make something up. I dunno, maybe we call it 'a study of hypnotherapy as an effective, holistic approach to adapting the conscious critical faculty and its behavioural norms'. Makes it sound a bit more positive, right?"

"Keep talking." Jordan continued scraping around what was left on his plate.

"We do all the tedious research that the tutors want to read about and carry out some surveys. Then we can bang on about methodology and data until we're blue in the face. That way, we're covered."

"And in the meantime? What? We're undertaking this secret, highly unethical study in the background?" He pointed at my leftover sandwich. "Are you going to eat that?"

"Seriously?" I pulled a face at him, pushing over what was left. "Just imagine if we can pull it out of the bag, though. It'd be a massive fait accompli. Our careers when we leave here could go stratospheric. Students would be studying *our* experiment at university for years to come. Forget Freud and Jung. It'd be Haines and Torrance."

Jordan grinned around a piece of wholemeal bread crust and I played my final card.

"I know it's a risky strategy, but the rewards could be massive." I paused. "I'll understand if you don't want to be involved, though. In fact, look…forget it, Jordan. I shouldn't have put you in this position. Maybe I'll ask someone else." I looked away from him, ostensibly letting my eyes wander around the room, but not before noticing the panic on his face.

Jordan took his glasses off and started cleaning the lenses with the edge of his shirt. A habit of his that he often did while he was pondering something deeply. I had no idea how bad his eyes were. I'd sometimes thought about pulling a face, just to see what his reaction was, or if there'd be one at all, but I'd managed not to so far.

Reaching a conclusion, he put the metal rims back in position and looked squarely at me. "It could be a phenomenal study," he said quietly.

"So, are you in?" I felt a surge of excitement as triumph started to bubble in my veins.

"Yes…I mean no. Well, yes. It would all be faked, obviously, wouldn't it? I mean, for starters, it's not like we can just walk into a shop and buy a gun. It would all have to be set up. We'd be in control, the victim would be aware of what was happening, and we could give the subject a toy gun or a plastic knife or, I dunno, a bit of polystyrene to bash someone with. But the essence of it is that we would be able to prove or disprove the Kennedy assassination claims."

"Are you saying what I think you're saying?" I asked him.

"Sure. I think I am. Let's do it."

I couldn't help smiling. I'd told Leigh only this week that the reasons I liked Jordan were that he was decent and kind, both of which were true. What I hadn't told her was that the main reason I liked him was that he was very easily led. "Are you sure?" I asked him. "I don't want you to feel like I've pushed you into this."

"Don't be daft. It really is a brilliant idea." Jordan held out his right hand, offering a handshake. "Let's try and hypnotise someone to commit murder."

I took his proffered hand and we shook just as Seb sidled up to the side of the table, no doubt trying to earwig on our conversation.

"Hey, guys." He pulled a chair round so he could sit on it backwards, facing the table. "What's going on over here with the secret handshake, then?"

"Not a secret, Seb. Just a handshake."

I used to be amazed that Seb could even tie his laces in the morning, let alone do a degree. I'd wanted to slate him for being a thick Sports Science student, but when I'd found out about the amount of biochemistry and physiology on the curriculum it proved that he couldn't be that bloody stupid. Still, he did a good job of making out he was most of the time. I guessed it fitted his image.

"What's happening, then? Whose murder are you planning?"

"Nobody's." Jordan shot me a warning glance.

Damn it. Bloody Seb had obviously overheard enough of our conversation already, and to deny him the chance of being involved would just risk him blabbing about what he did know. I started to wonder if he could actually be useful to us. I had a feeling he could be pretty good at keeping secrets based on his extra-curricular activities as a low-key dope dealer. What was that phrase? Keep your friends close, and your enemies closer.

Ignoring Jordan's obvious horror, I filled Seb in on what we were planning, watching his expression carefully. It started with mild curiosity, working its way through incredulity, and finally ended on being impressed.

"So, what do you think?" I asked him.

"It's a pretty cool idea, man," he admitted, drumming his fingers on the peeling Formica tabletop. "Wish I'd thought of it."

Chance would be a fine thing, I thought to myself. His idea of a good study would undoubtedly be based on the differentiating muscle strength of women dependant on breast size.

"Oh man, you know what this reminds me of?" Seb paused from his drumming. "Remember that old movie from the '90s where those students kill each other and bring themselves back from the dead? What was it? They did that really crap remake."

"You mean *Flatliners*?" Jordan started tearing strips from around the edge of his cardboard cup.

"Yeah man, that's it. Only when they came back from the dead, they brought all sorts of bad stuff back with them…demons and stuff."

Jordan turned to look at me and I raised my eyebrows back at him. "Oh my God, this is totally different. No one's actually killing anyone – or resurrecting them. And demons? Are you kidding me?" I started to re-evaluate my opinion of Seb once again.

"Well, you can count me in, anyway." Seb held his hand out to Jordan, for another handshake I could only assume. Probably one of those where you make complicated movements and end on a fist bump.

Looking confused, Jordan left Seb's hand hanging. "Thanks, mate, but we couldn't actually use you now even if we wanted to.

Whoever we use as a subject literally can't have a clue what he's involved in, otherwise, it means the results will be skewed. Sorry."

Seb looked truly gutted as his hand dropped back down to the back of the chair. Handshake denied.

"Actually..." I spoke up, taking my time to sip my drink and making sure that both Jordan and Seb gave me their full attention. "We *can* use you, Seb."

Seb's eyes lit up and Jordan asked, "How?"

Laughing, I put my drink back on the table. "We're going to need a victim."

5

TOM

When Tom opened his eyes, he found himself lying in what could only be a hospital bed. His body was covered with clean but worn sheets which felt both rough and soft at the same time and clung damply to him. He must have been sweating in his sleep as the air around him felt icy against his skin. His head rested on a thin pillow and his hands clenched the metal rails on either side of his resting place.

Mind swirling with confusion, his eyes darted around the darkened ward, picking out objects around him; a cabinet, a chair for visitors, and a bed tray down by his feet. A privacy curtain enclosed his immediate space, for which he was grateful as he had undoubtedly been thrashing around in his sleep as normal.

Tom's head hurt. No, it didn't just hurt, it pounded. And his stomach, God, it felt as though someone had reached inside it and pulled out his intestines before folding them up and shoving them back in with no due care as to where they landed.

The familiar hospital smell of disinfectant hit his senses, alongside the underlying smells of sickness, pharmaceuticals and the many ethyl alcohol dispensers which lined the walls of every ward.

The joining forces made his stomach roil and his head spin as though he'd just climbed off a roundabout. A groan left his lips with the realisation that this time maybe he'd drunk too much.

Was that it? Had Gemma come home to find him lying unconscious in a pool of his own vomit? Had she tried to revive him and ended up calling for an ambulance to come and get him? Oh, God, he felt sick with self-loathing and the fear that he could reach such levels of utter shit. It wasn't supposed to be like this.

He swallowed a sob, his throat raw at the effort, and his head aching. He'd undoubtedly had his stomach pumped. He knew the score. Pipe crudely shoved down the throat into the guts and then suction applied to drag up the contents of what he'd tried to numb his pain with.

Other than a small child crying somewhere down the hall, the ward was silent. Unusual in any hospital at night-time. There were normally the noises of disrupted sleep around you, the squeak of a rubber-soled shoe against linoleum, a phone ringing at the nurse's station. Although unlikely, perhaps he was alone in his ward.

The weeping from down the hall had risen a level and Tom was surprised that no one was on hand to comfort the infant. It was compounding the pain in his head and he wondered if he could get some relief by summoning a nurse. Trying to push himself up, he pulled his arms back towards him to rest on his elbows, only to find they would only move so far. He felt a tightening around his wrists and there was a dull clunk of metal against metal.

Brain thumping inside his skull, he looked down at his hands and his sleep-addled mind took a moment to comprehend that his wrists were encased in steel. A short but solid link chain joining to another bracelet looped around the side rails of the bed. Jesus Christ! What the fuck had happened? What the hell had he done to be handcuffed to a hospital bed? Fear clenched his heart tightly in its grip, squeezing each beat out faster and faster.

The child's cries had now ramped up to an almighty wail which made Tom's head want to split open in agony. Why wasn't anyone coming? Where the hell was everybody?

Taking a deep breath, he tested his voice which was nothing but a hoarse whisper. "Hello? Nurse?"

He coughed and swallowed, trying to lubricate his inflamed throat with what little saliva he had.

"Hey! Is anyone there?" he managed to rasp, no match to the screaming which continued from another ward.

Claustrophobia swirled tightly about him in an unwanted embrace and Tom didn't think he could bear the pain in his head any longer. The intensity matched only by the rising level of panic at being constrained without knowledge or reason. The screeching and waves of nausea came in tandem, and skull-splitting pain grew and grew.

And then the noise just stopped. Stopped dead. Tom's initial reaction was of absolute relief as he tried to get his agitated breathing back under control. The noise of his hammering heart filling the void that the screams had left. Just as loud in his ears.

Only as the echo of the cries subsided completely did Tom hear the footsteps making their way down the hallway. A heavy tread, somewhat muffled on the hospital flooring as it approached. Swallowing again, Tom tried calling out once more. "Hello? Could you help me, please?"

There was no response, and no other sounds from the rest of the hospital residents, just the footsteps continuing on their journey, same pace, same tread, but definitely coming in his direction. Slow, steady, determined. Echoing their warning as they came ever closer.

Something about this wasn't right. No, nothing about this was right. Tom yanked his wrists against their constraints, the metal clanking once more against the bed rails. He achieved nothing other than a new and insistent pain as the metal cut into his skin.

Tom's breath came rapidly as the footsteps got closer and closer still, and he knew that whoever was now stood on the other side of the privacy curtain would be able to hear his breath uncontrollably rasping, jagged from his lips.

Eyes fully accustomed to the darkness of the room, Tom saw a hand take hold of the edge of the curtain, and he felt a warm, damp trickle against his belly and thigh where his bladder had let itself go.

Without haste, the hand started to draw back the curtain and Tom's breath came in great gulps of disinfected air, his heart threatening to explode. Fighting and failing to stop the urge to close his eyes and shut out what was in front of him.

"You did this," a familiar voice spoke to Tom's cowering form.

His eyes stuttered open, widening in shocked recognition of the person stood still at the side of his bed. Nurse's uniform covered in blood and vomit, face bloated beyond recognition, but still undoubtedly his own.

For the second time that night, Tom's ears were full of screaming, but this time they were his own, ripping from the raw skin of his throat. He watched his body thrashing and flailing on the bed as best it could, bearing in mind its metal constraints, as his own mind, wrapped in madness, floated up above the hospital bed. An onlooker of the unbearable insanity and terror beneath him.

And then he woke up.

TOM FOUND himself alone in a tangled heap amongst drenched bed covers. A weird, guttural moan escaped his lips as his heart shocked him back into consciousness as if he'd mainlined adrenaline. His pulse was racing so hard, he felt absolutely sure his heart would explode within the confines of his chest. His eyes darted around the room searching for visible remnants of the nightmare that still clung to him like cobwebs.

Once he recognised the familiar surroundings of his bedroom, Tom allowed himself to move his limbs. One at a time, and ever so slowly, not wanting to draw any unwanted attention to himself, even though he was pretty sure the room was empty of threat. Sometimes, he couldn't tell whether he was awake or still sleeping, and the consequences of that were never good.

Reaching across to the bedside table, he flicked on the lamp, which cast a comforting glow around him, and he then pushed the sodden covers away. His skin, recently so hot and profusely sweating, had cooled, allowing the perspiration to chill him, gooseflesh pimpling his skin.

Swinging his legs over the side of the bed, he dropped his head into his hands and wept. The residue of terror stayed with him, as it always did for a while afterwards. It was like being haunted by a persistent spirit night after night with no exorcism able to rid him of his possession.

Gemma used to comfort him when his night terrors started. She'd touch his arm to reassure him, or drowsily ask if he was ok before falling back asleep. Sometimes, just to hear her breathing was comfort enough. But now he often slept alone in the spare room when she was on a day shift so she could get some rest. His thrashing about and screaming had become too much for Gemma to handle, and to his shame, he'd even lashed out at her on a couple of occasions when she'd tried to wake him in the middle of his nightmares.

It killed him to think about it. The last thing he would ever do in his right mind would be to hurt his wife, but it was the night terrors, they took away all his control. The first time, she'd managed to dodge his flying fist, but the second time it had landed firmly on her cheekbone causing some pretty dramatic bruising. Gem had managed to cover it up pretty well with makeup, but he felt sure there would still have been whispers at work in the cloakroom about how those marks had come about. No one really walks into an open cupboard door, do they?

"It's fine," she'd told him, but he could see the difference in the way she'd looked at him afterwards. The slight flinch behind her eyes when he came close, particularly when they argued, which, sadly, was often.

Wiping his eyes, Tom pushed himself up from the bed and made his way to the bathroom, switching on lights as he went so the shadows withdrew from around him. He stood in front of the mirrored cabinet above the sink and stared long and hard at his reflection. His eyes were still wide following the intensity of his dream and his pupils so dilated that not even the fluorescent bathroom lights had been able to contract them.

He ran his hands under the cold tap and splashed some water on his face before grabbing his dressing gown from the hook on the back of the door. It already smelt pretty stale so one more night of wear wasn't going to make any difference.

Slowly, he shuffled downstairs, leaning his weight heavily on the bannister as he went, still wanting to solidify himself to his surroundings.

They'd said he was suffering from PTSD. The doctors that Gemma had forced him to go and see. He couldn't quite get his head around that, though. PTSD sounded like it should only apply to men who'd been in combat, not run of the mill fools like him. But there you go; you couldn't argue with the men in white coats, could you?

Incurable too, they'd said. Of course, therapy might help, and medication. He'd tried both. The therapy was shit and the medication, well… the best he'd found so far was sat in a whiskey bottle in the cupboard.

Without hesitation, Tom headed to the drinks' cupboard, wishing a little that he'd put something on his feet as the chill from the wooden flooring downstairs travelled up through his toes. He took a glass and a bottle of whiskey from the depths of the cupboard. One day, he was pretty sure Gemma would start to try and hide the alcohol from him. He'd already planned for that event, though, with a bottle stashed away in the depths of his wardrobe. For now, it remained unopened.

The heating wasn't set to come on until 6 am during the winter months, so the house had a chill to it and Tom didn't think to turn on the thermostat. Taking his stash into the lounge, he sat on the sofa, wrapping his dressing-gown tighter around himself, and reached for a hand-knitted blanket that Gemma had spent many hours creating before displaying it for adulation on Facebook. Fair play to her, it was nice, and, more importantly right now, it was warm.

As Tom poured out a couple of fingers of whiskey, its sweet, heady smell soothed him straight away with the knowledge that everything would be better soon. He swirled the drink in his glass before knocking it back in one and pouring a second.

Using the remote control, he flicked on the television to be rewarded with a late-night shopping channel. Perfect, soporific viewing for insomniacs and shopaholics alike. He sipped a little slower at his second drink, watching the smarmy host trying to promote the virtues of an extremely ugly fake emerald necklace.

Second glass down and the necklace all but sold out, Tom started to feel the anaesthetic effects of the whiskey on his troubled mind. Baloo came and joined him after his evening of carousing, curling up on his bed beneath the television screen. Before long, he was fast asleep, his tail twitching every now and then as he undoubtedly heard the clink of bottle against glass each time Tom poured another.

By the time the bottle was three-quarters empty, the shopping channel host had started trying to sell fitness equipment to his invisible audience. There was a suggestion of light starting to filter through from around the edges of the curtains and Tom had finally fallen back into a fragmented sleep.

6

BETHANY

"Thanks for lending me the book," I said, handing over the volume about Robert Kennedy to my counsellor as I entered the warmth of her office. I'd practically inhaled it in one sitting after I'd left last week.

"You're welcome," she said, taking it from me. "Come on in and make yourself comfortable." She motioned me over to the regular seating area which had a new piece of artwork positioned behind her usual spot.

I say artwork, but it actually looked like a black and white photograph of a human brain sliced in half, showing its inner workings. Not the cheeriest image for all us troubled kids, I thought, wondering why on earth she would choose something so off-kilter to put on the wall. Surely, a nice picture of a boat in pastels would be a bit more...uplifting. Still, I supposed we were all entitled to our own choices. After all, I'd certainly made some pretty dodgy ones in the past and they were much worse than hanging up an image of a sliced brain. In its own way, it was even quite entrancing.

Taking off my winter coat and laying it over the back of one of the armchairs, I plonked myself down, waiting for Leigh to join me while she hummed to herself and faffed about with the paperwork on her desk.

"Did you enjoy it?" she asked as she joined me, book in hand. "Sorry about all my scribbles and underlinings in it, but it's been a really useful reference book over the years."

"It was fascinating," I told her, moving my eyes away from the photograph, unable to contain the words which were normally bound and gagged inside my head. "In fact, it's given me an idea for a project."

Leigh lowered herself into the chair opposite mine, removing her watch as usual and placing it on the small table in front of me. As she leant forward, I noticed she'd had her roots done. She must have felt me looking, as she patted her hair self-consciously. "Well, that is wonderful news, Bethany. Would you like to tell me about it?"

Normally, she would've had to crowbar any information out of me, but if I spoke about this instead, it meant I could get away with not talking about my past for yet another session. It was the perfect way to fill the next fifty minutes. Not that I was going to tell her the whole truth anyway as I could just imagine her professional and ethical values being somewhat upset by my idea. "We…Jordan and I thought it would be interesting to see if we could bypass the conscious critical faculty of a subject using hypnosis. We want to see whether their subconscious mind will allow us to change their moral code."

I sat back in my chair, for once not folding my arms across my chest in my usual closed defence mechanism. Instead, my hands rested open and wide on the arms of the chair, inviting questions about the project that I was so proud of.

Leigh matched my open posture and I wondered if she was doing it on purpose, trying to make me feel more comfortable.

"Tell me more." She obliged me with a smile as she played distractedly with her necklace. She always wore it, I'd noticed. A pretty little gold locket. One of those that opened up so you could put a photo in it. I wondered briefly whose image she had in hers before dismissing the thought and focusing on what we were talking about.

This was where I had to be careful of letting my mouth run away with me. Not that it should be a problem as I was well-rehearsed in being tight-lipped in Leigh's counselling room. For once, though, I found myself wanting to share more, wanting to get some kind of seal of approval. It was a new feeling and I wasn't sure it sat comfortably yet. "I can't go into too much detail as I don't want to jinx it, but the idea is to see if we can convince our subject to commit an unsocial behaviour."

Every single counsellor I'd ever had was well trained in disguising their own emotions while they're in session, probably so they can act as giant sponges to soak up those of their clients before wringing themselves out at the end of the day. I could have sworn that this time, I saw the faintest twitch of a well-manicured eyebrow, though. It was probably the best reaction I was likely to get to be honest.

"Ah," she said.

"Nothing quite as dramatic as assassinating the Prime Minister, though, clearly," I said with a laugh. A fake one.

"Clearly." She fake-laughed back. That was fine. "What's the unsocial behaviour that you're thinking of?"

"We haven't decided yet," I lied.

I set out elements of the plan that Jordan and I had put together over the last few days and Leigh listened intently to everything I put forward about the study, continuing to hide any surprise very well and even nodding in what I took to be approval in certain places.

"Wow. Full marks for having such an adventurous idea," she said once I'd finished.

I waited for the 'but'. There was always a 'but'.

"It's certainly a bold experiment that you want to take on."

I nodded.

"With plenty of risks."

I shrugged.

"Have you thought about how you're going to get your participants?" she asked, turning the book over in her hands.

"We were thinking about placing an ad on Facebook and then asking people to share it."

"Absolutely," said Leigh. "But what I mean is, you need to narrow it down a little. Maybe look at a specific group of people."

That was something I hadn't yet thought about. I remembered my mother being hypnotised years ago to give up smoking. She'd come back with a new air of importance, insisting she was 'not a slave to nicotine!' It had worked…ish. She'd given up her twenty-a-day habit and, to my knowledge, only ever had the odd one on nights out now. Just a part-time slave to nicotine, then.

"What, like people who want to give up smoking?" I asked.

"Exactly," said Leigh. "Although, not so many people smoke these days, so you need to look at something more common. Maybe read through some other studies for ideas." She patted the cover of the book and slotted it back into its home in the bookcase beside us.

"Hmm, true." I turned my lip ring over and over while I contemplated Leigh's words. Anxiety and depression were pretty common these days, but the last thing I wanted was to put a gun in the hand of someone who was bi-polar, even if it was a fake one. My eyes alighted on the tome next to the book she'd replaced. 'Counting Sheep.' I felt a jolt of excitement. "What about sleep disorders? There must be loads of people out there who can't sleep due to all that blue light at night from checking social media in bed."

"There certainly is, and I'd probably make a good candidate!" Leigh laughed. "Just make sure you don't offer any false hope of miracle cures as it wouldn't be ethical to promise anything like that."

I wasn't sure what emotion I was feeling, but her words, full of enthusiasm for my idea even though she'd only had a half-truth, gave me a heightened sense of confidence that it could really work. I didn't have to offer a cure as such, but maybe we could still hint at it.

"Anyway, we've still got some time left, Bethany. Did you want to talk about anything else today?"

See, this was what happened when you started opening up and talking about things. I cursed myself for letting her a bit further in.

"Did you want to talk about Daniel, maybe?"

I shook my head and cast my eyes around for a change of topic. Anything but that. I was drawn back towards the photograph on the wall. "That's not one of your old patients, is it?" I asked her.

"Hmm?" She followed my gaze towards the image of the poor sod whose head had been cut in half. "Oh, my new picture!" She smiled. "Quite bold, isn't it. Probably not everyone's cup of tea I expect. It's a CAT scan of the brain, which I find absolutely fascinating, as you might have already guessed."

"Sure," I told her, my expression undoubtedly giving away my opinion without the need for words. "Isn't it called topography?" I felt the need to show off my intellect to her for some reason as I imagined it was probably higher than most of her patients. It made me feel better about my own shortcomings.

"Ah, no, close. That's the study of the shape and features of the land. This is *tom*ography. Computed Axial *Tom*ography. It's where the word CAT comes from in a CAT scan, or a CT scan as they're called now."

"That's what I meant." I nodded, feeling angry for making myself look foolish but not wanting to admit the fact.

"Easy mistake to make. Oh, while I remember, let me write down some websites that might be useful for your project." She tore a page from her notepad and quickly wrote out some addresses.

I took the sheet of paper from Leigh's proffered hand and thanked her for her help. She might be part of the constitution, but so far, she was the best of a bad bunch and, for a fleeting moment, I wanted to be honest with her. "You know I don't like talking about my past, don't you?"

"I do, Bethany. It's ok. We can talk about your present until you're ready." She picked up her watch from the table. "Why don't we end it there for today."

I couldn't believe how quickly the session had gone. I guessed talking about something I was interested in made the time just go so much faster. I stood up and started gathering my stuff together and my head spun a little, making me fall back down on the armchair.

"Are you ok, Bethany?" Leigh looked concerned.

"Yeah, fine," I told her. "Just stood up too fast."

"Not just keen to leave, then?" My counsellor's attempt at a joke caused embarrassment to coat my smile.

As I LEFT the bright lighting of the office block, it underlined just how dark it was outside even though it was still only mid-afternoon. Roll on Spring, I thought as I pulled my stripy bobble hat firmly on my head, the chunky knit making my forehead itch straight away. As I searched my bag for my gloves, I heard the familiar ping of my phone which meant I'd received a WhatsApp message.

I eventually found the familiar shape of my iPhone amongst all the crap I felt necessary to lug around in my bag on a daily basis. Retrieving it, I could see all the latest social media notifications lined up, ready for me to look at. At the top of the list was WhatsApp, which had a bundle of messages waiting. Ah, Jordan.

Where have you been all afternoon? he'd written with a silly face emoji on the end. *Been looking for you everywhere.* Another emoji, this time one with a little monocle on its round yellow face. I rolled my eyes. He was so bloody needy.

I'd never told Jordan about my weekly counselling sessions. I didn't want the pity, or the absolute aggro that would unleash itself if I let him into my secret. It would mean having to explain why I had the sessions and the fact that I didn't have any choice in them. He would think I was a freak, a nutter, and I wasn't. At least, *I* didn't think so, even if everyone back home did.

I didn't feel like being drawn into a conversation right now, but he could tell I'd seen his messages now I'd opened them up, so I typed back *What's up?*

Straight away, three little dots appeared on the screen, bouncing up and down like an excited caterpillar as Jordan typed his response. *Been putting an advert together for our study. Need some help.* Then, *Where ARE you?*

I rolled my eyes for the second time, letting a puff of air escape from my lips in frustration. It bloomed in front of my face as it hit the cold air, looking like an exhalation of smoke. *I'm in the library.* I told him.

That's weird, he came back. *I've been here for the last couple of hours and I never saw you.*

Shit. Of course. I would have been better off telling him I was somewhere he was far less likely to be. I soothed him with the fact that it was the town library as opposed to the university one, walking as I typed with my thumbs on my phone, keen to get to the bus stop in time to get a ride back to my room. I didn't fancy pounding the rain-slicked pavements in this weather.

I hated the walk to the bus stop after my sessions. Leigh's consulting rooms weren't in the nicest area of town and the journey was full of shadowy doorways which reeked of piss and tobacco. Hearing the hocking up of phlegm nearby, I pocketed my phone and picked up my pace until I reached the relative safety of the shelter.

Seated on the cold metal perch in the glow of an advert for a McDonald's Meal Deal, my stomach rumbled and I remembered I hadn't eaten lunch today. I could kill for a big juicy burger right now. Not that they ever looked like the adverts in reality. More likely to be a sad, squashed little patty dressed unbecomingly with limp lettuce leaves and half a tonne of gherkins that no one ever wanted.

With the side of the bus stop thankfully blocking most of the chilly wind, I pulled my phone back out and typed out a long message to Jordan, filling him in on a couple of thoughts for our project before going through my other notifications. The same old boring crap on Instagram from bloody Hayley. Why she thought that continually pouting into a soft-focus filter was a good idea, I would never know. God, she was vacuous.

Even with the unrealistic Meal Deal wind block, my hands were freezing and I made a mental note to get some of those gloves you could still use your phone with. My current ones were useless for that, even though they were a lovely grey leather and probably really expensive too. Nice present from my mother for Christmas. Not much thought behind them, obviously, but hey.

As I was about to go onto Facebook, I saw out of the corner of my eye that my bus was finally approaching. Thank God for that, as the cold was really starting to bite through my layers of clothing now. The yellow glow from the interior of the bus was like something that I wanted to hold out my hands to, as though its weak fluorescence would warm up my goosebumps.

I hopped on board and exchanged the expected pleasantries with the driver before finding myself a well-worn seat halfway down the almost empty bus. It wasn't quite time for people to be going home from work just yet I supposed, which explained the lack of people riding the number 508 that afternoon.

I turned towards the window, seeing nothing but a dulled version of my own image reflected back at me in the fogged-up glass. I took off my itchy hat, scratching at my forehead again. Then, like a child, I traced a set of initials on the glass with my finger before confining them inside a heart shape.

I missed him.

Turning back to my phone, I typed his name into the Facebook search bar, like I had done every single day for the last few months. And just as it had done every single day for the last few months, Facebook crossed its arms and shook its head. I was still blocked.

Momentary anger fizzed underneath my skin. It wasn't even like I'd done anything wrong. Everything had been just fine until *she'd* stuck her oar in.

I was about to try searching another platform when WhatsApp pinged at me again. The distraction was timely, and I opened the latest message from Jordan.

What do you think? he wrote.

> ### Research Subjects Wanted
> *We are looking for volunteers who are experiencing any form of sleep disorder to participate in a psychological study. Whilst we cannot guarantee that your condition will be cured, some symptoms may be greatly improved. Subjects will be hypnotised under surveillance and asked to perform a number of tests to gauge their suitability. If chosen for the study, subjects must be available one evening a week for the next month.*
> *If you are interested in participating, please email Jordan or Bethany for more information.*
> *(Jordanhaines02@gmail.com or btorrance@gmail.com)*

He'd been busy.

I hastily replied, conveniently ignoring the fact we were blatantly offering a dangling carrot to any subjects that chose to come on board. It was subtle enough to swerve any liability.

Perfect, but we only need one point of contact, so just take my name off, Jordan. Let's keep it simple.

7

TOM

The last few days had been even more hellish than usual for Tom while Gemma had been on nights. Even with their relationship as sour as it was, her presence around the house in the evenings still managed to soften the reality of being awake. So, her absence just served as an excuse to use something else to take the edge off.

Tom wondered if it would be worth him getting a night shift job himself. After all, there'd be plenty going at the supermarket where he now spent most of his days stacking shelves and moving items from right to left across a bar code reader. Jesus Christ, no wonder he needed a drink in the evenings.

He didn't really mind the shelf stacking, to be honest. The monotony of loading piles of tinned fruit from trolly to shelf was calming in a weird way. Much better that, than being stuck on the tills having to listen to a never-ending line of old dears making small talk about their various ailments.

Today, he'd been put on till number nine, which was his least favourite as it faced both the far wall and Lydia on till number ten who always had a face like a slapped arse. He supposed he was a fine one to talk.

"Hi, Lyd," he called over to her as he took his place on the hot seat that morning. It was literally hot, too, after Sharon had vacated it. It always creeped him out a bit that her buttocks managed to create such a warm spot that he then had to meld his own into.

Lydia blew a strand of bleached hair out of her eyes and glared over at him as if he'd sworn at her, which he then did under his breath.

"Miserable cow."

"Right then," said Sharon, still hovering in the vicinity as he adjusted the height of the seat. "There should be enough change in the drawer."

"Great."

"Everything ok, Thomas? You're looking a bit pale today."

Hardly surprising, he thought, based on his sleep patterns combined with the unflattering orange uniform he had to wear. "I'm fine. Thanks for asking."

"Late night, was it?" She did all but wink at him, undoubtedly trying to elicit some juicy titbits to pull apart in the staff room later.

Tom reached into the depths of his psyche and managed to extract a smile for her. "No, just didn't sleep too well."

"Oh, poor you." She cocked her head to one side with a sympathetic look on her face. "You should maybe try putting some lavender oil on your pillow."

Oh, for fuck's sake. "I'll try that, Sharon. Thank you. I'd better crack on though, eh?" He gestured with his eyes towards a customer who had thankfully spotted the empty till and was now busily loading items onto the conveyor belt.

"Of course." She smiled. "I'll let you get to it." Patting his shoulder, her gold-plated bracelets jangling in his ear, she turned and headed off to the staff room.

Tom sighed and started the conveyor belt up. Truth be told, he missed his old job terribly. It was hard leaving behind a career that you loved and which made you want to get up in the mornings, to replace it with this drudgery day in and day out. The epitome of Groundhog Day.

He'd been a nurse for nine years and, despite the long hours and the low pay, he had never once regretted it. Well, not until it had all gone horribly wrong, that is. He'd had nine years of feeling like he had a purpose, making a difference to other peoples' lives, and there was nothing on earth like it. He'd absolutely found his calling and how fortunate was that? Most people worked a lifetime and never had that honour. Then, one stupid mistake had changed everything. Everything.

Sometimes, he was surprised that Gemma had carried on working as a nurse after what had happened at the hospital. While he couldn't blame her for continuing with her vocation, there was a small part of him that secretly thought it might have been more loyal for her to show some solidarity to him and hand in her notice. After all, it hadn't just been his decision that had started the ball rolling, had it? She'd let him do it.

Still, she hadn't left her job, and while she was no longer at the same hospital, she had still managed to get a transfer to a different oncology department when they'd had to up sticks and move.

"That'll be forty-three pounds and fifty pence please," he informed his silent customer who was busily loading up his bags for life.

He supposed he was jealous of his wife. Jealous that she still got to do the thing she loved, that they both used to love, while he had no choice but to be a till tart in a budget supermarket.

"Would you like a receipt?" he asked as the shopper retrieved his bank card from the card reader. Tom felt like a tired old stage actor reciting from a script each time he opened his mouth. The customers didn't always pick up the cues though, and this one shuffled off silently stage left, leaving Tom alone once again.

He looked across at Lydia whose head was bent over her mobile phone, fingers swiping angrily at the screen. Poor bastard that she decided to swipe right on, he thought.

It was going to be a long morning.

By the time Tom made it to the staff room for his coffee break, he'd swiped left on about twelve pints of milk, five loaves of bread, and had an enlightening conversation with an elderly lady about her recent colonoscopy. All he knew was that he was dying for some caffeine and he never, ever wanted to experience a camera being inserted into his backside.

He joined Lydia and a couple of the packing guys in the sad little box room out the back of the store. It housed a coffee machine, five chairs, and a tiny wall-mounted television which was constantly set to Sky News with the sound muted.

The other staff members were already sat, heads bent in the usual position over their phones. None of them spoke to each other, preferring instead to be part of the cyber world. Fine by Tom as he had nothing to speak to them about anyway. He selected what could be loosely described as a cappuccino from the machine, took a seat and retrieved his phone from his pocket. If you can't beat them, you might as well join them, he thought to himself.

To his surprise, Gemma had sent him a message. It happened so rarely these days that he felt what was almost like a little frisson of first date excitement as he opened it up. His wife had thought about him. Thought about him *and* wanted to contact him. Please God, don't let her be asking for a divorce, he thought to himself.

He scrolled through her message and opened the attachment she'd sent before he realised he'd been holding his breath. Letting it out in a loud puff, he became conscious of the other three looking up at him, briefly distracted from their fake worlds by the noise.

"Sorry," said Tom. "Coffee's a bit hot." He blew at the muddy brown water in its plastic cup as if to prove a point, then placed it on the table next to him. They went back to their screens, as did Tom, re-reading Gemma's message.

I've been thinking, it said. That wasn't always a good thing, in Tom's experience. *And I feel we owe it to ourselves to have one last try to make things better.* Tom swallowed. Surely, that must mean Ash hadn't got a proper hold on her yet. The message continued. *I know you feel like you've tried everything already to help you get past what's happened, and I know that nothing seems to have worked, but I've come across this advertisement for a sleep study, and I think it's worth one last try, don't you?*

He clicked on the attachment again, taking the words in a bit more. Tom groaned inwardly, conscious not to disturb the others from their screen time. The ad was asking for volunteers who suffered from sleep disorders to come in and be experimented on like lab rats, by the sound of it. There were no grandiose claims of curing conditions. The blind would not see, the lame would not walk, and the nightmares would probably not become dreamscapes.

Tom rubbed his hand over his eyes, practically able to feel the scratchy tiredness underneath the lids. If he was honest, he believed it would be one massive waste of time. But Gemma had sent it to him. Gemma had read that advertisement and thought of him, and while she still had the tiniest bit of faith in him, then he should really give it a go, shouldn't he?

Where did you find this Gem? he typed out slowly with one finger, unlike his roommates who seemed to have double-jointed thumbs for typing at the speed of light.

Gemma replied straight away telling him she'd seen it dotted around on some Facebook groups before it had been forwarded to her by a friend.

Immediately, Tom wondered exactly which friend had forwarded it to her. Like him, she didn't stay in touch with that many of their acquaintances from before. It did his head in that she talked about him to other people, discussed their private life, things he didn't want other people knowing, especially people like Ash.

Not that he was likely to meet any of her online friends any time soon. Could you even really classify someone as a friend if you'd never met them face to face? What did it matter if someone from an online self-help group knew that Gemma's husband suffered from amnesia and night terrors? Who in the online cat-lovers group would give a crap that he drank in the evenings to medicate himself? And was there really a single yummy mummy in the Hemsfield Local Buy & Sell group that would even recognise him as someone who lived on their estate? That's why they'd moved there, after all. To be anonymous.

Good for Gemma if she found solace in her online world of fake friends. Let them talk about their cats and their babies and their hippy-dippy massage techniques to promote better health. Let her ask for advice from people she didn't really know and who didn't really care about her and her problems. While they were all eager to be keyboard warriors, spouting 'useful' advice, he could bet that not one of them would actually get off their arses to come and do something helpful.

Her constant interaction with these people had always exhausted him, but if that was where she found the comfort that she craved, then who was he to complain? He had his own comfort.

Who sent it to you, Gem? he typed. The dots returned, then paused. Tom waited.

It doesn't matter who sent it.

Tom's heart sunk. Gemma had always been a bad liar, and by not giving a straight answer, he knew Ash was involved.

What would be the harm in trying?

Good question, thought Tom, as he took a sip of his coffee. It proved to be as rancid as it looked, and he pulled a face as he put the cup back down, sloshing some over his fingers. At least it wasn't hot.

He wiped his hand on his work trousers and stared up at the newsreader on the TV who was mouthing something at the camera. The writing on the newsreel tape on a constant loop around the bottom of the screen was so small that he couldn't make out any of the day's news. For all he knew, there could be a world war erupting and he'd be none the wiser. Maybe it was time he got some glasses, he thought. If only his other problems could be solved that easily.

Tom hated the fact that this unknown quantity was getting involved in Gemma's life – and now, by proxy, his life, too. Undoubtedly parading as someone who cared and whispering orchestrations into the ear of a desperate woman. And it was Tom's fault, wasn't it? His fault that his wife had felt the need to lean on someone else's shoulder as he'd moved his own out of reach. Fuck it.

Tom? Another message from Gemma. *Please?*

He sighed deeply, letting his head fall back to his shoulders and closed his eyes. God, he was tired. What if it could help? What if there was the slimmest chance that something could be triggered while they were poking around inside his head? Could it be worth a try, and really, what was the worst that could happen?

Not only that, but maybe Ash had expected him to say no to the idea out of spite. Expected him to kick off again so that Gemma would have to go running into his arms for solace. Sod that. Tom refused to fall for his pathetic reverse psychology tricks. With only five minutes left of his break, he opened his eyes, made a decision and tapped back a quick response to Gemma.

I'll do it.

As though she'd been poised, waiting for his response, she replied to him straight away. *Thank you.* She'd even added a kiss, which was something he hadn't realised he'd missed until he saw it sitting there against the white screen. He closed his eyes again, and he could still see that kiss, now white against the dark screen of his eyelids.

Not giving himself enough time to change his mind, Tom looked back at the advertisement. One click on the email link and he had put himself forward for the trial. He wondered if he'd be the only applicant, or maybe there'd be so many of them that he wouldn't even get picked. Only time would tell, he guessed.

Pushing himself up from the chair, Tom took his cup over to the sink, poured the liquid away and dropped the plastic into the overflowing bin. He had a strange feeling in the pit of his stomach, one that he supposed could be described as hope. He dampened it down, not wanting to allow the feeling to grow into a fully-fledged emotion. He'd been there before and it always seemed to go pear-shaped, so better not to get his hopes up. Still…

As he opened the staff room door to leave, his phone pinged from the confines of his pocket. He wondered if it could be another message from Gemma and wasted no time pulling it out to have a look. This time though, an automated email from someone called Jordan. The heading announced itself as *Research Experiment.*

Tom opened it up as he walked through the doorway, pausing to lean on the other side of the wall. None of the others were heading back yet, so he could have a quick look at what he'd signed up to before heading back to the shop floor.

The body of the email contained some standard blurb, thanking him for putting himself forward. Once again, it stated that a cure wasn't necessarily on offer, but that the researchers may be able to help with some of his symptoms. Some were better than nothing, Tom re-confirmed to himself, and read on.

The following is a conditioned response questionnaire designed to help us assist you more thoroughly with our hypnosis, and therefore your sleep condition. It is important that you answer the questions truthfully, keeping in mind that there are no 'right' or 'wrong' answers. Go with the first answer that comes to mind after you read the question. Please also be aware that your answers are private and confidential, and for use only within this research.

Tom scrolled down.

Have you ever sleepwalked during your adult life?

Have you ever awakened in the night and felt that you couldn't move your body?

Do you prefer reading fiction rather than non-fiction?

This wouldn't take long at all, he thought to himself as he scrolled on.

How many units of alcohol do you drink on a daily basis?

In an argument, do you have any feelings of intense anger?

Staring to feel a little uncomfortable, Tom scrolled further.

Do you have any prior convictions? If so, please provide details.

Shit.

The small fledgling of hope in Tom's heart was gone, replaced in one fell swoop with crushing dismay.

The door from the staff room suddenly opened beside him, heralding the return of Lydia to the shop front. Glancing at him as she brushed past, he saw her usual mask of general contempt slip, to be replaced with something that verged on concern. It was almost as unnerving as what he'd just read.

"Are you…?"

"I'm… I'll be…" Tom managed as he pushed past her to the toilets.

Slamming through the door, he was relieved to find the cubicle in the men's room empty. He locked the stall door behind him and pulled the toilet lid down, sitting on the edge of the cheap plastic and breathing hard. In through the nose, out through the mouth, in through the nose, out through the mouth.

It was too much. How the hell could he possibly go any further with this trial? Dredge up everything that he was trying so hard to run away from? He couldn't do it, he just couldn't. It would kill him.

But Gemma…. If he didn't do this, it would be all over for them. The final nail in the coffin of their relationship. He knew that deep in his heart.

And no matter how much he drank to soften the edges or how fast he ran to escape, he was never going to be drunk enough or fast enough to get away from what had happened. He was going to be stuck in his nightmare, both awake and asleep until he couldn't bear it anymore. And that moment was already snapping at his heels.

He knew what he had to do.

8

BETHANY

"This place is great, Jordan. How on earth did you manage to get it?"

I couldn't believe that my mild-mannered friend had pulled somewhere so great out of the bag for us to hold the sessions for our experiment.

The small annexe to the village library was perfect for what we needed. It had its own entrance, toilets, a tiny kitchen, and a great space for all our applicants to fill with their enthusiasm. I offloaded my bags full of paperwork and equipment onto a table and walked around our new hub.

"It's where my sister's gospel group rehearses," Jordan explained.

Christ, that was pretty cool. I really didn't expect that of anyone related to Jordan.

"They've cleared it with the library, and as long as we keep it tidy and lock up after we leave, they're happy to let us use it on Wednesday nights for the next few weeks."

"That's pretty trustworthy of them."

"Yeah. They're good people."

Stacked up against the far wall were lots of chairs and Jordan started to set them out on the main floor space, ready for our applicants to turn up.

"How many do we need, again?" he asked me.

"Well, we've had eighteen responders to the questionnaire, so I guess let's just get that number of chairs out."

"In rows, do you think? Or a circle?"

"Shit, Jordan, it's not a bloody AA meeting. Let's go for rows."

I looked up at the standard-issue plastic clock on the wall which read five thirty-five. Not long until the subjects started turning up at the allocated time of six. Well, I hoped they'd turn up, anyway. I took off my coat and laid it across the top of one of the stacks of chairs against the wall, then busied myself setting up a small tripod on top of a table, ready to attach my phone to it.

Jordan had thought it would be a good idea to video all the processes leading up to the final experiment so we had a record to refer to when we were writing up our notes. It was fine by me as long as I didn't have to appear on it.

By the time I'd finished, Jordan was only halfway through setting out the chairs, so I helped him position them into two curved rows of nine that faced the tripod. We both then pulled the blinds down, shutting out the gloom of the weak setting sun and giving us some privacy so that the subjects felt a little more secure.

"How long have we got?" asked Jordan, finally shrugging out of his parka.

"Fifteen minutes."

"Shit."

Jordan started banging and crashing around inside the small kitchen, I presumed setting out cups ready to offer tea and coffee when people arrived. I went back to my bags on the table by the door and got out everything we would need for the session. This included the completed questionnaires and waivers for the participants to sign allowing us to use video footage of them and any findings that we got from the study.

I could feel the excitement building up inside of me, gently fizzing like an Alka-Seltzer plunged into water. Excitement, but controlled within the confines of the glass. Jordan, on the other hand, seemed full of nervous energy, proving my thoughts right as I heard something smash.

"Shit." From the kitchen again.

"Jordan, just calm down," I told him. "You'll end up making everyone nervous."

"It's cool. I'm fine."

Just then, I felt a rush of cold air as the outside door opened emitting two women in the throes of conversation. They entered backwards, the edges of their coats damp, and both shaking their umbrellas free from raindrops.

Ten to six. They were keen.

I stuck my most amiable smile on my face and welcomed them in, suggesting they might like to leave their wet things on the coat rack, which they gladly did. Jordan's head poked out from the kitchen doorway and I could see him mentally composing himself.

"Ooh, this is so exciting," said one woman to the other as they came towards me. Her friend giggled in response as she patted her windswept hair back into place.

"It is, isn't it?" I agreed with them. "Would you mind just giving me your names and popping on a name badge for me?" I gave them the waiver forms to sign and directed them over to Jordan to get a hot drink before settling in their seats. Eager to be chosen, I knew they'd pick chairs in the front row, and I was right. I watched them tucking their bags underneath their chairs, continuing to chatter about their grown-up children. There was no way in hell that either of them would pass the suggestibility tests. They wanted it too badly.

Just as I was learning by proxy about Anwen's daughter and her blighted relationship with her boyfriend, Lennon, three more people came through the door in quick succession. First of all, two men, one of whom was probably deep into his retirement, and the other maybe in his late forties and looking as though retirement couldn't come quick enough. This was more like it. These two looked tired.

As the door had started to close behind the second man, he suddenly turned and pulled it back open for a woman who scuttled in apologetically. She thanked him and looked wildly around for somewhere to put her soaking umbrella. We were getting quite an interesting collection now, both of candidates, and umbrellas.

All ushered over to Jordan for refreshments, I looked through my list of who we had so far. Anwen and Sue, the two friends who were clearly here for a fun evening, which would probably be followed up by a glass or two of Prosecco at the pub down the road afterwards. The old chap was Joseph, who, I learned from his questionnaire had lost his wife not long ago and had been finding it hard to sleep ever since. Insomniac Mark was an estate agent who had ignored his calling as an archaeologist and now found himself working long hours and fighting the urge to book a ticket to Egypt and dig up some artefacts. Then there was Sally. In her late thirties, a single parent managing to survive on about three hours sleep a night.

Next through the door came a tall, skinny young man who looked as though a slight breeze could knock him over. He introduced himself as Andrew and his application form told me that we were the same age at twenty-one, but he only looked about fifteen. He suffered from sleepwalking and apparently, his girlfriend had suggested he take part in the study after she found him having a wee in her wardrobe in the middle of the night while fast asleep. I'd made sure to keep a straight face as I'd welcomed him in, remembering how I'd laughed aloud when reading his application.

It was nearly ten past six now, and there were still twelve more people that were supposed to be here. I'd expected a few no-shows but that was quite a lot. More importantly, the two I was really interested in after reading their questionnaires were yet to arrive. I looked over at Jordan who returned my gaze, then looked pointedly at his watch.

"Five more minutes," I mouthed at him, holding up my hand, fingers spread at the same time. It was ok to wait a bit longer while people finished their drinks and made awkward conversation with each other.

The door swung open again, introducing a brightly coloured raincoat which was wrapped rather snugly around a full-figured body. This had to be Melanie. Extremely overweight and, unsurprisingly, suffering from sleep apnoea. After removing her coat and pinning a name badge to her jumper, she ambled over to Jordan, probably in the hope that there would be biscuits to go with the hot drinks. I rolled my eyes.

As the long hand on the clock hit quarter past, one more person came bursting through the door, causing everyone to turn and look as though they were regulars in a small countryside pub, eyeing up a new arrival.

"God! Sorry! I'm late. I *am* late, aren't I? I put the wrong postcode in my SatNav, then the traffic was awful. It's the weather, I suppose, isn't it? Anyway, I'm here now. I hope I haven't held you all up!"

"It's fine," I assured the jittering woman as she placed her Starbucks coffee cup down on the table to fill in the waiver form. I wondered if maybe the reason she couldn't sleep could just be due to too much caffeine consumption. This was Lisa, single, workaholic, and insomniac. One of the two candidates I'd been interested in after reading their applications. Now I'd seen her, I wasn't so sure.

As she made her way straight over to the seats, I gave Jordan the nod. It was pushing twenty-past six now, so it looked like we were only going to get half our number. Pretty crap, but still enough to hopefully get a good subject from.

Jordan started clearing his throat and I went over to the door to lock it, just to make sure we weren't disturbed. As I was about to turn the key, I saw a man running down the path towards the library. As he passed beneath a streetlight, I could see he held a newspaper over his head, obviously trying to protect himself from the rain.

I pulled the door open as he came closer, ready to greet him, but as he lifted the paper away from his face, my throat squeezed the words back down my throat.

9

TOM

Tom hadn't been sure whether he was actually going to turn up to the first meeting, even as he'd pulled into the car park beforehand.

He'd forced himself to fill in the questionnaire that he'd been sent from Jordan with the bare minimum of information and, after a horrible hour and fifteen minutes of self-torture, he'd pressed send. He liked to think he'd been honest with his answers. Well, honest-ish.

Now, sitting in his car outside the library annexe, mind full of doubt, he'd seen a couple of women turn up, their excitement about the evening ahead obvious in their demeanour. If he hadn't been wavering beforehand, he certainly was now.

It was only ten to six, so he had another few minutes to make up his mind, and he was sure he'd seen a pub just around the corner before he came into the car park. Maybe he could just have a little something to settle his nerves. Grabbing his phone and wallet from the centre console of the car, he trotted down the path and turned the corner to find the welcome glow from the Red Lion.

Still early, and only midweek, Tom was fortunate to get served straight away by a bored-looking bartender who surely couldn't be old enough to work there. He took his pint over to a small wooden table by the window, where its last occupant had thoughtfully left a newspaper behind.

Tom settled himself and took a long draught from his glass, feeling his shoulders drop straight away. There was a fire burning in a grate just behind him, warming his back, and a good story on page two of the paper about a politician who'd been caught with his pants down. He didn't need to go anywhere. He could just stay here for a pint or two before heading home.

Home. Gemma would be waiting for him there, wanting to know how it had gone. He had no choice. Sighing, Tom skim-read the rest of the two-page article about the disgraced Member of Parliament before draining his glass and placing it back on its beer mat. He had to go.

Grabbing the newspaper to use as a makeshift umbrella to shield himself from the rain which had started falling, he left the comfortable familiarity of an unfamiliar pub behind him and jogged back down the path to the library room. As he reached the door, it was opened for him and he crossed the threshold, lowering the newspaper which immediately started dripping on the cheap carpet squares.

He thought he saw a moment of recognition in the eyes of the young woman who had opened the door for him, which made his heart kick up a beat. That was the last thing he could cope with, having someone recognise him from the disaster at the hospital.

He must have imagined it, though, as in the time it took to blink, her expression had changed from what looked like shock to something more like keen interest. It was a little unnerving to be honest, but as she welcomed him into the room and wrote out a name tag for him to wear, he found himself passing it off as a trick of the light. His usual damn paranoia.

The other participants were in the process of settling themselves into their seats and after signing a waiver, Tom sidled into the nearest chair to the door, at the back on the left-hand side. Not that he thought he would need to make a quick getaway, but he just didn't want to draw too much attention to himself. To the right of him, with a respectable gap of one chair between them, was a woman who also looked as though she'd rather be anywhere else but there. Tom tried to look at her name tag but couldn't quite make it out from the side. Oh well.

At the front of the room stood a young man who was adjusting an iPhone on a tripod. Not looking up at the gathered group, he seemed even more nervous than the participants, and Tom could only assume that this was Jordan who had sent out the emails. After a moment, he was joined by the young woman who had let Tom in, and he could literally see the adoration in Jordan's eyes behind his glasses. Poor sod, he had no hope.

The pair conferred in whispers for a moment, and then the woman stepped forward and spoke to her assembly.

"Thanks for coming, everyone. I'm Bethany and this is Jordan." She indicated her partner, who immediately dropped his eyes to the floor with a shy grin. "As you're all aware, we're undertaking a psychological study involving sleep disorders. As we stated in our initial advertisement, we can't guarantee that your individual conditions will be cured, but we do hope to be able to alleviate some of your symptoms if you do become our final subject."

The group looked on, waiting for her to continue. Probably all in the same boat as Tom, he assumed, waiting for her to produce the loaves and fishes…a miracle.

"As part of this study involves hypnosis, we'll first have to ascertain how susceptible each one of you is to suggestion and hypnosis, and to do this, we need to carry out some suggestibility tests."

The two women sitting in front of Tom turned to each other with a look of anticipation, and he felt like they should be sitting in the audience at the Palladium as opposed to an over-heated library annexe in Hemsfield.

"Now, don't worry, this first test won't induce hypnosis just yet, but as the evening goes on, they will serve as a guide for us to find the most suitable candidate for the final study. Jordan?"

Jordan stepped forward and managed to drag his eyes up from the ground. Public speaking was obviously way out of his comfort zone. "Ok, can I ask you all to just interlock your fingers in front of you, and then turn your hands outwards, so that your thumbs are pointing downwards." Jordan demonstrated as he spoke, which was a good job, as he was pretty quiet. "Now, keeping them turned outwards, raise them above your head."

"Sorry, young man, but I can't do that," the old man from the front row spoke up. "Got a dodgy shoulder, I'm afraid."

Clearly not expecting interaction, Jordan looked a bit panicked before reigning back control. "No problem, we'll try it another way. If you could all clasp your hands together in front of you instead, please."

"Keeping our fingers linked together?" asked the lady directly in front of Tom.

"No, you can just clasp them like this," demonstrated Jordan. "Now, I want you to press your hands together tightly. Really tightly, so that you can feel the palms of your hands pushing against each other."

Tom complied, his palms a little moist, no doubt caused by a combination of the warmth in the annexe and the exertion of jogging.

"Those hands are becoming locked together so tightly that they feel as though they're stuck together with superglue. They're just so tightly and securely locked together. The harder you press those hands together, the tighter they stick, and the more securely locked the hands become."

Jordan paused. From the expressions on the rest of the group's faces that Tom could see, it looked like they were all doing exactly as Jordan had requested, the woman next to him even gritting her teeth a little.

"Now, in a moment I'm going to ask you to try and open your hands. You'll try to open them, but they won't open at all because they are so tightly stuck together."

Tom closed his eyes and waited.

"Ok, so try to pull your hands apart now. Try really hard, and you'll notice that your hands are just too tightly clasped together, they don't open at all."

Tom made to pull his hands apart and nothing happened other than a slight pulse of effort in his upper arms. Amazed that they hadn't just opened like they normally would when instructed by his nerve endings, Tom opened his eyes in absolute wonderment to gaze at his clasped hands.

"The harder you try to open them, the tighter they feel."

Tom couldn't believe it. It was just as Jordan had said – his hands felt like they were superglued together. Part of him was completely freaked out, while the other part was full of wonderment, bringing what felt like a dopey grin to his face. Around him were gasps and sighs from some of the others, and the woman next to him turned to him, eyes wide and hands tightly bonded.

Past her, he could see the younger man on his row looking disappointed, hands already resting on his legs once more. On the front row, there seemed to be two more success stories - the old boy, and one of the pair of women who'd arrived together, who looked like her head was about to explode in excitement. Her friend tried, rather badly, to hide her disappointment at her own open palms.

"Ok," said Jordan, clearing his throat in the hope of regaining everyone's attention. "Now relax the hands. Stop *trying* to open them, and just let them open. Let them open easily, and the hands are moving apart. There. They're opening easily now."

Dropping his hands down to rest on his legs, Tom relaxed his muscles and watched open-mouthed as his hands fell apart.

"Well done, everyone," said Bethany from the side of the room. "Pretty incredible stuff, isn't it?" The group muttered their responses. "Now, we have Sue and Joseph from the front row, and at the back, Mark, Sally, and Tom." Tom felt her eyes on him again. "For those of you that weren't successful, you can head off now, if you wish, but you're more than welcome to stay and join in if you'd like to."

Jordan and Bethany spoke briefly with one another, and no one moved from their seats, making Tom wonder if they'd all been superglued to their chairs, as well. Then Jordan stepped forward again while Bethany adjusted the iPhone, making Tom realise that they were all being videoed. He chastised himself for not reading the waiver properly before signing it and ducked back a bit, obscuring himself behind the two friends in the front row.

"Right then, we're going to try a snap induction," said Jordan, who was coming across a lot more confidently now. "All this basically means is that we will try to put you into a quick hypnotic trance. So, I'd like you all to close your eyes and relax."

Tom did as he was told and waited for the next instruction.

"Keep your breathing nice and normal, in and out, nice and slow. Now, tense up. Your whole body should be tense."

Tom's limbs did as they were told, as though in a line up before a Sergeant Major.

"And now relax. You can feel yourself going into a state of sleep and, as you do, I want you to focus on my voice." There was a calm, rhythmical tone to Jordan's words now. "Think about how far you can drift into sleep, how far you can float, all the way until you're sound asleep."

Although Tom felt unbelievably relaxed, he felt sure he couldn't be hypnotised as how could he still be able to hear Jordan's voice? Hey, he thought to himself, if this didn't work, maybe he could pay

Jordan to do a recording of himself talking to help him drop off to sleep at night.

"When you wake up, after I count down to one, you will no longer remember your own name. Three, two, one. Now open your eyes. You, sir…" Jordan pointed directly at Tom. "Please tell me your name."

Startled, Tom went momentarily blank. "It's…" Damn. For the life of him, he couldn't remember. It was right there, on the tip of his tongue, but he just couldn't reach it.

"Madam?" Jordan had taken his gaze away from Tom and was now directing it to a woman on the front row. "Tell me your name, please."

"…I can't!" she blurted out.

Tom was gobsmacked. How the hell could he not remember his name? The test continued around him, like background noise, while he desperately went through the alphabet, testing each letter to see if one felt at home in his mouth. None did.

"Ok, everyone…take a deep breath in and fall asleep." Jordan gave a click of his fingers.

Tom's eyes closed and he felt his head drop, but Jordan's words were still clear.

"Now, stop *trying* to remember your name. Let your name come to you easily. There it is. There. Now, I'd like you to wake up on my count, and turn to your neighbour and introduce yourself, please. Three, two, one."

When Tom opened his eyes again, the room was in a hubbub. Everyone speaking at once, names tripping off tongues as easy as pie. "I'm Tom," he said as he turned to his neighbour, holding out his hand in time-honoured tradition.

"Lisa," she replied, taking hold of his hand with her own. "I never expected this, did you?"

"Not really, no," said Tom, shaking his head in disbelief.

"Ok, everybody," came Bethany's voice from the side of the

room once again, trying to regain order over her newly introduced group. "We now have Sue, Joseph, Tom and Sally. Sorry, Mark."

Mark, at the other end of the back row, held his hands up, shaking his head with a grin on his face.

"We have one final test to carry out this evening. One which was first used in the 1950s to see how hypnotism could make a subject do something that they wouldn't normally do. I'd like our final four to please stand and come to the front of the room."

Tom pushed himself up and walked over to the front of the room as instructed, trying to keep his back to the camera. He felt pretty uncomfortable with so many eyes on him and immediately itched for a drink to calm his nerves.

"Now, if we could have four volunteers to come and stand in front of each of our subjects, please?"

Immediately, Sue's friend jumped up and stood in front of her, clearly pleased to be a part of proceedings once again. She was followed by the two men on the back row, and the other woman from the front row. Tom could see her name tag read 'Melanie' as she positioned herself in front of him with a big smile.

Jordan handed each of the test subjects a pair of safety goggles and gloves, asking them to put them on. Doing as they were told, he then gave the four of them a glass beaker to hold.

As he was handing out the elements for the test, Bethany explained that they were going to carry out something called an Acid Test which was first used in the 1950s. Donning gloves and safety goggles herself, she took what looked like a small chemistry set from inside a box kept beneath the table.

"The best way to test for hydrochloric acid," she explained, "is with silver nitrate solution." With a dropper, she introduced a clear liquid to a test tube that she'd positioned in a rack on the table. "If a white precipitate forms when I add silver nitrate, then the acid is in evidence."

A second dropper released its contents into the test tube and, as

Tom watched, he could see a swirl of white substance forming in the glass tube in front of his eyes. Impressive, but he couldn't see what this had to do with the rest of the study.

"Of course, another way to tell if hydrochloric acid is present is to see if it melts through metal." Bethany now took an empty glass beaker and laid a sheet of tin foil over the top. "Watch what happens when the liquid hits the foil."

She squeezed the second dropper once more, and a perfectly formed bead of liquid fell to land on the foil where it fizzed briefly before melting its way through the shiny surface into the beaker below.

"Powerful stuff, right?"

There was a muttering amongst the gathered participants, all no doubt suddenly wondering where this was going. Tom too felt a grip of uncertainty in his guts, but not wanting to be the first to show fear, he swallowed it down and kept quiet.

Jordan was positioned at the furthest point from where Tom was standing, and he watched him walk slowly and deliberately down the line of volunteers. His first stop was with Joseph, where he clicked his fingers in front of his face and said just one word. "Sleep."

Unbelievably, Tom watched the old man's head lower, his loose chins coming to rest on the top of his thick roll neck jumper. The rest of his body remained in position, upright, other than a slight stoop, his right arm still at a ninety-degree angle, holding his empty beaker.

Jordan continued down the line, next sending Sue and then Sally into the land of nod before he reached Tom, whose heartbeat had kicked up a notch in anticipation. Tom watched Jordan's hand come up in front of his eyes, saw his fingers click a beat, and heard one of his least and most favourite words.

"Sleep."

Overcome with a sudden tiredness, Tom felt his head fall. He could feel his breath coming slow and calm as Jordan's soothing words washed over him.

"Once you've woken up, we are going to put some hydrochloric acid inside your beakers. In front of you is a volunteer who you've already met. That person is your target. When you wake up, you will hear a bell ring shortly afterwards. As soon as you hear that bell, you will throw your beaker of acid over the target standing in front of you. And in three…two…one…you're wide awake."

Tom's eyes opened and he found himself still standing, facing Melanie. Jordan slowly walked back down the line of subjects pouring a substance up to the halfway point into each of their beakers.

"Well done," he told them all. "You're doing great."

From behind him, Tom heard a tinkling bell, reminiscent of the kind that sat upon the handlebars of a bicycle. Without hesitation, he drew his arm in and then flung it back outwards completely involuntarily, sending the contents of his beaker flying over Melanie. Her friendly smile was gone.

10

BETHANY

"**I** honestly didn't expect it to work!"

For the first time, I was actually verging on enjoying my session with Leigh. Ok, so *enjoying* it was a bit strong, but the days were getting fractionally longer and while it was still mostly cold and damp, today had been bright and almost Spring-like in its demeanour. That, coupled with stage one of the project going so well, had put me in a rare good mood.

My walk to Leigh's place from the bus stop had been almost blinding with the sun bouncing off rain-slicked pavements, and I had to squint to be able to see where I was going. It was ok though, even when I trod in a puddle that sent splashes of muddy water over my boots. I felt as though I finally had something else to focus my energy on.

Now, in the over-warm consulting room, I found myself unusually spilling my guts to Leigh. I could tell she was thrilled to bits, even though she tried to hide it behind the professional mask that she always wore. I could see how pleased she was in the misguided thought that we'd finally made some kind of breakthrough in our sessions.

"Why wouldn't you expect it to work?" she asked me as she twisted the chain of her necklace around her finger. "Did you have a look at those websites I wrote down for you?"

"Yeah, yeah, I did. I hadn't heard of some of them before, but they gave me some great pointers." She almost looked smug to be the provider of knowledge that had helped someone on their path. "Although Jordan thought it would be better to replace the water in the beakers with confetti. He didn't want to piss anyone off."

"Good idea." Leigh laughed, the show of unprofessional joviality not looking as though it sat too comfortably on her face.

I'd had to agree with Jordan. It wasn't often that I did, but the thought of having to deal with angry volunteers who were soaked with water wasn't that appealing.

"Honestly, though, you should have seen their faces! Both the subjects *and* their targets. It was hilarious."

"I bet." Leigh smiled in her more usual, and much safer, non-committal way.

God, I wasn't even sure if I was supposed to be sharing sensitive things about other people with Leigh. Surely there was some weird client confidentiality thing in effect though. Our subjects had signed their secrets over to us, and in turn, my counsellor was bound to a confidentiality agreement with me. It had to be ok, didn't it?

"It's safe to share your thoughts with me, Bethany. If you want to, of course. Nothing will leave these four walls."

This was obviously why she got paid the big bucks by my mother. She could tell what I was thinking without me even having to say anything at all. Straight away, the thought of my mother put me on edge. I'd been seeing Leigh ever since I'd been forced to change universities. All my mother's idea, obviously, as were my regular counselling sessions.

It wasn't that she actually cared about me. She'd never cared about me. It was purely to get me out of her hair so that I would stop being a nuisance in her perfect manicured life. This was a quick fix for her. Throw money at the problem so that it goes away. And usually, it did.

Jesus Christ, even thinking about her made the raised skin of my scars start to itch, and I involuntarily started to scratch at my arm through the thin sleeve of my sweatshirt.

"Bethany?"

"Do you ever tell my mother anything about me?" I stared at Leigh, my eyes undoubtedly portraying my misdirected anger. "I mean, I know she pays for these sessions, so does that mean you have to report back to her?" I knew the answer already. Knew it was a stupid question, but just needed her to confirm it for me, I supposed.

"No, Bethany. As I said, this is a safe place for you to speak openly. Did you want to talk about your mother?"

I couldn't help but release a bark of laughter. What a cliché. I started to pick at one of my scars underneath my sleeve.

"Why is that funny to you, Bethany?"

"It's just all so clichéd, isn't it? You might as well have asked me to talk about my childhood. Done a whole Freudian number on me."

"Do you want to talk about your childhood?"

"What? You mean about how my father totally abandoned us? How my mother preferred my sister to me? Until she left me, that is, so, technically, my sister abandoned me, too. You'd think my mother would have liked me then, but she decided it was my fault Katie left. She took it out on me ever since, and I eventually turned into the complete and utter fuck-up that's sitting in front of you."

"Why do you feel like a fuck-up?"

Those words didn't sound right coming out of Leigh's mouth. It was like hearing a priest swearing. Crazy, I know, she probably swore like a navvy down at the pub at the weekend or had a black belt in cage fighting for all I knew, but right here in her warm cosy office, it just seemed off-kilter.

"You know why. You know what happened with the police and everything."

"I only know the basics, Bethany. I know what was in the police report that was provided to me, but why don't you tell me your side of things? Maybe I can help. Maybe I can help you understand what happened and how you can move past it."

I stopped picking at my arm, noticing a spot of blood blooming on my sleeve, and dropped my head into my hands. How could things have turned so completely and utterly shit over the course of the last hour? I'd been so excited earlier about the way forward, and now it had been flipped upside-down. This was why I didn't like to talk about stuff. It was easier to just keep things to myself. Forget about them.

Leigh had obviously noticed the stain on my sleeve too, as she quietly got up to retrieve a small green tin with a white cross on it from a drawer in her desk, knocking over the framed photo of her cat as she did so.

"Is he yours?" I asked as she righted the frame. Stupid bloody question - why would she have a photo of someone else's cat on her desk?

"Yes. Do you like cats?"

"They're ok. What's his name?"

"It's quite unimaginative, really." She laughed self-deprecatingly as she removed some items from her tin. "He's called Thomas. Thomas Hardy. I tell people he's named after the famous poet, but truthfully, it's just because he's a ginger Tom and I have a massive crush on Tom Hardy. Terrible, isn't it?"

I couldn't help but smile. Tom Hardy was pretty hot. I'd always liked older men. My mind slipped briefly back to the previous evening at the library annexe. Tom had been the other participant that I'd hoped would show up, and I was doubly pleased he had. Not only was he completely susceptible, but he was, well... I nodded in agreement. "He's very cute, though."

"Yes, he is," she said, and I wasn't sure if she was referring to the cat or the actor. She added, in a stage whisper, "Although, if I could, I'd rather have a dog."

I knew it.

"Here," she said gently, holding out some antiseptic cream and a plaster.

Why the hell did she have to be so bloody nice? I wasn't used to liking any of my counsellors, but Leigh was verging on being a human instead of just another nodding dog therapist. It made me realise that, for all I knew, she might go home lonely every night to her cat and eat a microwave meal for one while watching Coronation Street and sipping on a Chardonnay. We all had our crosses to bear.

I rolled up my sleeve, keeping an eye on her face as I did so. As much as I was always conscious about covering up the latticework on my arms to others, sometimes I couldn't help but take pleasure in seeing the shock in their eyes when I revealed my scars. Leigh didn't flinch, denying me my satisfaction this time. She'd seen it all before, no doubt, and worse.

Part of me wished I could stop giving her such a hard time, but it was so difficult. I didn't like forming bonds with other people, because at some point I knew that the relationship was going to be ripped to shreds and I'd end up being on my own again. It was much easier not to bother in the first place. Not only that, but I had to remember that whatever connection I created with her wasn't real, anyway. She was paid to care.

I dabbed antiseptic on my arm, letting it soak into the skin a little before positioning the plaster over the top and rolling my sleeve back down. I took my time, letting the pinpricks of moisture in my eyes seep back inside their tear ducts before she could see them. The last thing I wanted was to be offered a tissue from the ever-present box on the table. Leigh held out her hand for me to drop the plaster backing into it.

"Why don't we talk about your project some more?" she suggested. "You can talk me through it in our last few minutes." It was more of a statement than a question, but it was safe ground.

I nodded. Why not? I'd had enough of thinking about the reasons that had got me here in the first place. As usual, I knew I would find it far easier to talk about the reasons that would get me away from here, instead.

"So, what happens next? It all sounds very exciting."

"I suppose so." I sniffed, looking up at her encouraging expression. "Well, we've got three subjects to choose from, actually." I felt my equilibrium returning a little with the change of subject back to present day.

I couldn't believe we had that many to pick and choose from bearing in mind the limited number that had turned up and, already, I was leaning towards one of them more than the others. Sue, Joseph and Tom had all thrown the contents of the beaker over their targets. Tom and Joseph almost immediately when the bell had sounded, and Sue just fractionally afterwards.

In my head, I'd pretty much discounted Sue already as, first of all, she was pretty bloody annoying, and I wasn't sure whether or not she'd go blabbing about everything to her friend after each session. Secondly, I had a sneaking feeling that she hadn't really gone into a trance at all. The way she'd thrown the confetti slightly later than the other two looked, well, like she was just copying what they were doing. Like I'd thought in the beginning, she just wanted it too much.

Leigh nodded sagely as I explained this. "So, that leaves the two men?"

"Yeah."

"Does Jordan have a preference?" she asked.

"He wants to use the older man," I told her. "I think he feels sorry for him. He's lost his wife and Jordan just wants to make life better for him."

"And you don't?"

"I just… I think we should use the other guy."

"Why?"

"I don't know, exactly." I felt my face getting hot. "He just feels right."

Leigh nodded. "Go on."

"Anyway, next, we need to get him in for conditioning. We need to condition him into thinking that he can do what we want him to do, even if it goes against his natural belief system."

I had to think quickly about how I phrased this to Leigh. I was pretty sure I'd never been wholly honest about the full experiment, as I'd expected her to talk me out of it. That was the problem with white lies, you had to continually keep on top of them.

"And what makes you think you can do that?" she asked.

I thought back to the questionnaire Tom had submitted. Short, elusive answers which alluded to something dreadful in his past that he still carried with him. Something that had caused him to have a criminal record and problems with control. He was far from perfect, but ironically, that made him perfect for what I needed. "His suggestibility is through the roof," I told her.

"He sounds ideal," said Leigh. "Have you got your triggers that will induce and remove the hypnotic state all sorted out? Sights? Sounds? Smells, even?"

This was something else Jordan and I still needed to discuss, but I'd been giving it some thought already. "What's your favourite song, Leigh? Maybe I could use that? Other than Stormzy, obviously?"

Leigh laughed for the third time in the session, pushing a strand of hair back behind her ear. While the frivolity sat uncomfortably on her face, it suited her, nonetheless. She should do it more often. Perhaps people felt the same about me.

"Nothing wrong with a bit of Stormzy," she said.

Maybe I'd misjudged her before. Nice clothes, expensive

perfume and an age range of thirty to thirty-five didn't mean that you couldn't like grime music, did it? We all had our weird hang-ups after all, and people in glass houses, like me, really shouldn't throw stones.

"I do like Simon and Garfunkel, although they would be well before your time."

I'd heard the names before but couldn't relate them to any music I'd ever heard. No doubt the kind of easy listening crap my mother played on Magic FM. I looked at her, my expression probably conveying my lack of interest.

Leigh distractedly stroked her locket as she spoke, and I wondered fleetingly if the song reminded her of whoever's photo was tucked inside. "Interestingly, it's said that they were inspired to write one of their songs following the assassination of JFK, Bobby Kennedy's brother."

That had my attention. "Seriously?"

"Seriously. I don't know how true it is, but yes, ostensibly 'The Sound of Silence' was written as a tribute. It's a beautiful song. Very deep. I think you might like it."

My mind whirred and I took out my phone to tap it into YouTube. I skipped past the annoying adverts and was initially surprised not to find a music video. Instead, there was just the cover of an old album which morphed into a black and white image of two men that I presumed must be Simon and Garfunkel.

I wasn't prepared in the slightest for what I heard. Two voices and a guitar, and the words... powerful, haunting. I closed my eyes and listened until the final notes echoed from my smartphone. It made me want to cry.

"Maybe that would be a good place for us to stop for today, Bethany." Leigh's voice brought me back from that other world. "You've done really well."

I opened my eyes to see her pick up her watch and fasten it around her slender, unmarked wrist. I became aware of my tongue twirling around my lip piercing as I battled internally with how I was feeling. For once, I wasn't pulling my coat on, desperate to leave. I found myself wanting to trust her, to tell her more. It was a disorientating feeling and words swum in my head as I tried to form them concisely, without giving them total free rein to spill over.

"I loved him, you know?" The words were out before I could cut them off.

"Who do you mean, Bethany?"

"Daniel. My boyfriend back home."

"I'm sure you did love him, Bethany. Do you not love him anymore?"

I was aware that Leigh kept using my name, trying to force familiarity between us, trying to lure more from me, but I didn't care. "I...I don't know. She tried to steal him from me. Make him leave me, just like everyone else leaves me."

"Who did, Bethany?"

"His wife."

11

TOM

Tom walked through the front door after another mind-numbing day at work. He didn't normally get wound up when he wasn't drinking, but Jesus Christ, he could have swung for bloody Lydia today. Sometimes it felt as though her whole reason for being was to make his life a misery for eight hours a day. So far, she was doing a great job.

He'd tried to shrug off his annoyance on the way home, but it clung to him like shit on a blanket. Urgh. If he was honest with himself, his bad mood was probably partially down to the fact that he hadn't heard anything from Jordan and Bethany yet.

They'd told everyone they'd be in touch in the next twenty-four hours to let them know the final selection. It was now nearly forty-eight hours later and he felt like he was getting RSI in his fingers from checking his emails and text messages on his phone every few minutes. Still, at least he felt like he fitted in with the other phone addicts when he had his coffee break in the staff room.

Shrugging his coat off, Tom made his way to the fridge to grab a cold beer. He knew Gemma wouldn't be back for a little while yet, so he could down it quickly before she walked through the door and gave him an earful.

Beer in hand, he got the bottle opener from the drawer and released the hops with a satisfying sssst noise. He aimed the metal cap at the bin against the far wall, missing as usual, and leaned back against the sink, retrieving his phone from his back pocket after it clunked against the cupboard below.

As he placed it on the side, he noticed that there'd been a missed call from a number he didn't recognise. Putting the bottle down, Tom wiped his wet fingers against the leg of his jeans. He couldn't believe he'd forgotten that his phone had been on silent for the whole journey home after he'd been so obsessive about checking it all day.

Swiping against the voicemail icon, he held the phone to his ear and waited for the robotic message to finish from his service provider. Could it be any slower as it spelt out the phone number and the time of the call? Finally, the actual message clicked in.

"Hi, it's um Jordan."

Tom felt a little jolt of excitement tripping through his heart, and he held the phone closer to his ear, not wanting to miss his quiet tone.

"I'm just ringing to let you know that we'd really like to have you as the subject for our research study...if you were still interested?"

Closing his eyes, Tom wasn't sure what emotion he was feeling. A strange mixture of hope and fear, excitement and relief. There wasn't a name for it that he could think of.

"Um...well, if you could give me a call back just to let me know, and then we can arrange our next session with you. Um...yeah, that'd be great. Thanks. Bye."

Tom realised he'd been holding his breath throughout the whole message and he let it out slowly between clenched teeth. He hadn't thought much further ahead than the initial meeting at the library, unsure as to whether he would even be selected to continue with the research. He'd wanted it, sure, if for no other reason than to appease Gemma; but now it was being handed to him, he felt pretty nervous, too.

He reached for his beer and as he did so, his phone vibrated in his other hand, still on silent. It was Gemma and he answered straight away, keen to share some good news for a change.

"Hiya, it's me."

"Everything ok?" he asked.

"Yeah." A sigh. "Just letting you know I'm running a bit late."

"Ok, no worries." He paused, tracing a drop of condensation with the tip of his finger as it worked its way down the side of the beer bottle. "Gem?"

"Yeah?"

"I just heard about the research project."

There was a brief silence, loaded with expectation. "And?"

"I got through, Gem. They want to use me for the research." The phone went quiet again for a beat, just long enough for Tom to think he'd lost her. "Gem?"

"I'm still here, Tom, I just…I just needed a second. That's… that's great news! Are you pleased?"

"I think so."

"It's going to work, Tom. I have a good feeling about this."

"But what if it doesn't?" Tom was working the beer bottle round and round on the kitchen worktop with his fingers, watching a water ring slowly forming beneath it.

"If it doesn't, then at least we tried, eh?"

"Yeah."

"Look, why don't I grab us a takeaway on the way home? We can celebrate."

"Sure, why not. That'd be good."

Gemma ended the call and Tom was left standing in front of the sink, beer bottle in hand, looking at his image reflected back at him from the backdrop of darkness kept at bay on the other side of the windowpane.

This meant so much to her, he knew. It showed that she still cared and that she still had hope for them. For Gemma, it must have been like wrestling with a deranged soul some nights as he'd battled with sleep, and alcohol, and anger; and yet she was still here. The fact that she'd even sent him the advertisement for the study in the first place meant there was a glimmer of hope for them to work things out.

Keeping hold of his own gaze in the windowpane, Tom made a decision and swallowed hard before pouring the contents of the bottle down the sink. Breathing deeply, he caught the heady whiff of fermented yeast as it fizzed and swirled its way down the plughole, but he maintained eye contact with himself.

"You've got this."

GEMMA WALKED through the door about half an hour later, her heavy coat bringing inside the freshness of the chilly evening, which was in turn engulfed by the aromas of sweet and sour pork and crispy chilli beef. Tom's mouth watered and Baloo suddenly appeared, his nose twitching as he wound his way around the legs of his favourite person. Gemma dropped the bag of food on the kitchen counter and scooped the cat up in her arms, covering his head in kisses while he stared balefully at the cartons of food that Tom pulled from the bag.

"Not for you, mate," Tom told him.

"It's not fair, is it baby?" Gemma crooned before putting him back down on the floor and shrugging off her coat.

As Tom served up the food, Gemma broke into the thin bag which held the prawn crackers captive and started munching on one straight away.

"God, I'm starving." She covered her mouth as she spoke.

How Tom wished they were a normal couple, about to spend a regular evening together. They could crack open a bottle of wine and compare their respective workdays, moaning about how tough it was to work in nursing, while still knowing they would never choose to do anything else in a million years.

"How was your journey home?" he asked, chickening out.

"Fine," she told him, pulling out a stool at the kitchen counter. "Lots of traffic though." Gemma filled her mouth with another prawn cracker and Tom followed suit, the uncomfortable silence accompanied by the noise of chewing. This was what they did now, when they spoke at all.

"Drink?" Tom asked as he reached behind him to the fridge. "We have still or sparkling."

"Sparkling please." Gemma gave a self-conscious grin, no doubt awkward in what could be construed as a reference to alcohol.

Tom was taken back to the first night that they'd started living together, sat on the floor of their flat, surrounded by boxes, eating Chinese food straight from the cartons and clinking Styrofoam cups full of Prosecco. They'd been so happy and filled with optimism, and he could remember the twinkle in Gemma's eyes. There was a faint echo of that same sparkle now.

Grabbing a bottle of fizzy water, Tom filled their glasses. They ate accompanied by the sounds of a local radio station, the DJ bemoaning the coldness of the day and valiantly trying to lift his listeners' spirits with cheesy songs from the eighties. It was comforting to know that the day to day lives of other people were carrying on in the world outside their own four walls.

Tom could tell that Gemma wanted to talk about the research study but undoubtedly didn't want to push him on it just in case it ruined the delicate armistice they had achieved. He knew she wouldn't be able to hold off for long though, and decided to save her from her awkwardness.

"Good news then, eh? About the research." He saw her shoulders drop a little.

"Are you ok with it?" She toyed with the noodles on her plate. "I mean, I know you weren't keen and I talked you into it, but you know I only did it for us, don't you?"

"Yeah, I do."

"Ok, good."

Gemma's phone pinged from the confines of her bag and their two sets of eyes travelled over towards it before coming back to rest on each other.

"You can check it if you want," Tom told her.

"It'll keep." Gemma put her fork down and held out her hand to her husband. He could see her eyes still shining, but now with tears instead of happiness. Her emotions were always so easy to read.

"Gemma, what is it?" Tom asked, taking her opened palm in both of his hands. A tiny, injured bird held safely. "We're celebrating, aren't we?" He felt desperate to keep the mood up, keep the memory alive of sparkling eyes and the future full of hope. It wasn't the time for emotion and soul searching. Not now. Not yet. Not when he'd poured beer down the sink, ready to take on the world, to take the first steps. He needed Gemma on board, too.

"We are." She swiped at her eyes with her other hand. "Of course, we are. It's just all a bit emotional, you know?"

Tom nodded, his eyes sliding away from hers, knowing instinctively that her pain was about to surface, ugly and unwelcome, and aware that he wouldn't be able to cope with it on fizzy water alone.

"I just want it to work so much."

He knew that if he looked at her, he'd see her chin quivering and her eyes about to spill over with a cascade of tears. Behind her, another ping came from her bag and Tom grasped on the excuse for a change of subject, unable to bear the shame of where the current one was taking him.

"Someone wants you," he pointed out.

"It doesn't matter. We're talking here, aren't we?"

Tom felt chastised and pulled his hands back away from hers. Why did everything always have to be talked about? Regurgitated again and again, when surely it would be so much easier to sweep under the proverbial carpet and click reboot? He was doing what she wanted with the research study and that was pretty much all he had to offer at the moment.

"Please, Tom?"

He risked a look at his wife and saw two tracks running down her cheeks from her eyes. If he was honest with himself, he was surprised that those tracks hadn't formed natural gullies over the last few months and he hated himself that little bit more. Her phone pinged twice in quick succession.

"Jesus! Why don't you just check your phone?" Tom was aware he was turning his anger at himself onto his wife, but he couldn't help it.

"It's probably just work," she placated him. "It's not important. *This* is what's important." Gemma's hands opened up to him in supplication. "Please, Tom, can't we just talk?"

She was openly crying now, and Tom was torn between offering comfort to the person he loved the most, and anger for the shame she was unwittingly heaping upon him. He chose the second option.

"You're an oncology nurse, for fuck's sake. How can you think that isn't important?" Tom stood, grabbing their plates and taking them to the sink. He felt like an absolute tosser the minute the words were out of his mouth, but he kept going nonetheless with his back to his wife. "You should feel grateful to still be able to do the job that you love."

He heard her sharp intake of breath. "Tom, that's not fair."

He stood silently, still facing away from her. She was right, it wasn't fair, but nothing about their situation was fair. He felt like weeping too, if he had any more tears. Gemma's stool scraped against the lino and Tom raised his head, watching her reflection retreating in the window.

He heard her footsteps running upstairs and the door to the bedroom closing. Tom could picture his wife lying, sobbing on the bed and he hated himself for his inability to be able to comfort her the way she needed him to. But he had no comfort to give, not even for himself. He sighed and started to scrape the leftover food into the bin.

Gemma's phone pinged again from inside her bag. Someone really wanted to get hold of her. Wiping his hands on his jeans, Tom reached inside and pulled out the phone just as the screen went dark.

Before thinking twice, Tom pressed the button at the bottom of the phone, watching the screen light up once more. There had been five missed text messages, all from the same person. Before his brain registered what his fingers were doing, Tom had tapped on the icon, revealing its contents, each one stacked below like a family of Russian Dolls.

Hello, lovely.

Are you there?

Just thinking about you and hoping you're ok x

Remember, you've done everything you can now

I'm here for you x

Tom's heart stuttered in his chest.

Ash.

12

BETHANY

Daniel's wife was a bitch.

I'd never actually met the woman, but she'd managed to ruin my life, even more than it was ruined already. I couldn't believe that she was still doing it from so far away.

I'd stomped all the way home after my session with Leigh instead of taking the bus like normal. I didn't care that it was dark and that the streets were pretty desolate. I just needed to clear my head. This morning seemed like light years away when I'd splashed through puddles, excited about what was to come. Now, I just felt like shit and while it had briefly felt good to let Leigh in, it had also opened up a great big can of worms inside my head. One that I'd kept tightly sealed and tucked away under lock and key. Now the can was wide open and there were worms everywhere. Damn it.

I hadn't meant to tell her anything and I couldn't understand why I'd let her in so easily. It was almost like she'd snuck up on me by coming through the back door, and before I knew it, I was blabbing about things that had no good reason to be taken out for an airing. At the time it had felt right, but now, the more I thought about it, it just felt uncomfortable to have shared so much.

She'd seen it in my eyes afterwards. The uncertainty. And, well versed in listening to a million sad songs, she'd given me her mobile number just as I was leaving. No doubt worried she'd pushed me too far and that I was about to go and do something stupid. But my whole life had been something stupid, so why stop now? I'd taken her number, typing the digits into my phone as she read them out and giving her a personal ringtone. 'Blinded by Your Grace', of course. It had to be. She'd smiled as I told her that, our little joke, all the while pressing on me to call her if I felt I needed to. We both knew I wouldn't, though.

I made it back to my student accommodation ok, briefly popping into the local corner shop to buy a bag of crisps and a small bottle of vodka to wash them down with. I could hear my mother's clipped voice in my head as I'd placed my goods on the counter, saying "You should never drink alone." It made me change my mind and ask the shop assistant for a bigger bottle instead.

Back in my darkened room I purposely left the harsh overhead light off, choosing instead to switch on the desk lamp. Through the window at the far end of the room, all I could see was night and a few lighted windows from the apartments across the road which glowed, bragging of the happy lives carrying on behind them. I pulled the cheap green curtains closed briskly and turned back to my own crappy life.

My small wooden desk was covered with papers and books that I was using for my studies and my laptop sat open amongst them with a garland of post-it notes framing its screen. I couldn't wait for my course to be over so I could get on with things. Get some money and stop being beholden to the woman that had given birth to me.

I put my stash on top of a pile of folders and looked around for something to mix my vodka with. All I had was an old bottle of orange squash, but I didn't want to risk bumping into anyone in the shared kitchen so it would have to do. I poured myself a shot, followed by a dash of squash, and sipped. It was pretty foul, as I'd suspected it would be, but I didn't care. It was better than nothing.

Sitting down on my red duvet which was decorated with white appliqué flowers, I tried not to look in the direction of my bedside cabinet. Instead, I took my phone out of my bag to distract myself. I tried to tell myself that I wasn't going to look for updates about Daniel, but that lasted for all of about ten seconds.

I'd thought I was doing pretty well in gradually getting over him during the last few months. Of course, most of that involved pretending we were still together to anyone that asked, namely Jordan. I even sometimes pretended to myself. But today's session with Leigh had made me remember the truth, and how empty I felt without him. It was a familiar feeling, emptiness. One that had been my companion throughout most of my life.

My first port of call was Instagram. Not that I had access to his account anymore as it had been set to private, and I'd been removed from the honoured few who could see photos of his filtered life. His wife had made sure of that. Instead, I'd followed a few of his friends' pages who didn't recognise my username and now and again posted their own filtered images. Sometimes he cropped up in them, but mostly he didn't. There hadn't been any for a while.

I tried Facebook next. It was bound to be a wild goose chase as usual, but you never knew. One day, he might just realise that his wife was an absolute control freak and that he'd stupidly thrown away something really special with me. Then he would unblock me and beg me to go back to him. I'd make him wait for a while, obviously, just to teach him a lesson, but I'd go back to him in a heartbeat. I'd spent so many hours just daydreaming about him wanting me back. Different scenarios, different words, different outfits, even. But all of them involved me sinking into his arms and basically living happily ever after. My dreams were living, breathing Disney films.

To my shame, I'd even tried to look at his wife's profile. I'd felt sick when I did it the first time, but she'd obviously blocked me, too. Like I wanted to look at her stupid face anyway!

There were no new images that I could find of him anywhere on social media so I had to make do with scrolling back through some old pictures of him on my phone. He wasn't one for posing for photos, so most of the images were when I managed to catch him unawares, just gazing into the distance, his brown eyes far away. I loved them.

Not one of the photos showed the two of us together. Not by any choice of mine, obviously. I would have loved to have a proper picture of the two of us, but he was always really careful not to let that happen, just in case his wife ever saw them. He never said that, but I knew it was what he was thinking.

I knew when we first got together that he was married, so it's not like I went into the relationship blindly. But I also knew he wasn't happy. I wasn't happy either, so it was like two lost souls finding each other. A meeting of minds. We were magnetised with no choice but to pull together. "Written in the stars," he'd said.

A tear fell unattended from my eye and landed with a tiny splash against the cracked screen of my phone, only serving to remind me how real my pain was in losing him. How could it still be so raw after all this time and all this distance? It hurt… so…much.

Heart feeling as brittle as the most fragile glass, I knew I had to do something before the pain smashed it completely, creating piercing shards that would undoubtedly kill me. It ached and throbbed so badly, and there was only one way to ease the anguish: turning it into a physical thing. I reached for the drawer in my bedside cabinet, pulling it open to reveal its contents.

My hands scrabbled around inside, emptying books, hair grips, lip salves and other crap that had manifested in there. Tucked away at the back, I found what I was looking for. A small white envelope, which I wasted no time in ripping open. Inside lay three razor blades, their metal glinting against the glow from my lamp.

Rolling back one of my sleeves to reveal the scarring that decorated my forearm, I wasted no time in taking out my tiny weapon and holding it against the skin. I didn't need to press too heavily before being rewarded with a small red dot. A tiny pinprick against a pale backdrop. Snow White made flesh and…blood. I pulled the blade across my arm a couple of inches, watching the pin prick become a thin trail, and I felt the agony in my chest lighten, replaced instead by the physical pain in my arm. Now I could see it realised, it felt better, safer, tangible.

I lay back on my bed with my eyes closed, feeling a sense of relief. I didn't bother to wipe away the blood. I hadn't cut too deep, so I wasn't worried. I just allowed the pain from my stinging arm to wash over me like a balm and draw out the poison from my heart. I visualised that it was almost like having someone sucking the venom from me following a snake bite.

I knew it wouldn't last long, sadly. Like a hit of heroin, the feeling of calm would wear off all too quickly, leaving me consumed with guilt and disappointment in myself for being so weak. That was the way it worked, the pattern that never deviated. It was exhausting.

Before the downer could kick in, I knew I needed to take action. Opening my eyes once again, I looked up at my cork board which was pinned above my bed. I'd decorated it without much thought. Timetables, receipts, letters and cards all jostled for attention, but my eyes bypassed all of them to land on the one photo of Daniel that I'd printed off and kept so that I felt he was always with me while I slept. I'd thought about framing it, but that *really* would have made me nuts. It was bad enough having to see a shrink as it was, let alone having a framed photo of my ex on show.

Sitting back up, I swung my legs off the side of the bed, once again facing my cluttered desk. At the front of it sat the profiles of the research subjects that Jordan and I had spent hours pouring over the day before, bickering about who we were going to use for our final choice. To give him his credit, Jordan had put up a bit of a fight to use Joseph, which was really unlike him, but I'd gotten my own way in the end, as I knew I would. All that unrequited love used to my advantage.

On the top of the pile was Tom's profile. The filmy plastic wallet contained his questionnaire and the copious notes that I'd drawn up following the first session at the library. On the very top was a Photo Booth picture of him attached with a green plastic paperclip. If I glanced at it quickly, or squinted, he looked a little bit like Daniel. Similar hair style and face shape, and around the same age, too. I'd noticed it that night at the library, but I'd managed to pull myself together and not stare too much.

Twisting around and reaching behind me, I pulled out the little yellow bobble-headed pin that held the photo of Daniel in place on the cork board. The paper fluttered down to land next to me on my duvet. I picked it up and held it in my hand, looking between the two images.

What was I doing? Why was I clinging onto a man who didn't want me? Without giving myself a moment more of hesitation, I ripped the glossy image of Daniel in half, and then into quarters, the noise satisfying to my ears. I dropped the shredded photograph into my wastepaper basket where it came to rest on top of my used razor blade, covering up the evidence.

Purposefully turning my back on it, I let my gaze return to Tom's image. It was time to move on.

13

TOM

Tom had always thought that when someone was hypnotized, they just fell into a 'deep sleep'. After all, that's what all the old stage hypnotists said wasn't it? "You're falling into a deep sleep," then, blam, that person would completely zonk out. In reality, it was more like closing your eyes for forty winks, and, during the whole process, you could still hear and be aware of most of what was going on around you. The first session had proved that to him, which was why he wasn't quite so worried second time around.

He'd been summoned once again to the library annexe to have his first private session with Bethany and Jordan, and instead of taking a diversion to the pub as he'd done previously, he'd bravely gone straight there.

Arriving on time, he could see Bethany illuminated through the windows, head bent over a laptop and her hair falling forwards, partially covering her face. As he approached, she pulled it back and tied it up loosely with a hairband from her wrist. She'd be a pretty girl if it wasn't for that hideous lip ring. He'd never understood why anyone wanted to deface themselves like that. He hadn't been keen when Gemma had wanted a tattoo, even though it was only a small one on her hip. She'd gone ahead and done it anyway, though, so he'd had to put up with it.

She'd texted him earlier to wish him luck, obviously still uncertain as to whether he'd go through with the next step of the research after their failed attempt at a celebration. *Thanks*, he'd replied, cautious that his words would be relayed back to the omnipresent Ash. It really did feel like the last hope, for both of them.

As he pushed through the door, Bethany looked up from what she was doing, a smile spreading across her face as she came over to greet him.

"Hey, you made it. That's great."

"Of course," said Tom. "I'm looking forward to you guys helping me to get a good night's sleep at last."

"Well, we'll certainly see what we can do." She touched his shoulder warmly. "Come on in. Would you like a cup of tea or anything? I've just asked Jordan to go and grab some biscuits."

"Ah no, thanks. I'm fine."

"Ok. Well, grab a seat."

Tom did as he was told, feeling a little bit like a bug under a microscope with Bethany's gaze on him.

"Have you had a good day?" she asked, returning to her laptop.

"Um, yeah." Tom shrugged. "Although, this is probably the highlight so far." He noticed Bethany's face colouring and hoped she hadn't thought he was referring to anything other than getting started on the trial. Before he could say otherwise, Jordan blew in through the door in a bundle of oversized Puffa jacket, carrying a selection of packets of biscuits, one of which fell on the floor.

"Oops. Sorry. Anyone for a smashed-up digestive?" he asked with a shy grin.

Tom laughed, feeling like he needed to put Jordan at ease

instead of the other way around. "Go on, then. And maybe I will have a cup of tea, after all."

Five minutes later, and all three were sitting around one of the cheap plastic topped tables, having a lukewarm cup of tea and a biscuit. Bethany had made the tea far too weak for Tom's taste, but there was something comforting about its sweet milky flavour, and as they made small talk, he could feel his shoulders drop slightly.

Tom was somewhat despondent to see that Jordan had once again set up his iPhone to record the session, but, other than that and the laptop, he didn't see any other equipment or beakers of confetti acid lying around, which was somewhat relieving.

Trying to subtly look up at the clock without appearing too ungracious he saw that he'd already been there for half an hour and he wondered when they were going to get started.

"Um, I don't mean to be rude but—" he began.

"I know, times ticking on isn't it," said Bethany.

"Yeah, a bit."

"Don't worry." That disarming smile again. "We've already started."

Tom couldn't help but feel a bit disconcerted. Was he in a trance without knowing? No, that was just daft. "Um, ok."

"Do you remember the last time you had amnesia?" Bethany had gotten up from her chair and moved around behind it, hands on the back, blue eyes still firmly on Tom.

"Um…" He didn't know how to answer that.

"Do you know how to drive a car?"

Ok, that was a weird sidestep. Tom decided to just go with it. "Yes."

"And do you know that feeling when you're driving and you just forget what you're doing?"

Tom laughed, relieved that the questions were starting to tie up. "Yes."

"And you sort of just forget where you are?"

"Yes."

"Ok, great," said Jordan. "I'd like you to remember that feeling."

Tom found himself immediately remembering the almost trance like state of driving along in his car, mind totally blank to surroundings and motions and feelings. That moment before his mind remembered the job it was supposed to be doing in its conscious state and clicked back in to make him think *where on earth am I?*

"Now, Tom," continued Jordan slowly and calmly. "I'm going to show you a pattern on the laptop, and whenever you see that particular pattern, in these particular colours, you will find yourself falling into a trance state, although your eyes will stay open."

Tom felt himself nodding as Jordan opened the laptop in front of him and carried on in his soft tone of voice.

"You won't have any memory of what happens when you're in that trance state, Tom. And whenever you see this pattern that I'm showing you now, whether it's on a screen like this, or anywhere else, you will immediately go into this trance state, quite comfortably."

Other than Jordan's voice, Tom was only aware of the small monochrome dots on the screen in front of him, and his breathing, slow and relaxed.

"When the pattern is removed from your field of vision, it will feel like you're being counted awake from five to one, and you'll have no memory of what happened when you were in the trance state. Now, I'm going to close the laptop."

Tom felt so relaxed that he would've agreed to pretty much anything at that point, and when the laptop closed with a snap, he felt almost bereft to be brought back to full awareness again. He blinked his eyes a couple of times and regarded the others.

"Hey, Tom," said Bethany.

He focused on her, letting Jordan slip into his peripheral vision.

"Can you tell me how long you think you were looking at the screen for?" she asked.

"Um, I'm not sure. Maybe around twenty seconds?"

Jordan and Bethany both looked at each other, trying and failing to disguise massive shit-eating grins, before turning back to him.

"It was actually ten minutes," Jordan informed him. Tom's face must have registered disbelief, as Jordan continued. "If you don't believe me, take another look at the clock. You checked it just before I showed you the pattern on the screen, remember?"

Tom turned, this time not trying to hide his time keeping. The clock read six forty-two. What the-? How the hell was that even possible? Where had the time gone? His mind struggled to focus.

"And Tom?" He turned back to them. "Are you missing anything?"

Tom patted his trouser pockets and checked those on the inside of his coat, mentally ticking off his wallet, phone and keys in his head. "Nope, I don't think so."

"Are you sure about that?" asked Bethany, her eyes once again boring into him.

"No. I mean yes. I don't think so."

"Aren't your feet cold?"

"Eh?"

Tom looked down, drawing his feet out from under his chair where they had been crossed over each other. To his absolute disbelief, he was only wearing his socks. Dark green socks, pretty worn at the toes and which should have been tucked firmly into his trainers.

"Jesus!" Tom whipped his head back up and felt his brain taking a while to follow.

"Ah, you can just call me Jordan," said the young student, pushing his glasses up the bridge of his nose, clearly chuffed to bits with himself.

"Where the hell are my trainers?" Tom cast his eyes about him, half expecting to see them kicked off beneath his chair. They were nowhere in sight.

"Don't worry, they're just in the kitchen," Jordan told him. "I'll grab them for you."

Open-mouthed, Tom watched him retrieve his battered, and probably smelly, trainers from the other room and stupidly felt relieved it hadn't been Bethany handling them.

"How the hell did they get there?" he asked as Jordan handed them over.

"Well, you undid them and gave them to me when I asked. Although, I was the one who put them in the kitchen."

Tom crammed his feet back into his trainers and bent over to lace them back up, making sure to do a double knot, even though it was a bit like locking the stable door after the horse had bolted. "I just can't believe it," he said.

"Let me show you the video footage," Jordan said, connecting his phone to the laptop and pressing a few buttons to bring up Tom's image on the screen.

And, sure enough, there he was, eyes wide open and seemingly fully aware, pulling off those same trainers and handing them over to Jordan who stood in front of him, hands ready to receive them, before walking over to the kitchen. Tom had no memory of it whatsoever.

14

BETHANY

"You seem different today, Bethany."

Leigh was appraising me, head tilted to one side, silver pen tapping against her painted lip. It wasn't a question that she'd asked, but it really was. I left it hanging in the air like a balloon, its string dangling down enticingly, waiting for me to grab hold of it before it blew away. I let it go.

I wasn't quite sure why I didn't want to answer, other than the fact that I'd probably shared way too much last time I was here. Instead, I smiled. Leigh would have probably described it as a secretive smile, and I suppose it was. I was full of secrets.

Blinking herself out of her gaze, Leigh gave me a thin smile and put her pen down on the low table between us next to her pad and her watch. We were in our usual spot, bookcase to the left of me, escape route to the right. As I said the words in my head, I was reminded of that song, 'Stuck in the Middle with You,' and I smiled again at the irony.

Leigh was still quiet, obviously waiting for some kind of revelation from me. It was such an old hack's trick, waiting for me to fill the uncomfortable silence with words. It was like playing a game of chicken, and I wondered how long I could hold out. Seemingly unphased, Leigh untied the silk scarf which she wore around her neck and draped it over the arm of her chair. My eyes fell to her necklace and I made a mental note to ask her about it when I was feeling more communicative.

"What would you like to talk about today, Bethany?" She tried a change of tack. I had to give her credit for the open question.

It wasn't that I didn't want to talk to her. I actually kind of did, but after the last time, all it had done was to open up old wounds, literally. Surely that must prove that talking about the past wasn't always the best idea. Much safer to stay in the present.

"The project's going well," I offered.

"That's great. Why don't you tell me a bit about it? Did you use..." she paused to look at the notes on her pad "...Tom in the end?"

"Yes, we did."

"And? Did you make the right decision, do you think?"

She seemed honestly interested, so I relented in my mission to only share what was absolutely necessary.

It was nice to talk about the project with someone other than Jordan, to be honest. He had such set ideas on how we should be doing things and it felt like a bit of a battle sometimes. Leigh just listened and didn't try and push her opinions on me. I knew that was what she was paid to do, but nevertheless.

I enjoyed seeing her interest in what I was doing. It felt encouraging and nurturing, and I couldn't help but wonder what it would be like to have a mother like her instead of the crappy one that I really had. I hadn't even spoken to my mother in weeks and when I did, it was never by choice. She'd call every couple of months, just to check I was still alive and not causing any embarrassment. Toeing the line like a good girl.

Leigh would be too young to be my mother anyway, unless she'd been knocked up as a teenager. I supposed she'd be more like a much older sister. Luckily, there was a spot for one of those in my life, too. I'd idolised my sister, putting her on higher and higher pedestals as we got older. It wasn't my fault she was scared of heights.

"Bethany?" Leigh was looking at me curiously. I must have wandered a bit off track onto memory lane.

"Sorry."

"What were you thinking about?" she asked.

"Why does everyone leave me?" I answered her question with a question, another thing that drove my mother mad.

"Who's left you, Bethany?"

God, my mother would be going nuts with this conversation. "Basically everyone. My dad, my sister, Daniel."

"Why do you think they left?"

It did my head in that counsellors never just gave you straight answers. It was down to you, the patient, to work things through yourself and come up with your own solutions. It clearly hadn't worked that well for me so far. "My last counsellor thought I might have borderline personality disorder."

Leigh frowned at my comment. Counsellors weren't supposed to have thoughts, or, at least, they weren't supposed to vocalise them, especially to their patients. "And what do you think?"

"I dunno." I started picking at a loose thread on my sleeve, which unravelled a bit of seam. "I suppose I struggle with some stuff."

Leigh tucked her hair behind her ear, as if that would help her to hear better. She asked me to carry on.

"I just, I dunno, I just feel things really intensely."

"That's a very brave thing to admit to."

"Is it?" I smirked and pressed down on my legs which were jittering up and down, anxious to take flight.

"Yes, it is." She smiled. "You can get up and move around if you'd like to." Leigh had obviously noticed my discomfort.

"Yeah, thanks. I will." I stood and walked over to the window by her desk. It had been a pretty cloudy day and dusk was starting to crowd us, jostling around the edges of the windowpane. At least the days were starting to get a bit longer now and, even though it was still only just March, Spring must surely be getting itself ready. I could imagine the legion of bulbs below the ground in their soil jackets, cautiously sending out shoots to the surface as if testing the temperature of a bath before jumping in. I willed them on and then turned back to the room, gobsmacked that Leigh had once again managed to get inside my head and make me open up to her. Oh, to hell with it.

"I *am* feeling happier today," I told her, moving back to my seat on the sofa.

"That's wonderful news. Can you pinpoint the reason why?"

"I guess I've just decided it's time to move on with my life," I told her.

"Tell me more."

"Well, the project is going great, and Jordan and I are working well together, when he's not doing my head in, that is."

"Why does he do your head in?"

"He likes me."

"Isn't that a good thing?"

"No, I mean, he *likes* me."

"Ah, I see. And you don't feel the same way?"

"He's just a friend."

It wasn't that I didn't care about Jordan, and he wasn't a total minger either. Well, he wouldn't be if he ever cleaned the bloody smudges from the lenses of his glasses.

"Friendships form the best foundations in relationships." Leigh looked a little wistful as she spoke and her hands fluttered to the locket around her neck, making me wonder again about her home situation.

"Maybe." My voice sounded sulky even to my ears.

Leigh looked as though she was concentrating hard for a moment, giving herself a strict and silent talking to, before turning her high beams back onto me again. "So, tell me how else you're moving on with your life, Bethany. Do you think you can accept and get past how you felt about Daniel?"

"I think so, yes. It's probably time to meet someone else, isn't it?" I wasn't looking for approval as I'd already decided.

"You could try to come to an understanding of why you had such intense feelings for someone who didn't return them."

"You make it sound like he never loved me." That pissed me off. Just when I'd started warming to her as well.

"Do you think he did love you?" Leigh asked, pushing that damn bit of hair behind her ear again. She should get it cut if it was annoying her that much. It was certainly getting on my nerves.

I knew she had to ask me these questions, that was the worst of it, and to be fair, she was going about it in a much kinder way than my last counsellor who had just been far too blatant in his opinion. I supposed his method had been tough love, but it just felt like he didn't really like me.

"Of course Daniel loved me," I insisted, feeling a lump starting to form in my throat. A small speed bump well-positioned to slow me down.

"What was it that makes you certain?"

"I don't know. I just know it was real."

I didn't like where she was pushing this conversation to go. It felt wrong, like it was tainting my memory of our beautiful time together. I couldn't bring myself to question his feelings for me as they had been chiselled into stone in my mind. Worst of all, if I thought he'd never cared about me, I'd have to put him in the same box as my mother.

"He loved me."

Leigh didn't respond immediately to my words, but instead adjusted her pen and pad next to her watch on the table, no doubt giving me time to re-evaluate. The only thing I was re-evaluating was whether she should be the one in counselling as she clearly had OCD. Her insinuating silence pissed me off. I kept quiet, playing her at her own game.

"Maybe that's a good place to stop for today, Bethany." Leigh picked up her Radley and strapped it back to her wrist, pulling her sleeve smartly down over the top of it. The quick movement unbalanced me for a moment and I couldn't believe my hour was up already.

I say hour, but I suppose the sessions really only consisted of forty minutes of useful time. Ten minutes were taken up in the beginning to get settled and talk about the weather, then forty minutes of session time. The final ten minutes were to tie up any loose ends and get me out of the door before the next patient arrived. Leigh ran a tight ship as I always found myself in the corridor on the other side of the door before the next mixed-up person arrived. I guess time flew when you were having fun.

In the entryway to the office building, I pulled on my gloves. Spring may well be on its way but according to the weather app on my phone, it was still only five degrees Celsius outside. I adjusted my bag on my shoulder and put my weight against the revolving door, just as a woman did the same from the outside. As we passed in a semicircle, I wondered if she was Leigh's next patient or whether she was just here for one of the other small businesses that hired space in the building.

The door pushed me out into the flat grey sky as she was deposited inside in perfect synchronicity. Not for the first time, I wondered how Leigh coped, taking on so many problems from other people. One in, one out, just like me and that lady, passing through a revolving door of mental issues.

The woman passed by Leigh's door without pause, making her way further down the hall. Oh well, it looked like Leigh had scheduled a toilet break for herself. I dabbed at the corners of my eyes which were watering from the cold wind as it whipped my hair around my face before setting off towards the bus stop.

As my feet fell on their familiar route, I went over parts of my conversation with Leigh. I guessed that she was just trying to help me get over my feelings for Daniel by making me question his love for me, so, while it was irritating, I couldn't let it upset me. No matter what she thought, I *knew* he had loved me. Loved me deeply. And nothing would ever change that.

Even when he'd blocked me on social media, I knew he'd only done it to protect me from his wife's retributions. And when he told me fuck off and stop calling him, I knew he didn't mean it. No doubt his wife had been standing over him, monitoring what he said. If she hadn't stuck her oar in, we could've been happy. I felt my anger starting to bubble up and I pushed it back down quickly. I had other things to focus on now.

15

TOM

When Tom arrived at the library annexe for his next session, he was surprised to find a Red Cross employee there. He'd seen the ambulance in the car park but had just assumed its occupants must be attending an emergency somewhere in the town.

He came in hesitantly, tapping lightly on the glass of the second door which led into the annexe room, unsure as to whether or not he was gatecrashing. The uniformed woman looked up from the massive bag that she had on the table. Her sleeves were rolled up to the Red Cross badges on the upper arms, and both hands were deep inside the bag as if performing some kind of bizarre heart surgery.

"Hi there," she chirped, retrieving a rubber head and torso from the bag, almost like a magician pulling a rabbit from a hat, but with slightly less of a flourish. The bag sagged without its contents, and Tom felt pretty much like doing the same. He hadn't slept much the night before and, to his shame, he'd ended up on the sofa with the whiskey bottle for company once more. All his resolve from the week before feeling completely unachievable.

"Hi," he returned. "Have I got the right evening?"

"Tom! Hi." It was Bethany. "We were just in the kitchen making tea. Did you want one?"

"Um yeah, sure. Thanks."

"Hannah? Did you want sugar?" Bethany addressed the other woman.

"No thanks, I'm sweet enough."

"Good for you," said Bethany with a smile that didn't quite reach her eyes. Jordan gave him a small wave from behind her retreating figure and Tom returned the gesture. He then grabbed one of the chairs stacked up against the wall and sat at the table with Hannah and the contents of her bag. He watched as she smoothed a wet wipe over her dummy's expressionless face.

From the kitchen, he could hear angry whispers and then a spoon clanking against china as tea was vociferously stirred. Before long, Jordan and Bethany joined them around the table. They had the air of a couple who'd had a disagreement of some sort, both unwilling to meet the others' eyes and overcompensating with everyone else.

"I expect you're wondering what's happening this evening?" Jordan addressed Tom, unusually taking the lead as he dunked a digestive into his drink.

"Well…"

"Absolutely nothing to worry about," continued Jordan, looking crestfallen as half of the biscuit fell into his tea with a small splash. He fished about with the other half, but it was too little too late and his dismayed expression brought a good-natured smile to Tom's lips, which felt nice. Jordan seemed to Tom to be one of life's good guys and he couldn't help but like him.

"While my partner here messes around with his tea, we're just going to ask Hannah to check your resting heart rate for us if that's ok?" Bethany took over the baton which Jordan had dropped, along with the biscuit.

On cue, Hannah took Tom's right hand. She turned it over and clipped a small device on the end of his middle finger, watching the digital numbers on its screen change before settling. "Hmm, not bad," she said as she placed his hand sunny side down back on his knee with a small pat. "Not good, mind, but not bad." She made a note on a piece of paper and Bethany continued.

"You might remember that on your initial questionnaire, one of the questions asked you about any fears you have?"

Tom had just taken a sip of his drink and her question stopped him in his tracks, the tea held slightly longer in his mouth than normal as his throat constricted. He forced himself to swallow. "Yeah."

"Well, part of our process which will ultimately, we hope, help you with your sleeping difficulties, is to get you to face that fear and realise that you can have control over it. Does that make sense?"

"Yeah."

The reality of Tom's situation was starting to hit home. Why the hell hadn't he written that his greatest fear was spiders instead of choking? He wasn't keen on them either, with Gemma having to dispose of any eight-legged creatures that decided to visit their house – if Baloo didn't get them first. Even so, he would much rather be sitting at a table with a zookeeper and a tarantula in a glass case than Hannah and the unspoken threat of choking.

"Are you ok, Tom?" Bethany was touching his knee and staring at him, concern etched on her face. Next to him, Hannah stiffened like a runner at the blocks, ready to dive into action.

"I'm…I'm ok," he managed.

"You kinda went a bit pale there," Jordan said, shooting a look at Bethany that Tom couldn't read.

"I'm...no, seriously. I'm ok."

"Ok, well, if you're sure?" Bethany's hand was still on his knee and as he looked down, he caught sight of a raised scar that wrapped around her wrist like a bracelet. He guessed she'd seen him register it as she removed her hand, stretching her sleeve down to grasp it in the fingers of the same hand. She didn't meet his eyes when he looked back up and instead nodded at Hannah, who dutifully checked his pulse once more.

"I'm sure," Tom confirmed, and Bethany nodded briskly, once again letting Jordan take the lead.

"We've asked Hannah along just to go through a bit of an emergency first aid session with us. She's going to talk through some issues such as choking, seizures, and what to do when someone is unresponsive."

"Ok." Tom felt his heart rate thankfully taking a step back, falling into line with its regular rhythm, like a good soldier. He could deal with a first aid session. It was just words, after all. Words that he knew already and couldn't hurt him. It would be like sucking eggs with his background, wouldn't it? When he'd filled in the questionnaire, they'd only asked for details about his current job and not the one before, so they would not have a clue that he could probably tell them more about first aid than Hannah ever could.

"I think we'll just pop a heart rate monitor on you if that's ok, Tom? Otherwise, it'll be tricky for Hannah to keep checking your pulse while she talks things through."

"Um yeah, sure. No worries." Tom took the proffered piece of equipment from Jordan and excused himself to go and put it on, not wanting to bear his naked torso in front of an audience.

The toilets were pretty chilly, but he pulled his layers of clothing up and clipped the device around his chest, turning it round so that it sat snugly against his skin with the monitor facing outwards at the front.

Back in the annexe room, Jordan already had his face buried in his mobile phone, studying whatever his screen was telling him. "Alright, Tom." He looked up briefly. "Just getting your heart rate reading coming through on the app now."

Hannah, who had one sturdy looking buttock perched on the

table, put her mug of tea down and looked towards Bethany and Jordan. "I'm ready when you are."

The pair sat themselves down with Tom and Hannah launched into what must be a regular spiel that she provided for groups of office workers around the country.

Tom had seen it a hundred times before, he'd even been a part of demonstrations in the past when called upon, and as a nurse, he'd been called upon a lot. He knew how to wrap a bandage, he knew how to deal with seizures, burns and allergic reactions. He supposed he should maybe have said something about his background on his application form, but they hadn't asked and the last thing he wanted to do was to go into depth about his past, especially after what had happened.

Instead, he sat there, glued to his seat, while Hannah went through her repertoire, interspersed with regular questions from Bethany and Jordan. Her words washed over him and the warmth of the room conspired to lull him into a doze, especially after his lack of sleep the night before. But then, as he shifted in his chair, forcing his eyes to stay open, Hannah mentioned the magic word that would bring Tom crashing out of his relaxed state.

"Any ideas on how we would deal with a choking situation?"

Tom noticed Jordan's head whipping down towards the screen of his phone, and imagined his heart rate monitor had just transmitted some interesting data over to it.

Not really expecting answers from her small assembly, Hannah ploughed onwards. "Well, if someone is clutching at their chest or neck and unable to speak, breathe or cough, they may well be in that situation, and what you need to do immediately is to hit them firmly on their back between their shoulder blades."

She turned her dummy around to point out the area which would need pummelling.

"This will help to dislodge any blockages, as it should create a pressure or vibration in the airway, allowing them to breathe again."

"What if it doesn't work?" Bethany piped up.

"Well, in that case, you'll need to try an abdominal thrust. You must stand behind them and join your hands around their stomach so that they form a fist." Hannah took hold of her rubber torso and held him in an embrace. "Pull your hands inwards and upwards, and repeat up to five times."

"And what if it still doesn't work?" asked Bethany. "What if they pass out?"

"You'll need to lower them to the ground and call the emergency services straight away. If you can't do it, you should get someone else to."

And what if the emergency services are no bloody use? thought Tom. He didn't need to see Jordan's reaction to his phone app to know that his heart was beating faster. They couldn't know who he was, surely? There was no way.

"Now, if the person choking is a child, you can treat them in the same way as you would an adult. You would need to give them five firm blows on the back, but with slightly less force."

Tom desperately tried to steady his breathing and focus on a point on the far wall. Breathe in, breathe out, breath in, breathe out. He felt bile rising in his throat. Breathe in, breathe out. She couldn't know him.

"But what if it's a baby?"

"If the child is under a year old, they should be positioned face down along your thigh, making sure that their head is lower than their bottom. You should then hit them firmly on their back five times."

Tom was past pretending now. His skin felt cold yet sweaty and his breath came faster and faster, verging on a panic attack. The room around him started to slowly circle, speeding up faster and faster until it spun completely out of control, taking his breath away with it. He was going to throw up.

Tom leaned against the tiled wall in the toilet with his eyes closed, one arm up over his forehead, letting the coolness from the ceramic work its way into his skin, until a chill rose goosebumps on his clammy body.

That had certainly been unexpected. Although, bearing in mind the combination of no sleep, half a bottle of whiskey and Hannah's presentation, it wasn't any wonder, in hindsight. He opened his eyes and pushed himself off the wall and over to the sink, which he gripped on either side, looking at himself in the mirror. Dark stubble offset the paleness of his cheeks. It wasn't his best look.

Twisting the stiff faucet, he stooped to scoop water into his mouth before spitting it back out. No matter how many times he did it, the sour taste of vomit wasn't going anywhere fast.

There was a knock at the door, which opened a crack, revealing Jordan's concerned face.

"Are you ok?" he asked.

"Yeah. I'm fine." Tom answered. "I'm fine." He wiped his sleeve across his mouth and then delved into his pocket to see if he had any chewing gum or mints. Nothing.

"Shall I get you a cup of tea?" asked Jordan.

Tom's stomach lurched again at the thought of another lukewarm milky tea. "Could I maybe just have some water please?"

"Of course." Jordan scurried off once more, seemingly happy to have a task to carry out.

Tom exhaled deeply and pulled open the door, following Jordan a few steps behind, back into the warmth of the annexe. As he entered he heard Jordan speaking in a hushed voice to Bethany about whether it was a good idea for them to carry on with the rest of the evening.

"I would certainly question it," Hannah interjected.

"Let's see how he feels." Bethany looked up at Tom as he came in, the blueness of her eyes a distraction from her words.

"I'm absolutely fine," Tom told them. "Honestly, I actually feel ok."

"I'm really not sure," said Jordan. "I wouldn't want to make you feel worse."

"Hey, no pain, no gain, right?" Tom plonked himself back down in his recently vacated seat and took the glass of water proffered by Jordan. "Seriously. Let's just crack on."

"Ok, well, look, Hannah's here on standby anyway, so all you have to do is shout if you start feeling rough again, ok?" Jordan looked over at Hannah.

"Fine by me."

"Right then." Jordan pulled over another chair which he placed in front of Tom and took a seat. Bethany retrieved the glass of water from Tom and then stood to one side with Hannah, waiting for Jordan to start.

"How are you feeling now, Tom?" he asked.

"I'm fine."

"That's great." Jordan held his hand out. "Just press your hand down on my open palm."

Tom did as he was told.

"Now, close your eyes."

Tom complied.

"Now, go into 'that sleep'."

He heard Jordan's words washing over him, some registering in his mind and some having little meaning whatsoever. Jordan spoke slowly and quietly and each time he counted down, Tom felt himself feeling safer and more relaxed.

He loosely registered the sound of someone, a woman, coughing and then a song being played. Something familiar, but not enough to be able to name it.

And then, before long, he could hear Jordan counting again, this time in reverse. Other than a slight feeling of regret that he had to leave such a wonderfully relaxed state, he felt completely refreshed, his eyes pinging open instead of the usual hesitant half-lidded view of the world that he usually had upon waking. He hadn't felt this good in ages.

16

BETHANY

"I heard it all got a bit intense last night, man," announced Seb as he slid himself onto the seat next to me whilst we waited for the lecture hall to fill up. He leaned in conspiratorially, making me wish he hadn't been quite so generous with his aftershave that morning. Then I caught a whiff of dope lurking underneath it and understood why.

"Nothing we couldn't handle." I pulled back and raised an eyebrow, guessing that Hannah had filled him in on how things had panned out the night before. "It was really good of your cousin to help us out like she did, by the way."

"Yeah, she's alright. Likes a chat though, eh?"

I smiled indulgently. He wasn't kidding. It had taken a good half an hour to crowbar Hannah out of the building at the end of the session. Not convinced by the readings on the heart rate monitor, she'd insisted on checking Tom's pulse again herself, and even felt his forehead with the back of her hand. Like that was needed! Just wanting to touch him, no doubt, under a veiled disguise of healthcare. Not that I could say anything, as she had just done us a massive favour, giving up her time for free. Nevertheless, it pissed me off.

"Where's your fan club today, then?" Seb asked.

To be fair, I'd wondered that myself, too. Jordan was normally in the lecture room before me, dutifully saving me a seat next to him. Maybe he was ill. Surely, he couldn't still have the hump with me following on from the argument we'd had just before Tom turned up last night.

Saving me from answering, Seb's attention was momentarily distracted by Hayley's backside as it sashayed past his eye line and took its honoured place amongst the rest of the Kardashians. Unable to resist the lure of fake tan and cultivated eyebrows, Seb scooped up his bag and stood, ready to follow like one of Pavlov's dogs at dinnertime. God, men were predicable.

"I'll catch ya later, man," he said, not even glancing my way. Fine by me, as I wouldn't then have to explain the look of disdain on my face.

"Sure," I told him. "Are you still ok for next week, though?"

"Next week?" He glanced back at me, his sexual distraction obviously playing havoc with his thought processes. Either that, or it was the weed he'd smoked earlier.

"The hypnosis experiment, remember? You're our murder victim."

"Oh, yeah, totally."

Over Seb's shoulder, I saw Jordan coming through the doorway and spotting Seb talking to me, the frown on his face deepening. I had a feeling Jordan was going to enjoy having our intellectually challenged classmate bumped off.

I rolled my eyes at him before addressing Seb again. "Just go, before you start drooling down your shirt."

"What? I've got something on my shirt?"

"No, Seb. We'll talk later, ok?"

"Yeah, laters." He turned heel and was soon enveloped in the cloud of Vera Wang Princess perfume that Hayley was spraying around her. Between them, the pair smelled like the perfume counter at Selfridges.

"Alright?" Jordan asked as he joined me, filling the empty space that Seb had only just vacated.

"Yeah, I'm good. Are you alright?" I didn't need to ask the question as every fibre of Jordan's body exuded the fact that he was far from ok.

"I'm fine."

God, he was such a girl sometimes.

He was the one that had decided to start asking me stupid questions while we were making tea in the kitchen. It wasn't my fault he hadn't liked the answers.

17

TOM

Tom couldn't remember the last time that he and Gemma had been out to dinner together, and right now, as they sat opposite each other in Canalettos, he realised they probably should have done it a lot sooner.

The little Italian restaurant was buzzing with customers' conversations, and good-natured staff ducked between strings of garlic as they delivered fresh food from the kitchens to watering mouths. Candles held in plump wine bottles adorned each table, their wax drips never quite reaching their bell-bottoms, and every now and then, someone would call out 'Saluti,' which was followed by the clink of glasses.

Ignoring Gemma's protestations, Tom had ordered one, then a second bottle of Chianti to go with their food and, as the night wore on, he relaxed and chanced reaching across the red and white checked tablecloth to take Gemma's hand in his. He'd missed her touch a great deal and with the wine talking, he admitted as much to her.

"I've missed you, too," she told him, stroking the back of his hand with her thumb. He almost melted.

"I know we can't turn back the clock, Gem, but it's not too late, is it?" He'd do anything to make it better between them.

"I hope not." She looked down at her plate, swirls of Arrabiata sauce creating an inkblot image on the white china.

"Me too. There's only another week left until this research study is finished, and I'm really hopeful it's going to help, you know."

"Just remember they did say it might not work."

"Yeah, I know, but after the last session, I'm already feeling much better." He smiled, enjoying the feeling of being tipsy without underlying anger or despair for a change. He relished the fact that he was out in public with Gemma. "It'll work. I know it."

Gemma smiled and pulled her hand away as their waiter came to remove their plates, asking if they'd like anything for dessert. Tom looked over at Gemma who shook her head, and Tom declined for the both of them, just asking for the bill.

"Of course," said the waiter as he tipped the last few drops of wine into their glasses. "Perhaps some Limoncello as a nightcap before you leave us?"

"Why not?" Tom agreed, and the waiter all but clicked his heels together before leaving them to fetch some glasses.

"Maybe we shouldn't." A look of concern crossed Gemma's face as she ran her finger around the base of her wine glass. "I think maybe we've had enough."

"Ah, c'mon, don't be such a spoil sport." Tom drained his wine and pushed the glass into the centre of the table. "It'll do you good to relax."

Gemma shrugged, her wide-necked shirt slipping to reveal one beautiful shoulder. God, how Tom wanted to touch her skin, kiss her neck.

"You're beautiful," he told her, making her blush. An involuntary reaction that she'd always found mortifying, while he adored the fact that her body responded to his words. She pulled her top back in place as the waiter rejoined them, proffering two shot glasses full to the brim with Limoncello, and giving them his blessing with a "Saluti."

Tom lifted the drink, the stickiness of the alcohol that had spilt over the top bound his fingers to the tiny glass. "Let's drink to something."

"Like what?" Gemma raised her glass too.

"Let's drink to the future." Tom held his glass forwards.

"To the future," she repeated, dutifully clinking hers against it and taking a tiny sip while Tom threw his back.

"Come on, drink up," he encouraged her.

"I am, I am," she told him. "I just can't do it all in one go like you."

"Well, all the more time for me to have another, then." Tom raised his glass and their waiter homed in on it like a heat-seeking missile, bottle in hand.

"Tom…"

He could hear the warning tone in Gemma's voice but chose to ignore it. "Come on, Gem. Your turn to make some toast…do a toast." Whoops. That was the problem with good waiters, they kept on topping up your glass when your drink got low.

Gemma played around with her glass, looking uncertain. He noticed she hadn't finished her wine, either.

"Come on, Gem," he tried again. "What are we going to drink to?"

She lifted her glass, making it appear as though the tiny vessel weighed a tonne. She dragged her eyes up to meet his and suddenly, he knew what was coming, but it was too late to stop it.

"To family."

"Yours or mine?" Tom tried to veer her off course with his badly chosen joke.

"Ours," she stated, and clinked his motionless glass before throwing the contents of her own back. Oh, now, she chose to do that.

Tom felt his insides turn to ice as he watched her busily averting her gaze, looking anywhere but at him. Knowing full well that she'd ruined everything with one word. He downed his drink and signalled the waiter to pour another, wishing for something that tasted less like sherbet lemon. "You know that's never going to happen."

Her eyes sprung back up to meet his gaze, looking as though he'd physically hit her. "But why? We need to get over what happened. And you said yourself that you were hopeful for the future and that you're feeling so much better." She folded and unfolded her napkin with nervous fingers.

"I said no." Tom could feel himself scowling back at her. "I don't want to start a family. Not after what happened. I can never be around children again. I couldn't deal with it."

"We both lived through it, Tom." She was pleading now.

"Yes, but it was me, wasn't it?" He drained his glass, wincing now at the sickly sweetness of it. "It was all my fault."

"No, it wasn't. That was proved by the outcome of the legal proceedings. The hospital was negligent."

"Oh, for fuck's sake, Gemma, they didn't force me to do it." He held his glass out for another top up, but his wife grabbed it and pulled it out of the way of his grasping fingers.

"You've had enough," she told him.

"Damn right I've fucking had enough." He glared at her, noticing the waiter edging over to them, his earlier welcoming smile replaced with a look of concern.

"Is everything alright, sir? Madam? Can I help with anything?"

Tom rose from his seat, the movement causing the chair to fall onto its back, making sure that everyone in the restaurant who hadn't already invested in their drama, turned their heads to look. Tom was beyond caring. He pulled some cash out of his pocket and threw it on the table. "That should cover it. Come on, Gemma, we're going."

"But I…" She was crying now.

"Gemma, come on, get up."

Their waiter positioned himself between them and asked Gemma if she was ok. Tom could see the other three waiting staff moving in a formation towards him, whether protective of his wife or their restaurant, he wasn't sure.

"She's fine, mate," Tom answered him. "Come *on,* Gemma. Get up." He manoeuvred his way around the waiter, pulling his wife's coat from the back of her chair and pushing it at her. She flinched away from him as though he'd just flung a poisonous snake. "Suit your bloody self. I'll be outside getting a cab."

Tom grabbed his own coat, which had fallen to the floor along with his chair, and staggered a little as he stood back up. He could imagine all the other diners judging him, already thinking about what they would write on their social media posts later. He couldn't give a shit.

He pushed his way outside into the cold night, his breath billowing in front of him. Why the hell couldn't Gemma just let it drop? He was living proof that things did not get better with time.

He paced up and down the pavement in front of the restaurant, waiting for Gemma to follow him out. Where the fuck was she? Probably enveloped in the caring arms of some slick prick called Giovanni, or making a call from the ladies' toilet to her Facebook friend Ash. Fucking arsehole. Let him give her some bloody babies if that's what she wanted so badly. Tom's anger escalated a notch and before he knew what he was doing, he'd lifted his foot and kicked over a bin, causing litter to scatter across the pavement. It didn't make him feel any better.

He could feel the diners' eyes on him from the window now. No doubt alerted by the bloody racket he was making in the street, like a litter-raiding racoon. Despite the alcohol-induced bravado, he felt a moment of acute embarrassment at his actions and moved further down the road out of their sightline, where he leaned against a wall, wishing he smoked.

A few minutes passed and then Gemma stepped out from the doorway, light spilling briefly around her and pooling at her feet as the door closed behind her. She held a tissue in her hand which she dabbed at her eyes.

"They've ordered us a cab."

Tom shrugged.

"Jesus Tom, what's wrong with you?" She took a few steps towards him, then paused as a taxi came to a stop outside of the restaurant. Gemma leant down to the window to speak to the driver and then opened up the back door of the car. "Are you coming?" she directed at Tom.

Tom followed his wife into the taxi and folded his arms across his chest like a petulant child. It reeked of spices and something underlying, like old vomit, and he felt nauseous as the vehicle pulled away from the curb.

If only Gemma hadn't brought up the topic of having children again, then none of this would be happening. They would've had a good night, he wouldn't feel like a dickhead, and they'd be in a decent taxi that he would have ordered himself instead of this pile of shit with peeling faux-leather seats that smelled like a toilet. If Gemma hadn't pulled at that ever-present loose thread that they both ignored most of the time, he wouldn't be sitting here wanting to cry and argue and throw up all at the same time. He took a deep breath in, taking the noxious odour of the car with it, and exhaled.

"Tom?" Even his name on her lips annoyed him at the moment. "Talk to me. Please."

A little voice in the back of his head tried pointing out that maybe he should just leave well alone until the morning when they were both sober, but the devil on his shoulder jabbed at him with its pitchfork, making his negative thoughts swirl. Jab. Jab. Jab.

"You wanna talk, do you?" He turned to her.

Gemma nodded, raising the tissue to her eye again. Fucking crocodile tears.

"Well, I have a suggestion, Gemma." He knew he was about to hurt her even more, but at that point, he didn't care, as she would never hurt as much as he did. In the meantime, it was worth a try. Misery likes company, after all. "Maybe your mate Ash can help you with babies if that's what you want so much."

Tom saw his wife's eyes widen. He wasn't sure if it was surprise or guilt. He didn't care. "I'm sure he'd bloody love to help you out in that department, then you'll see if he'll always be there for you." He curled his index fingers to create crude quotation marks as he said the last five words, sarcasm heavy on his tongue.

Gemma's mouth started moving, obviously trying to find the words before her brain caught up enough to hand them over. "Are you kidding me?" Her hand holding the tissue fell to her lap. Her eyes now devoid of tears, chased away by her anger. "Ash is my friend, just my friend. I've got no one else to turn to. I have no real friends here at all and Ash is the only one who listens."

"Oh, please! He only listens because he wants to get in your bloody knickers!" There was no stopping him now.

"No, it's not like that. Seriously. We're just Facebook friends, Tom."

"Sure you are," Tom sneered at her.

"It's true. Jesus Christ, Tom, we met on a bloody Facebook support group. That's what we do…we support each other. That's all."

"Oh, come on Gemma. I might be a complete waste of space but I'm not fucking stupid. I've seen all those comments on your timeline, and the cute little texts he sends you, so don't treat me like a dick." Tom was breathing fast now, and he barely registered the taxi turning into more familiar streets.

"Well then, don't act like a dick." Gemma's response was quiet and tipped Tom over the edge. God, he could bloody well swing for her sometimes.

"Why don't you just piss off and leave me then, eh? Why stay with such a worthless waste of space?" Tom glared at her, his voice rising. "In fact, why don't you just run off into the distance with your mate, Ash? Go and fuck him for your bloody babies. Why are you bothering with me?"

Gemma sat in silence, looking down at the tissue in her hands which she was slowly shredding, small pieces scattering on and around her lap. Looking forward, Tom could see the cabbie glancing in the rear-view mirror at them, uncertain about what to do and probably wondering why he'd ever become a cab driver.

"Got a problem, mate?" Tom eyeballed him through the mirror until the other man looked away.

All three sat in silence as the car made another turn and arrived in their street.

"Just here, please." Gemma took some cash from her purse and handed it over to the driver while Tom crashed his way out of the back of the car onto the street. He watched her brush the shredded tissue from her skirt and head up the path to their house. Jesus, her silence was pissing him off even more. Why wouldn't she shout back?

He followed her into the house, with the beginnings of regret nudging at his anger, poking it back into its cage.

Gemma hung her coat in the hall and, without looking at him, spoke quietly. "I'm going to bed, and I don't want you anywhere near me. You can stay in the spare room from now on. Just leave me alone."

She walked off, leaving him in the kitchen. No doubt shaking her head when she heard the fridge door opening and the clink of a bottle. Fuck her. He sat at the breakfast bar, wanting to throw the bottle at the wall instead of drinking it, but just about holding it together.

He tried to put his chin in his hand, but his drunkenness knocked his elbow from the edge of the table, like an old lush sitting at a bar. The sober version of him knew it was the wrong thing to do, but the pisshead told him to send Gemma a message on Messenger. "Never go to bed on an argument," his dad always used to say. Although, that was generally after he'd slapped him and his mother around, and then sat in tears drowning in guilt. Jesus, no wonder I'm fucked up, thought Tom, not for the first time, as he clumsily opened the app on his phone.

There was Gemma's name right at the top, with a little image of her face snuggled up next to the cat. He could see the remnants of her last message to him saying she loved him, and he clicked it open. Shit, had he screwed up? Had he just literally poured acid over the last frayed threads that were holding them together?

As his addled mind played games, he saw the little green dot appear next to her name on the screen, telling him that she was online. Maybe she was going to message him? He sipped his drink and waited. Nothing. She wasn't writing anything. Not to him, anyway. And, bearing in mind she'd just told him she had no other friends to talk to, that left one person. He wanted to fucking kill her.

18

BETHANY

"**A**re you all set for the big finale of the experiment?" Leigh asked, rolling up her shirtsleeve to remove her watch.

How did she manage to wear smart clothes like that all day and not even get them creased? Maybe she ironed them between each client. Today's outfit consisted of tailored navy trousers and a crisp white shirt. She probably called it a blouse. My mother would have loved it. I twirled my lip ring with my tongue and wondered if maybe it was time I started making a bit more of an effort myself, especially now.

"I think so," I told her. "Our subject did have a bit of a meltdown at our last session, but I reckon we're going to be ok."

Leigh cocked her head to one side like a confused dog that doesn't quite understand the instruction it's been given. "What do you mean by a meltdown?" she asked, a fine line creasing her otherwise smooth forehead.

"He threw up!"

"Oh! Oh dear. That's…not good." She looked as though she'd smelled something really unpleasant.

"It's ok," I told her. "He still wanted to carry on and all the other elements are coming together really well, so I'm pretty sure it'll be all systems go."

"I thought you said he was the perfect applicant, that he had good suggestibility?" She unconsciously fingered the locket around her neck, which I was realising may well be her own form of reassurance. Bless her, she was actually showing concern for my project and it felt good to have her support.

"Oh, he does. He really *is* perfect." I couldn't resist a secret smile. He was perfect, but just not in the context that my counsellor was obviously thinking of.

"Ok, well, good. You make sure you keep at it and I'll keep everything crossed." She placed her watch in its usual position on the table and gave a small cough, covering her mouth with her perfectly manicured fingers.

Time to get down to business.

"How are you getting on with Jordan, now?" Leigh's face had reconfigured into its usual caring tableaux once again.

"Not great."

"Any particular reason why?"

"He thought it would be a good idea to ask me out."

"And it wasn't?"

"Er, no." I couldn't help an edge of sarcasm seeping into my voice. "I told you I don't see him that way. He should know that."

"Why should he know that, Bethany?"

"Because I've spent the last few months telling him I've got a boyfriend back home who I go and visit every weekend, for starters."

"I see." Leigh leaned forward a little, risking a crease in her crisp white shirt. "So, what changed, do you think?"

I rolled my eyes. "I told him we'd split up."

"Ah, I see." Leigh leaned back again, not a crease in sight. "So, Jordan saw it as an opportunity to ask you out before someone else swept you off your feet."

I must have looked at her like she was mad, as she carried on.

"You mentioned there might be someone else on the horizon last time we spoke."

"Did I?" God, sometimes I couldn't remember who I'd told what.

"Yes, you'd said it was time to move on with someone else."

I vaguely remembered saying something like that. Damn it, now she was going to ask me a million questions about it. Why did I have to start opening up to her? It was so much easier when I was maintaining my vow of silence.

Leigh continued to probe. "Did you tell Jordan that you've met someone new that you like?"

"Well, I had to, didn't I?"

"Why's that, Bethany?"

"I couldn't just say no when he asked me out, could I?"

"Why not?"

Oh my God, she was sounding like a toddler with all her questions. Why's the sky blue? Why's the earth round? Why? Why? Why?

Feeling a bit bullied into answering, I told her that Jordan hadn't exactly picked the best time to make his move. We'd just got Hannah all set up at the library annexe and we were in the kitchen making tea when he'd started on at me, asking how things were going with Daniel. I'd stopped talking about him quite so much lately, and Jordan had obviously got a sixth sense that all wasn't right in paradise.

It had really wound me up when he'd asked me out. Yes, I knew he fancied me, and, to be honest, that never really bothered me. It was actually pretty useful as I knew he'd be a devoted ally, one I didn't have to form an attachment to on my side. Now, he'd put me in a position where I had to do something mean. It didn't actually bother me being mean, but I didn't want him to think it. Was that weird?

The second I'd told him that things were over between me and

Daniel, I regretted it. I was still riding high after my decision to let go of the relationship, and the words had just tumbled out before I had time to think about what I was saying. I'd technically opened a door that before now had only ever been ajar, and I'd had no time to scoop the words back in before Jordan was asking to take me out to dinner. I mean, who does that anyway? Drinks maybe, not dinner!

"I can't," I'd told him, opening a kitchen cupboard to retrieve mugs and taking time rattling them around as a cover to hide my face from him. I might not be able to see his expression, but I could feel the disappointment emanating from him.

"Oh, right. Well, ok then." He was hurt.

I'd closed the cupboard again and turned to face him knowing that I had to do some damage control. "It's not that I wouldn't, Jordan." He'd looked at me, a glimmer of hope behind his smudged lenses. "It's just that I've kind of met someone else." The hope died.

"Wow, um…ok." Jordan had busied himself filling the kettle, drowning out my apology.

"What does *that* mean?" I'd asked him.

"What does what mean?"

"Wow. Why did you say 'wow'?"

"No reason." He'd flicked the switch on the kettle. "It's just a bit quick, isn't it?"

I had stood there staring at him, trying to get my brain to accept the fact that Jordan had just criticised me. That was a new situation and I was trying to get my head around it. I wasn't sure if I should be hurt or angry or both. I'd decided to go with both. I mean, Jesus, just because he hadn't had a girlfriend in God knows how long, it didn't mean he had the right to judge me.

"I don't think it's really any of your business," I'd told him. "Besides, you just asked me out yourself. Isn't that just as quick?" I'd been about to let rip on him when Tom's voice had filtered through into the kitchen, breaking up our argument with perfect timing.

Leigh was still looking at me, waiting for more. Maybe an

answer as to why I'd felt the need to tell Jordan I was seeing someone else. Or did she actually want to know why I thought it was time to start seeing someone else? I wasn't sure. I looked back at her, silently twirling my lip ring. My eyes felt dry and I blinked, slowly, breaking the game of chicken that seemed to be enveloping us.

"Do *you* think it's quick, Bethany?" Leigh asked, obviously repeating Jordan's words in a more generous re-phrasing.

"It's not like we're moving in together," I told her. "We're taking it slow."

"Well, that seems sensible. Have you thought about explaining that to Jordan?"

"No. I'm not sure he'd appreciate it," I told her. Leigh looked at me questioningly and I sighed, fighting the urge to make something up and realising I just didn't have the energy. "He's kind of with someone else."

"Kind of?" Leigh's plucked eyebrow had risen a fraction. Undetectable to the untrained eye, but I caught it creeping up her forehead, nonetheless.

"Ok, ok, he's *with* someone else."

"Bethany…I—"

"Look, I know what you're going to say, so please don't bother. This is different. He's not like Daniel. He couldn't be more different to him." Leigh let me continue, a look of resignation on her face. "I know he's not happy in his relationship. They just don't want the same things anymore."

"And what *does* he want Bethany?" Her eyes bored into me. "More importantly what do *you* want?"

"I really like him." I looked down at my hands.

"I'm sure you do." She looked at me and I could feel what I thought was pity in her tone. Pity, and acceptance of the inevitable. Knowledge that she was probably failing as a counsellor.

I knew what it'd look like to anyone on the outside. The crazy girl in therapy who had struggled to get over one man who couldn't leave his wife for her, and was now about to throw herself headlong down another rabbit hole. It wasn't like I'd done it on purpose, though. I didn't set out to like him. I really didn't. It just crept up on me. And it wasn't like I was the other woman or anything either. Not at all. We were just friends, for now, but I knew that he liked me just as much as I did him. He didn't even have to say the words, as he made me feel special just in the way he looked at me. He wanted to be with me, and as soon as things were finished with his wife, then we could be together properly.

"Have you explained any of this to Jordan?" Leigh asked me.

"No. It isn't his business, and the least said the better, otherwise it just all gets so complicated."

Leigh didn't look satisfied with my answer and instead tried a different tack to keep me talking. To keep me talking long enough so that she could try and persuade me not to jump out of the fire and into the frying pan. She had her work cut out for her.

"You mentioned previously about people always leaving you, Bethany."

I felt my arms start to itch and, even though the room was warm, I pulled my sleeves further down my arms, holding the edges firmly with my fingertips.

"Have you ever wondered if you could be pushing people away?"

I laughed out loud at that one. "Only the ones I don't want around."

19

TOM

Thanks to their shift patterns, Tom hadn't seen his wife at all since their argument. In the last four days, she'd managed to avoid him completely, and on the first morning after the bust-up, he'd stepped out of the spare room to find she'd packed up all his things from their shared bedroom and left them in piles out in the hallway. Baloo had already claimed a tower of sweaters for himself and rolled over as Tom emerged, probably hoping for a scratch of the belly. He was going to be out of luck.

Not for the first time since their argument in the restaurant, Tom asked himself if he should try and make amends with his wife. He knew it was highly likely that he'd jumped to the wrong conclusion about Ash, but his pride and a steady top-up of alcohol had kept him from backing down.

Now, in the cold light of yet another lonely day stretching ahead of him, he started to admit to himself that he'd probably had a few too many that night and, as usual, Gemma had managed to push all the right buttons to set him off. It was a toxic situation that they'd created between them.

Maybe Gemma was telling the truth about Ash, though. Maybe he *was* just a friend, otherwise, why would she have been so keen for them to work things out? Tom tried to think back to the messages he'd read. He knew they'd pissed him off with their familiarity, but could they have been written by a friend? Someone who was just caring, like Gemma claimed, as opposed to someone trying to manipulate their way into her affections?

Another layer of guilt laid itself down upon his shoulders and Tom made a move towards the bedroom at the end of the hall. The one where he used to be welcome. He paused as he heard a muted giggle coming from the other side of the door. Shit, was there someone else in there with her? Surely not.

Tom held his breath and tried to muffle his heartbeat which had started pounding loudly in his ears.

"You're right, we should definitely meet up." His wife's voice filtered through the wood panelling. Then a brief silence. "I'd really love that."

Tom allowed himself to breathe again. She was on the phone. That was all.

"God no! Of course not!"

What? What? Tom crept closer.

"No, don't worry…I wouldn't tell him in a million years."

She had to be talking about him.

"Me too. I know. I feel exactly the same."

Tom didn't hang around to hear any more. What was the old adage about eavesdropping? Something about never hearing anything good? Well, he'd proved that to be true, hadn't he? And Gemma had proved him right, too. He walked back down the hall and instead of picking up his clothes and carrying them into the spare room with him, Tom just kicked the last pile over in utter frustration before walking past the scattered mess to go downstairs and make himself some breakfast.

The kitchen was bright as he entered, and he squinted against the sunlight that played on the glass of the window. It bounced against a small crystal vase on the windowsill, which held some half-dead daffodils, and created a kaleidoscopic pattern on the far wall. Its frivolity annoyed him.

Reaching up, Tom grabbed the bottom of the blind, pulling it down to blot the cheeriness of the sunshine from the room. That was better. He put some week-old sliced bread in the toaster, picking off a couple of green spots of mould beforehand, and switched on the kettle to make a coffee. Moving over to the fridge to grab what he needed, he managed to tread on the cat, who had obviously followed him downstairs, his interest piqued by the possibility of food. Baloo let him know how unhappy he was with a hiss and a Freddy Krueger swipe at Tom's bare ankles.

"Bloody cat!" Tom bent to move him out of the way, but he was too slow and Baloo was gone in a clatter of the cat flap. Off into the garden, looking for smaller prey to rip into shreds, no doubt.

Tom unscrewed the top of the bottle of milk, and its acrid smell told him that it was definitely past its best. Like the bloody bread. He supposed they'd need to go shopping, but he wasn't exactly sure how that was going to work now. Would they both do their own and write their names on stuff before putting it away? God, this sucked. Instead of pouring the milk away, he put the lid back on and returned it to the fridge. Black coffee this morning, then. He'd think about making a list of things to get from the shop later.

He poured steaming water into his favourite mug. Gemma had bought it for him when they were first together. 'I Love You a Latte' it proclaimed on the front with a humanised picture of a cute cup of coffee. Like everything else seemed to be, those words were probably now out of date, too, he thought, the bitter smell of coffee snaking up into his nostrils and giving his brain a small hit.

A ping from his phone signalled a text message had just landed and he grabbed it from the pocket of his saggy jogging bottoms in the vain hope that it might be Gemma, even though he knew damn well it wouldn't be. She was otherwise occupied upstairs.

'Bethany & Jordan' it announced, and Tom swiped it open with a sigh.

How u doing? Still ok for lunch today?

Eh?

Drawing a blank, Tom thumbed a message back. *Sorry. Did we arrange to meet? Thought our next session was tomorrow.*

Within seconds, another text bounded in. *Yes, the other night. Remember? Look at ur texts. 12 pm at the Rose & Crown.* It always amazed Tom how quickly the younger generation could text. Maybe his fingers were just too fat and old.

The toast popped up in the toaster, making Tom jump, and he looked at the clock on the oven. It was ten-thirty already.

He scrolled back through the parade of messages on his phone and yes, there it was, the first one from him on Thursday night at 23.14. Closing his eyes, he briefly massaged his temples, wondering how he could have no recollection of sending it. And then the epiphany. His friend alcohol had hidden it away. He read the text.

Sorry guys. I'm going to have to bail on the last session. I can't do this anymore. Yes, he'd sent that. The argument with Gemma that night had made him want to jump ship. After all, what was the point if they weren't even going to be together anymore?

Tom sipped at his coffee, the hot liquid burning his tongue, and a whole storyboard emerged before his eyes as he scrolled through the messages from that night. He'd even told them about what had happened in the restaurant, well, parts of it. The ones that didn't make him look like a tosser. He'd managed to paint himself in a much more flattering light than he'd probably deserved. The indignation of a drunk man.

My marriage is over, he'd typed. *I can't give her what she wants.* He was mortified to read the comforting replies underneath. What must they think of him? He scrolled further down, letting the words blur as they sped past. And there it was, clear as day in a grey bubble:

Let's meet so we can talk about this. It was followed by today's date, the time and the location.

Ok, he'd finally replied with a sad face emoji.

He looked back at the clock, which still read only ten thirty-five. He had a choice to make. He blew on his coffee and took another sip, cooler this time. It would be so easy to just ignore the texts and walk away from everything. Dignity not even close to being intact. He could just butter his toast and take it into the lounge with his coffee and watch a bit of *This Morning* on TV. Holly and Phillip would do their best to cheer him up and he'd probably fall asleep in front of a segment about cooking the perfect cheesecake. It sounded appealing, other than the fact that he'd wake up again at some point and still be miserable, still be tired and still be feeling like he had nothing left to live for.

I'll be there, he typed.

20

BETHANY

He was still coming.

I'd had an early night last night and set my alarm to go off at eight o'clock. I wanted to be sure to get the first use of the bathroom before my housemates started dragging themselves out of their pits to go to lectures. Luckily, most of them were stereotypical students who didn't emerge during daylight hours unless they really had to.

I'd taken my time in the bathroom, even treating myself to a bubble bath and shaving my legs, just in case. I'd lain there, soaking for a good half an hour, daydreaming about how I hoped my lunch date would go and watching the tiny bubbles pop and fizz along my body.

My mother always used to complain when I had a bath instead of a shower, moaning that I was using all the hot water and not leaving any for anyone else. My housemates would probably do the same when they got up, but it didn't bother me. Each time the water started to dip in temperature a little, I'd top it up from the hot tap again, adding some more bubbles, too.

Hair squeaky clean and my skin at serious risk of puckering, I eventually got out of the tub and used my nice Sanctuary moisturiser over my whole body, humming 'Blinded by Your Grace' as I did so. Normally, I had to use my boring non-perfumed aqueous moisturiser on the scars on my arms, but today was a special day, so to hell with it. I'd always wanted someone to tell me that I smelled amazing and then ask what I was wearing so that I could then reply, "Nothing. It's just me." It would be a lie, of course, but what's a little white lie between friends?

I let the water drain from the tub, giving it a quick swish around with a cloth. I wasn't going to waste time cleaning it as I'd had to wash down the tidemark before I even got in. God, people were disgusting.

Wrapped in my fluffy dressing gown, I walked down the shabby carpeted hallway back to my room, just as a guy I'd never met before came down the stairs from one of the rooms above. He was clad only in a pair of grimy looking boxer shorts, his body thin and soft looking.

"Alright?" He shuffled awkwardly past. Obviously, he hadn't expected anyone to be up yet either.

I guessed that Steph, who rented the room above mine, had hooked up last night. I wondered if she regretted it yet, or if she was up there scratching yet another notch into her bedpost. It must look like a bloody toothpick by now if all the grunting and groaning I heard on a regular basis was anything to go by.

I turned the key in the lock to my room and entered my safe haven, flicking the catch behind me, just in case boxer short man got lost on his way back. It wouldn't be the first time that my door handle had started twisting and turning without invitation. Sometimes, this place was like living in a B-grade horror movie.

I hung my wash bag on the hook on the back of the door and then turned to my wardrobe. Last night, I'd hung up three different outfits on the front, and, as I contemplated them now, none of them seemed right. What had I been thinking?

The first one was way too slutty, the second one would be the kind of thing you'd wear to an interview. The third and final one, while not exactly setting the world on fire, would have to do. They were like the three bears of outfits. Although, Goldilocks, I was not.

I wasn't used to getting dressed up and it had been ages since I'd made an effort to look good for anyone. If anything, for the last few months, I'd tried my hardest to look inconspicuous so I could just blend into the background. I hadn't wanted to be noticed. It was easier that way.

Today was different, though. Today, I wanted to showcase myself in the best possible light. I wanted to appeal to every one of his senses. Sight, sound, smell, touch…even taste. I closed my eyes and imagined him kissing me. My lips parted at the thought of it and I traced their outline with my fingertip, feeling my heart pick up its pace. Losing myself in the world of my own creation, I allowed my hand to lower, to stray downwards towards the opening in my gown. It was warm in the room and it would be easy to just slip under the covers, momentarily living out my fantasies. It would be good practice, after all.

Just as my imaginary world was becoming more interesting, the real world interrupted with my door handle rattling up and down. Jesus Christ, I knew it.

"Wrong room!" I shouted at the door.

"Shit, sorry," came back a muffled reply.

I sighed and pulled the belt tighter around my dressing gown again. To be honest, it was probably for the best. I didn't have time to waste daydreaming when the real thing was becoming a possibility. I took my makeup bag from my bedside cabinet, pushing aside the envelope that held my secret stash of weaponry. I didn't think anything of it, but the visual made my arms tingle. I put it down to the perfume in the moisturiser.

Sitting on the small functional stool, at my small functional desk, I positioned my mirror in front of me. I was used to just putting on a lick of eyeliner and mascara most days, but today called for a bit more effort. I opened the bag and gazed inside at the place where makeup goes to die. The lining of the bag itself looked like it had been pebble-dashed with blusher, and I hoped it would look better on my face than on the saggy old material.

As I worked on my appearance, I thought about the conversation I'd had with Tom the other night, and just the memory of it made my heart go out to him. I'd got the gist previously that things weren't great at home, but his texts just confirmed it, divulging that he and his wife were still together, but may as well not be. She sounded like a right cow and I couldn't understand why she would want to treat him so badly.

He'd mentioned that the whole reason he'd signed up to our study in the first place was down to her insistence. For that, at least, I had to be thankful to her I supposed, as otherwise, I wouldn't have met him at all, and now I was in the position to help him.

In between the flurry of texts with Tom, I'd had a little look at his wife's Facebook profile, just to get a better image of the woman he was talking about. I'd had a peek before, but that was just out of curiosity. Now, it seemed more of a necessity. I wanted to know who my competition was.

She was probably early to mid-thirties, and pretty with her long curly red hair and green eyes, I'd give her that; but she looked distant, almost stuck up. Most importantly, she didn't look right for Tom. Their faces didn't fit together at all. I could only see a parade of profile pictures, unfortunately, due to her security settings, but it was amazing the information you could glean from those alone.

For example, most of the pictures were of her on her own, or her and her cat. Tom didn't feature in any of them for months on end, which seemed odd. She was either completely self-obsessed, or things had been over between them for a very long time. Poor Tom, having to put up with a woman who didn't really love him. It was about time he knew what real love was again.

Tom's texts to me had hinted that he thought she'd found someone else and lo and behold, I could see all their interactions whenever she changed her profile photo. There'd be a few likes, and one or two loves, always one from this Ash person. And generally, a comment, too. *Gorgeous* read one. *Wit woo* declared another. I took offence. No wonder Tom was so unhappy.

We'd never actually discussed the reasons behind why Tom had his sleep problems, but I was guessing this was a large part of it. Well, if his snotty wife didn't want him, and he was lonely and sad, then I would be more than happy to step up and show him how good life could be. I traced his cheek with my fingertip on an old image of him. The couple looked like they were wearing wedding outfits, which made his present situation even sadder to me.

Now, lipstick or no lipstick? I wondered. My mirror told me that I'd done a pretty good job with the makeup. Understated always took so much hard work, and I'd achieved it perfectly so far. I didn't want to ruin it all now. Besides, if he did kiss me, he wouldn't want lipstick all over his face, would he? I shivered at the thought. I knew in my heart that it was unlikely, but I couldn't count it out altogether. People do things they wouldn't normally do after a couple of daytime drinks, especially when they're emotional. I twirled my lip ring with my tongue and made a decision not to wear lipstick. Then, before I could change my mind, I removed the stainless-steel ring too, leaving a tiny little dent just below the pink of my lip. I didn't want any obstacles.

Ironically, just as that thought crossed my mind, my phone pinged with a WhatsApp from Jordan.

'Can we talk? Think we need to clear the air.'

I rolled my eyes. His timing was proving to be as rubbish as always.

Looking at my watch, I noted it was nearly eleven-thirty. Jordan would just have to wait if I was going to make it to the pub on time. I'd pre-booked a table at the Rose & Crown, which seemed perfect.

It was nice enough not to be full of uni students, but not so nice that it was over-priced. Best of all, due to the old style of the place, there were private nooks and crannies that we could tuck ourselves into and not be overheard by anyone else.

I pulled on my chosen outfit of jeans, heeled boots, and my long-sleeved cowl necked top which would show off just enough of my collar bones to be alluring, without being too obvious. It was only lunchtime, after all. I gave myself a quick spray of Body Shop perfume before collecting my bag and grabbing my coat from the back of the door. It was time to go and meet the man who was going to be my new boyfriend.

21

TOM

Tom pushed the heavy door of the pub open and stepped inside, the low lighting of the room in stark contrast to the brightness of the day. Momentarily blinded, he lifted his sunglasses, sliding them back to sit on the top of his head. He squinted around the room and spotted Bethany seated at a small table tucked around the side of the unlit fireplace. She was stroking a small dog who, on seeing Tom, jumped to its feet and barked at him.

"Hey, it's ok." Tom bent over, holding out his hand reassuringly. "Come here, boy."

The dog stayed where it was and continued its high-pitched yapping, seemingly displeased with the intruder.

"No wonder the dog doesn't like you. It's not a boy, it's a girl." Bethany laughed.

Tom raised a smile and tried again. "Here, girl."

The dog just looked at him scornfully and then trotted off on its stumpy legs behind the bar.

"Don't mind Poppy," the bartender told Tom as he straightened himself up again. "She's a bit of a grump. What can I get you?"

Tom eyed the draft lagers and plumped for a pint of Carlsberg. He gestured to Bethany to see if she wanted anything but she shook her head, a glass of white wine already on the table in front of her.

"It's ok, I'll bring it over, mate," the barman told Tom as he reached for his wallet. "The lady's set up a tab."

Tom thanked him and wound his way over to Bethany. They were the only people in the pub at the moment, but it was early. No doubt there'd be a few more people venturing in for scampi and chips soon.

Bethany stood up as he got to the table and Tom couldn't help but notice that she'd made an effort. Normally, she had her hair tied back, but today it was down around her shoulders. It made her look older, and more approachable somehow. He felt a bit underdressed in comparison. Still, it could have been worse if he'd been working today and had to turn up in his hideous orange uniform.

"How are you doing?" she asked as they both took their seats. Bethany leaned against the cushioned back of a bench and Tom perched precariously on a stool that had been built for someone much smaller than he was.

"I'm ok." Tom swapped the stool for a nearby chair. That was better. "I'm sorry about the other night. I...I wasn't in the best frame of mind." He shrugged his coat off and hung it over the back of his chair, just as his drink arrived at the table.

"Hey, don't worry. We've all been there, trust me." Bethany smiled.

"Hmm."

Tom wasn't sure that she could have a clue about what he was going through. She had to be what? Twenty-one? Twenty-two? Barely old enough to have experienced anything in life yet. His hand circled the pint of beer, fingers running down the sides of it, wiping droplets from the outside of the glass.

"Trust me," she repeated, her gaze resting firmly on his eyes.

Tom could have kicked himself. It didn't matter how old you

were when it came to pain. "Jordan not here yet, then?" he asked, looking around the empty room needlessly as if Jordan was about to jump out from behind a banquette shouting 'surprise!'

"We aren't joined at the hip, you know." Bethany laughed again, looking down at the table and seeming almost surprised that he'd asked the question.

"Sorry, it's just I thought…"

"He couldn't make it. Had some last-minute paperwork to get in, apparently, so I'm afraid you're stuck with just me."

"Not at all," Tom offered, feeling really awkward to be sat in an empty pub with an attractive young woman, one who he'd shared way too much with via text messages. Still, not one to learn quickly from his mistakes, he lifted his drink. "Cheers."

"Cheers," Bethany echoed, lifting her glass and taking a small sip.

Tom told himself he'd just have the one and then go. He felt completely lost as to what was expected of him in this situation and, as nice as Bethany seemed, and no matter how good her intentions were, this wasn't something that he wanted to pursue, not when he could be sitting at home and feeling sorry for himself on his day off. He still needed to get to the shops and buy some food, too. He took a long draught from his lager and looked out of the window, hoping for some inspiration to make conversation.

"How's the research going, then?" It was the best he could come up with.

Fortunately, the barman decided to put some music on, which filled the empty space and alleviated Tom from the earworm that had been dogging him all morning. Just the same snippet over and over again, but for the life of him he couldn't place the song and it had been driving him mad. This sounded like Amy Winehouse, which was just fine with Tom. Bethany seemed to like it too as her fingers started tapping against her glass.

"It's going well, thanks," said Bethany. "And a lot of that's down to you. We really appreciate it."

"Ah, that's good. And you're welcome." He took another drink while Bethany filled him in on some of the finer details, most of which went over the top of his head if he was honest. Out of the corner of his eye, he noticed an elderly couple coming through the door of the pub. At least they wouldn't be the only ones in there anymore.

By the time the new customers had been seated and served, Tom had finished his drink and Bethany was halfway down hers. He couldn't just leave her here to finish on her own, so Tom decided he'd just have one more to keep her company. He was a lot of things, but he still had some manners.

"Did you want to order some food?" The barman had materialised at their table.

"Ooh yes please," said Bethany. "I'm starving." She paused. "Fancy a quick bite, Tom?"

His stomach rumbled at the thought of it. "Um…"

"Go on. It's the least I can do, bearing in mind we can't afford to pay you for participating in the study."

He supposed it didn't matter, did it? And it wasn't like he had anything better to do right now other than indulging in his regular self-pity, and that was getting boring. Yes, this was a bit weird and he hardly knew the girl, but so what? It wasn't like he was doing anything wrong. Tom's mind flitted briefly to Gemma and that dickhead Ash who he still wasn't sure if she'd been carrying on with. God, he wished he had an image of Ash so that he had something better to focus his anger on. Prick.

"Oh, sod it, why not."

Menu choices made, and a fresh bottle of Pinot Grigio on the table with two glasses, Tom sat back and allowed his shoulders to drop a little. Bethany was proving to be decent company, and that was something he'd been starved of for a while. If it wasn't for the fact that her phone kept pinging every few minutes, you'd have thought she was much more mature than she actually was.

"Someone's popular." Tom nodded at her phone as it pinged again.

"Oh, God, I'm so sorry. I should've put it on silent." She picked it up and frowned at the screen before flicking a switch and putting it face down on the table.

"Everything ok?"

"It's fine. Just someone that won't take no for an answer."

"Ex-boyfriend?"

"Something like that."

She rubbed at her wrist and Tom was reminded of the scarring he'd caught a glimpse of on her arm at the last session. Her life was obviously more complex than he'd given her credit for, and he imagined the worst, hoping that she had the strength to get through whatever situation she had found herself in.

"Are you ok?" Tom asked her.

"I am now." She took a drink and looked at him with a mixture of what looked like sadness and hope in her eyes. "For a long time, I wasn't."

She looked lost and Tom wanted to do something to make it all better. She seemed such a strange mix of vulnerable youth and knowing maturity. Truth be told, he wanted to wrap her up in a bear hug, but he settled for patting her hand with his own. It felt small and cold underneath his warm palm.

Their food arrived and Bethany seemed relieved not to have to divulge any more information.

"Anyway, what about you?" she asked. "You never mentioned why you have problems sleeping?"

Tom's entire body tensed up again. His shoulders cranked back up to his ears, his jaw clenched, and his tongue glued itself to the roof of his mouth. "Ah, well. I don't tend to talk about it." He picked up his knife and fork and made a start on his lasagne. "You should eat up before it gets cold." He gestured to Bethany's salad, only realising his mistake after the words were out of his mouth.

She laughed kindly. "Well, you can talk to me, you know…if you want to."

"Thank you. That's very kind." Tom's smile made a concerted effort to reach his eyes but he suspected it didn't quite make it.

As they ate, Amy Winehouse finished up her last song on the *Back to Black* album and was replaced with another female crooner. Perfect background music for a midweek lunchtime. It was Adele, and Tom hoped it wasn't her first album. He never did understand the hype about Adele and he couldn't bear to listen to that album in particular nowadays although it was one of Gemma's favourites. He didn't feel that hungry anymore.

"I used to be a nurse." Tom put his fork down and replaced the empty space in his hand with his wine glass.

Bethany looked up at him, surprised, either at the news or at the fact that he'd spoken at all in their momentary silence. She finished chewing and looked at him questioningly.

"A paediatric nurse."

"Wow, that's an amazing job. I'm guessing the Red Cross talk was rather familiar the other night, then?" She laughed and popped a cherry tomato into her mouth, understandably not realising the gravity of Tom's admission. She chewed for a bit, then swallowed, her face registering the sweetness of the fruit, before looking back at him with some confusion. "Hang on though, you said your biggest fear was choking."

"Yes. It is. Hence my sprint to the toilet."

"But how did you manage as a nurse?" Bethany took a sip of her drink and carried on with her food, unaware of the trickle of sweat that was working its way down Tom's back.

"Until a couple of years ago, my biggest fear was spiders. I lost…" Tom paused and took a deep breath, causing Bethany to focus on him properly. "I lost someone in my care. An infant."

"Oh, Tom, no." Bethany started to rise.

"Please don't. Just...sit down." Tom was breathing heavily and he was glad he hadn't eaten too much of his lasagne as the few mouthfuls he'd taken were starting to shift around uncomfortably.

What the hell had possessed him to start sharing that information with Bethany? He barely knew her, but for some reason, the words just wanted to keep on coming of their own accord. He guessed there was some kind of truth in the ease of sharing with strangers. Bethany sat still and silent in front of him, her eyes wide.

"How did they...?" She didn't finish the sentence. There was no need to.

"He choked." Tom put his face in his hands, his breath coming raggedly from his lungs as they struggled to keep up with his rising panic. He couldn't let it claim him. He couldn't make a scene in another restaurant again. It was becoming a habit.

"Tom?"

"It was my fault. I should never have left him." He spoke from behind his hands, using them like a shield so she couldn't see his eyes. "If I'd been there...if I hadn't been so tired. Such a fucking idiot."

He felt Bethany's hands coming to rest on his forearms, their coolness calming, like a cold flannel to a fever, and he allowed his arms to be lowered. She had reached so far across the table that her sleeves had ridden up and he could clearly see her scars, not just on one, but both her arms. There were so many of them, mostly small and neat, but some longer, jagged, heartbreaking.

She'd followed his sightline with her eyes and pulled her arms back to her own side of the table, tucking them underneath, out of sight.

"I'm sorry," she said.

"What for?"

"For your pain."

Tom held his hand out to her across the table. "I'm sorry for your pain, too."

Bethany paused for a moment and then took his hand, the pair sitting in silent acknowledgement.

"Everything ok with your meals?" A member of staff stood at the side of their table enquiring over their half-eaten dishes and Tom reflexively pulled back, breaking whatever spell had been cast between them with such minimal speech.

Both Tom and Bethany made an effort to assure the waitress that the food was absolutely fine and that they'd just lost their appetites. She shrugged and took away their plates, undoubtedly not giving a damn what their excuses were as long as there was still a tip on the table when they left.

At a loss for words and feeling his initial awkwardness creeping back a little, Tom allowed his gaze to return to the window, noticing how full the car park had become. He hadn't been aware of the pub filling up behind him. The clatter of cutlery and the low ebb and flow of conversation that had gradually drowned out the rest of the Adele CD, which had now been replaced with the greatest hits of George Michael.

The waitress returned with the bill and Tom grabbed hold of it before Bethany could. Even though she'd said this was hers and Jordan's thank you treat, he didn't feel it was right that she paid, especially as she was just a student. The least he could do was pay for the uneaten meal.

They both stood and gathered up their things, Tom calling out a thank you to the barman on the way to the door, which he held open for Bethany.

"Well, you'll have to let me pay next time," she offered as she pulled her bag up to her shoulder, and Tom joined in with what was obviously a comment made in jest.

"Sure, why not."

She smiled at him and Tom could see that she really was a pretty girl. He'd not noticed before. Maybe it was because his marriage was all but dead and buried now. Maybe it was the wine. Maybe it was because she'd done something different to her hair, her face? Her face!

"Hey," he exclaimed. "You've lost your lip ring."

"Yeah, I'd had enough of it."

"I like it. I mean I like you without it."

"Really?" She touched her lip, looking pleased.

"Really."

Tom held out his hand again, and she took it, leaning up towards him, her other hand alighting on his shoulder and her lips lightly brushing against his unshaved cheek. Surprised at the contact, and very much out of practice, Tom reciprocated by jabbing his lips out and making contact with an area slightly to the back of Bethany's ear.

"So, I guess I'll see you for the final part of the project tomorrow, then," he muttered, trying to cover his embarrassment as they parted.

"Absolutely, so make sure you get a good night's sleep beforehand."

Tom laughed. "I'll try."

Heading off down the road, Tom put his sunglasses back on, even though the brightness of the morning had now been eclipsed by the usual cloud cover. He liked the anonymity they gave him.

He didn't quite know how to feel. Other than Gemma and a few counselling sessions, this was the first time he'd come even close to opening up to anyone. While it had been somewhat therapeutic to be honest about his past for a change, he couldn't help but feel a bit like kicking himself for sharing too much information to this girl that he barely knew; and who obviously had enough problems of her own. What on earth had possessed him to do it?

In fact, he was amazed that once he'd started talking, Bethany hadn't recognised him from all the news reports that had come out at the time, painting him as the devil incarnate. The stories so damning that even he believed some of them.

Maybe she had recognised him and didn't want to be rude, or maybe she didn't care. Maybe she had her own agenda that he wasn't even aware of.

He slowed his pace, turning to check the traffic before crossing the road, and caught sight of Bethany still standing outside the pub, tapping furiously into her phone like her life depended on it.

That was it, then, wasn't it? She was probably Googling his name right now.

22

BETHANY

I watched Tom stroll down the road from the pub before retrieving my phone from the depths of my bag. Just as I'd thought, there were about half a dozen WhatsApp messages queued up from Jordan, clamouring for my attention. He was so needy. God, I could just imagine what it would be like in a relationship with him. He'd want to discuss everything, picking every little thing apart. He wore me out with his friendship, let alone anything else. Why couldn't he just chill?

Nevertheless, we still had some way to go with our project so I couldn't ditch him just yet. I fired off a quick response telling him that everything was ok and there were no hard feelings on my part. His response pinged back straight away. Jesus! Was he just sitting by his phone waiting for me to get in touch? And my mother called *me* obsessive! *Seriously, everything's fine,* I replied. *We can talk later.*

I decided not to bother going home, instead choosing to have a wander around the shops in town for a while before heading over to Leigh's office for my session. I never normally went window shopping as the thought of it just depressed me. What was the point of looking at things that I couldn't afford?

Today, though, was different and I enjoyed just wandering around people watching and pretending I had loads of money to spend. I was still hyped up from seeing Tom and the wine that I'd drunk made everything soft and fluffy around the edges. It was such a nice feeling to be on the brink, the precipice of falling for someone again, and I practically skipped to my afternoon appointment, determined not to let Leigh bring me down with her depressing reality.

Her room was as warm as ever, and the comfort of the sofa combined with the afterglow of the alcohol I'd drunk conspired to make me feel drowsy. Leigh wasted no time in getting to the point.

"Have you been drinking?" she asked.

"Yup." I grinned. "Mind if I take my shoes off?"

"Not at all."

I eased my boots off and massaged the soles of my feet. I wasn't used to wearing heels.

"Do you want to tell me about your day, Bethany?" Leigh looked bemused, unused to seeing me so unrestrained.

"Yes, I do," I told her, dragging out my words for maximum impact. "I…went…on…a…date!"

A smile furrowed its way onto Leigh's face. I could see her trying to suppress it, but it was no good. "Was this with your mystery man?" she asked, clicking the end of her biro in and out before placing it down on the table between us, perfectly lined up with notepad and watch, of course.

I smiled coyly, not wanting to reveal too much, especially bearing in mind she'd probably frown upon me dating my research subject. Ethics and all that.

"Well, you look lovely," she told me. "I see you've removed your lip ring, too?" She was more observant than Tom, but I guessed that was part of her job description, always observing, looking for clues.

I nodded, enjoying the compliment from the woman whose wardrobe looked like it was bulk bought from Chanel.

"It suits you," she said.

"He said the same thing."

"It went well then, I take it?"

"Oh my God, it went so well." I couldn't help myself. I didn't have any girlfriends to share this kind of thing with, and Jordan would rather poke needles in his eyes than hear the details of my date. Leigh would have to do.

She looked at me, her expression asking me to continue, which I did. I told her about how we'd held hands over the table, the kiss as we'd parted, and how I was sure he'd inhaled my scent as his lips had touched my neck. I relived each moment as I described them, probably boring her rigid with my Mills and Boon replay of a pub lunch.

"We've got so much in common. Our backgrounds are both flawed but that just makes it easier for us to understand one another. And the way he looked at me, it was like someone had seen me for the first time, like he actually saw me."

"That's an interesting choice of words, Bethany. Do you think he knows you well enough yet?"

"Well, of course not yet, but we've got loads of time. He's splitting up with his wife."

"He told you that?"

"Well, sort of. She's cruel to him."

"I see." She paused. "I don't want you to get hurt, Bethany."

I wanted to cry. What was she doing? Just pouring negativity on my perfect day. I should have known better and cancelled my stupid session or just kept my mouth shut. "It's not *me* that's going to get hurt," I blurted. "He cares about me, I can tell. She's the one that's going to wind up hurt, and it'll be her own stupid fault."

"How can you be so sure?" she asked.

I didn't know, for sure. But it wasn't going to be me that suffered this time. I'd been through enough in the past and I wasn't prepared to go through it again. I was a new person. I was stronger, and I was moving on with my life.

Why was Leigh trying to ruin things? I'd been on my own for so long with no one that really cared about me, and now I had an opportunity to be with someone who felt things as deeply as I did.

My father didn't want me, my mother barely contained her dislike for me, my sister moved away as soon as she could, and my ex-boyfriend decided to leave me and go back to his wife. The only reason Jordan wanted to be my friend was because he wanted to sleep with me. They were all arseholes, and so, now that I'd found someone amazing, why didn't I deserve a chance to be happy with him? This wonderful man who, like me, had suffered so much. We could help each other heal.

I opened my mouth to reply and, just as I did so, Leigh's mobile phone rang.

"I'm so sorry, Bethany. That's very unprofessional of me. Let me turn it off." She hurried to her desk, leaving me sitting on the sofa with my arms wrapped around my middle, staring up at her stupid tomography picture on the wall.

"Where were we?" she asked once she sat back down opposite, but the moment had passed and, wanting to change the subject, I pointed to the chain around her neck.

"I like your necklace."

"Oh." Her fingers touched the locket. "Thank you."

I leaned in closer, for the first time able to see some engraving on the front but not close enough to make out the letters. Pretty. Maybe I could get one. I could keep a photo of Tom in it.

Leigh picked up her watch as usual to signify the end of our session. "We should stop there for today," she said. "It's good to see you moving on, but make sure the decisions you make are the right ones for you."

"Oh, I will," I told her.

STILL NOT WANTING to go back to my room at the shared house after I left Leigh's office, I felt like walking instead of waiting for my usual bus. It was late afternoon but due to the brightness of the day, the sun was taking its time to set; and even though my feet protested, I just wanted to stay outside in the fresh air for a while longer before holing myself back up in my pokey room.

Mind still buzzing with excitement, I took my phone from my bag and called up Google Maps. I then pressed 'Directions' next to the postcode that I'd already typed in. I couldn't actually remember doing it, but I knew exactly where I wanted to go. I watched the little red pin drop into place. Not far from here at all. In fact, it was only a twelve-minute walk.

I knew I probably shouldn't be doing this, and anyone on the outside looking in would think it was quirky behaviour, but it wasn't going to hurt anyone, was it? Just a quick peek at the house to see what it was like and I'd be on my way. No one would be any the wiser.

I pressed 'Go' on the app and let it guide me street by street deeper into the estate until I turned onto a fairly nondescript road with a small row of terraced houses looking like they'd been plonked in the middle of it. It was getting darker now so it was hard to pick out details, but the gardens all looked pretty neat and I could just about make out the house numbers. There it was, number eight, right on the end of the row. It needed a bit more care than the others, the grass overly long with a couple of broken fence posts protesting their strange angle.

Feeling my heart speed up with excitement, I kept on walking past, not wanting to draw attention to myself. I crossed the road a bit further down, taking a narrow-gated alleyway into a small recreation area.

I sat down on a bench and watched an elderly man make a

circuit around the edge of the grass. He was accompanied by a panting Jack Russell that strained on the end of its leash, probably desperate to run around.

I could just see the front and partial side of the house from where I sat, and as I watched, an upstairs light came on, illuminating the room. The decor wasn't much to shout about that I could see. The usual magnolia-coloured walls and a standard shaped raspberry coloured lampshade hanging from the ceiling. I waited, hoping for someone to walk into view, but there was no movement that I could see from my angle and the light was turned off again, creating a negative image of the shape of the window in my retinas.

"Evening." The old man and his dog shuffled behind me on their trail.

"Evening." I blinked back at him.

It was getting colder and I shoved my hands back in my pockets, annoyed that I hadn't brought my gloves. I could only make out the outline of the house now against the deepening night, so I told myself I'd just give it five more minutes and then head off.

I watched the old man carry on his circuit and then pass beneath a streetlight on his way towards the exit of the park, pausing briefly at a poo bin to make a deposit. Other than him, the street was empty.

I sighed and pushed myself up, trying not to feel disheartened that I hadn't seen Tom. As I did so, a small car pulled up in front of number eight. I couldn't see what colour it was in the dark, and was unsure of the make, although it was a small car, maybe something like a Corsa. My knowledge of cars was rubbish.

I froze and watched as the headlights were turned off, followed by the engine, plunging the street back into silence. The driver must have removed the key from the ignition as the interior light came on. I don't know why I was surprised to see her, but I was.

It was Gemma. Tom's wife. Bundled up with a big scarf around her neck and her hair tied up in a ponytail. I wasn't close enough to read her expression, but I could see her typing something into her phone. Even when the interior light ran out of energy, she sat there for another few moments, the glow from the screen illuminating her face.

I stayed perfectly still, frozen in a solo game of musical statues, worried that any movement might break the spell. Tom's texts to me had clearly said that there was no love between him and his wife anymore and that he was sure she was cheating on him. I could just imagine her messaging her lover now, telling him how awful her husband was and how much she wanted to leave him. Maybe she'd just come from being with him while poor unsuspecting Tom was sat at home waiting for her.

No matter which, she sounded like an absolute cow and it was no wonder Tom had had enough the other night when he poured his heart out to me. It was no surprise that we had found each other, both of us having suffered so much. It was meant to be. Destiny. It was written in the stars.

23

TOM

Maybe he was nervous about the final research session the next day, but Tom was having one of the worst nights that he'd had in a while. He was also conscious that Gemma was literally just across the hallway from him in their bedroom, probably sleeping like a baby. He hated being stuck in the spare room like a lodger.

The last few days had passed with minimal contact between them, mainly down to Gemma who'd arranged to do more night shifts at the hospital, no doubt to keep out of his way. She wouldn't come home in the morning until he'd already left for work, and then she'd have the house to herself while he was working at the supermarket. The only time when there was a risk of bumping into each other was the late afternoon, but she managed to make herself scarce even then. Tom wondered where she went before her shift and found he didn't like where his mind took him.

He lay on his back staring up at the raspberry-coloured lampshade. He hated the decor in this room, but as they were only renting there wasn't much they could do about it. Gemma had asked the landlord several times in the past if they could redecorate, but the answer was always a resounding no. He supposed they'd have to talk about taking one of their names off the lease sooner rather than later, and guessed it would probably have to be him. No doubt he'd end up as some sad single bloke living in a one-bedroom flat with only a spider plant for company, and cirrhosis of the liver.

Turning to look at the radio alarm clock on the bedside table, he groaned. Three twenty-five. He'd seen every hour since the moment he'd taken himself up to bed at eleven and he was exhausted. He'd managed to drop off sometime around two but had woken back up again, wrapped in the chilling embrace of a newly familiar nightmare that had taken hold of him.

It had started the same as usual, waking up in that damn hospital bed, the thin sheets stuck to his damp skin. He was still handcuffed securely to the bed rails, but this time as the screams down the hallway got louder and the privacy screen was pulled back, all he could see was the bed in the next bay. Gemma lay on top of it, her body naked, her throat giving voice to screams of pleasure as she gave herself up to someone else. She was unaware of Tom's presence as the two bodies writhed together, her partner, faceless, yet still ugly.

Tom's head was held still so he couldn't look away, and his eyes were clamped painfully open with wire speculums that cut into his lids. He had no choice but to watch the scene unfold next to him, hearing his wife call out the name that he knew was coming. "Ash." It poured from her lips like honey as she curled her fingers in her lover's hair.

Tom had fought against his restraints, eventually giving up and trying to stare at a spot just past the couple, whilst reciting familiar song lyrics to try and block out what was happening in front of him. His voice was a whisper, although he could hear himself sobbing. He got halfway through the first verse and, as he mouthed the words, Gemma turned her head in his direction as though she'd heard something. His breath caught in his throat and he repeated the words. At that point, she looked him straight in the eye and laughed, and laughed, and laughed. Tom was filled with more rage than he even knew was possible.

He'd woken up at that point, his anger and devastation battling for supremacy while his heart hammered against his chest. He knew it was his mind playing tricks on him. All the thoughts that he'd had at his darkest moments had conspired against him while his body had felt safe enough to relax in sleep. It was like a private viewing of the most terrifying horror film he could imagine.

He'd never been a fan of scary movies, so it was ironic that his own mind seemed to want to show them to him. The first one he'd ever seen had pretty much put him off for life. What was it called? That one with Freddy Krueger in it, with knives for fingers. *Nightmare on Elm Street*. That was it. All the kids in it were getting killed in their nightmares by Freddy, until one of them, the girl, had decided to face her fear and take away his power. And, apparently, it was that easy. Just like that, it had worked. No more Freddy and no more nightmares. Well…until the sequel, anyway.

Tom's mind was filled with the thought of pouring himself a little something to soften the edges and ease him back into sleep, but he fought the urge with every fibre in him and instead pushed himself up and reached for his iPad which lay, charging, next to the clock radio.

Maybe there was something in the *Elm Street* storyline that was worth a try. Maybe, if he faced his fears, his demons would give him a moment's peace. He opened the iPad and, not for the first time, typed his name into Google.

24

BETHANY

I t felt as though it had taken ages for today to roll around. The culmination of our research experiment was finally here and, while I was excited about the outcome, I was even more excited just to be seeing Tom again.

I hadn't put my lip ring back in since the other day, knowing that Tom preferred me without it, and I guessed the little pinprick hole beneath my lip was starting to heal up. I'd not really thought about it until Jordan commented.

"Wow." He'd done a double-take when I arrived at the library. "Where's your face metal?"

My tongue had gone straight to its usual spot on the inside of my lip, and it had surprised me when it hadn't met its solid resistance. I'd forgotten it wasn't there. "I just decided it wasn't me anymore."

"You look much better without it," he said, making me bristle. It wasn't like I'd asked his opinion.

We'd managed to clear the air but there was still tension between us. I could tell Jordan felt put out that I wasn't interested in him and, in turn, I just couldn't be bothered to make an effort to cushion his feelings anymore. It wasn't my fault that I'd met someone else, was it?

"Did you bring the gun?" I asked him, itching to get things underway as soon as Seb and Tom turned up.

"Of course."

Jordan reached into the blue backpack that seemed to accompany him everywhere he went and pulled out a folded over carrier bag. "It's so lifelike. You won't believe it." He rummaged inside, first retrieving four red-tipped neon green rubber bullets and placing them on the table. His hand dipped back inside the bag and came out cradling what looked like an actual pistol.

"Oh my God. It's…*is* it real?" I reached out to touch it and my fingers met with plastic instead of the cool metal they had expected.

"Mad, isn't it?" Jordan was beaming with pride. "It's modelled on a Colt. It even has a real blowback style loading mechanism."

"I won't even pretend to know what that is. Is it safe?"

"Shit, man! That's what I'd like to know, too!" Seb had materialised in the doorway. Our willing victim, who was now looking a little bit dubious as Jordan swung around with the prop in his hand. "Whoa man, seriously, is that thing real?" Seb ducked back behind the frame of the door, making both Jordan and I catch each other's eye and allow ourselves a shared smile. I felt a little of the bad vibes easing between us again.

"It's totally safe," Jordan assured him. "It takes rubber bullets and they only fire a few feet. Look, I'll show you."

Seb crept back through the doorway and was now watching, rapt, as Jordan fiddled around loading the bullets.

"All our would-be murderer will need to do is pull the trigger and the bullet will fire. Here…" Jordan held the gun out to Seb, who took it in his hands as if it were a bomb that might explode at any minute. "Have a go. You can fire it at me. It really doesn't hurt."

Seb turned the gun over and held it in both hands, arms out straight, mimicking the hundreds of action heroes that he'd probably watched over the years in movies. Jordan positioned himself in front of him.

"Just try not to aim at my face or my nuts."

"Yeah, no worries."

Seb pulled the trigger and, as promised, the bullet made a half-hearted effort to travel at the speed of sound before running out of energy and cushioning into Jordan's chest.

I clapped my hands together, totally lost in the moment before realising I must look like one of Hayley's sad little Kardashian gang. I stopped, hoping neither Jordan nor Seb had noticed. I needn't have worried as the pair of them were too busy geeking out over their new toy.

"That's awesome, man. Where did you get it?" Seb was now turning in a circle and aiming at random points around the room like a wannabe Jason Statham.

"Amazon. Only £8.99." Jordan's chest puffed out with pride like a bloody pigeon.

"Gotta get me one of these bad boys." Seb turned the gun in my direction.

"Don't even think about it," I told him.

He grinned and lowered it back down. "What's the score then?"

Jordan confiscated the gun and collected up the little brightly coloured bullets that had been dispensed as we both started filling Seb in on what was going to happen.

"So, he's going to fire it at the back of my head then?" Seb asked.

"Yeah, don't worry. We wouldn't want to mess up that pretty face," I told him.

"I always knew you wanted me." A lopsided grin worked its way across Seb's mouth as he lunged forward to try and grab me in a hug. Even though Jordan was stood behind me, I could feel his distaste, no doubt wondering if I would stoop so low. I sidestepped

Seb's advances and he gave up on the chase quickly, proving that he was about as interested in me as I was in him.

"Ok." Jordan stepped in. "You'd better disappear before our subject turns up."

"Yeah, no worries, man. Just one question, though. Do you think he's actually going to do it? You know, pull the trigger?"

"We don't know." I shrugged. "For the past few weeks, he's been coming in for sessions with us and we've used hypnosis, elements of mind control and amnesia training so he can't remember what's happened. So far, he's done really well, but up till now we've only practised the shooting element with two bits of wood taped together with duct tape at a right angle."

"Bloody hell." Seb blew his fringe up out of his eyes. "So, did he fire it? The wood?"

"Well, he aimed it and tried to pull a trigger so, technically, yes. This is the first time we'll have tried it with an actual replica gun, though, so it's kind of make-or-break time. Either way, we're going to get some great findings, so it doesn't really matter if he pulls the trigger or not."

Jordan looked at me, shocked. "How come you've never mentioned that before? I thought that was what you wanted? To prove that it can be done."

I stopped in my tracks. He was right. Somehow, though, I'd let my feelings for Tom become more important to me than the project itself. Of course, I wanted a positive outcome, just not to the detriment of Tom's feelings for me.

With Seb out of the way, Jordan and I set up the room so that we were ready for when Tom arrived. We'd plugged my laptop into the mounted TV set and put out several chairs in random positioning to face it, figuring it would be easier for us all to watch the film on a bigger screen. We'd pushed a table underneath the television and Jordan's trusty iPhone sat on top on its side, balanced against some mugs, ready to record proceedings. We were good to go.

Just before Tom was due to arrive, I popped to the ladies and sprayed a little perfume on my neck. Not too much, but just enough to trigger Tom's senses, reminding him of the moment he'd kissed the side of my neck after lunch the day before. I shivered with pleasure at the memory and hoped it would elicit the same feeling in him.

It was another few minutes before Tom arrived, and when he did, my heart felt like it was hurling itself repeatedly against my chest. My breath came quickly as I walked over to him and said hello. The poor man looked exhausted, his skin pale, but half disguised beneath a couple of days' worth of stubble on his chin. He rubbed it distractedly as he came into the room.

"Bethany, hi," he said, before nodding over at Jordan. "Sorry you couldn't make it yesterday."

Jordan looked up from the laptop, confused.

"Do you mind if I grab a quick coffee? I'm shattered." Tom wandered off to the kitchen, leaving Jordan staring at me with massive question marks in his eyes.

Damn it. I'd been so caught up in my blossoming romance that I hadn't even thought of a cover story for Jordan. "I'll tell you later." I brushed it off, hoping that would satisfy him for now.

"We're supposed to be a team," he whispered angrily, the reproach clear in his face.

"We *are* a bloody team. I'll tell you later, I promise." I gave Jordan a weak smile, my brain trying to kick into gear to find a suitable story that I could fob him off with.

Jordan bent back over the laptop and I busied myself moving chairs around until Tom re-emerged with a mug of coffee in his hands. "Sorry, I should have asked if anyone else wanted one."

"Don't be silly," I told him. "Why don't you grab a seat and make yourself comfy."

Tom did as instructed, blowing at the liquid in his mug a few times before giving up and putting it on the floor to one side of his seat in the middle of the second row. There were a couple of chairs on either side of him and three others just in front. I looked at Jordan and smiled but he looked away from me again.

"Are we expecting anyone else tonight?" Tom asked gesturing at the empty seats.

"Yes, he'll be here shortly," Jordan explained. "Just a third, or, technically, fourth party to keep an impartial eye on the experiment."

We'd already arranged with Seb that he would turn up at a specific time, allowing Tom the opportunity to settle in and start to immerse himself in the film we were about to show him. He was supposed to make a noisy entrance and seat himself in the chair directly in front of Tom in the hope that this would spark an initial irritation in him. I just hoped Seb didn't get distracted by anything between now and the point of his arrival as he was quite often like a dog spotting a squirrel and forgetting all other information.

Tom rubbed his eyes and nodded, clearly not caring if our whole student year turned up to watch. He just looked as if he wanted to lie down and fall asleep. I wondered if he and his wife had been up arguing all night. Maybe he'd left her. Maybe he'd left her for me. It was only a matter of time.

I sat down on one side of him, still making sure to be out of view of the iPhone. The urge to reach across and take his hand was almost insurmountable, especially when he looked across at me and smiled bleakly. "Well, I'm ready when you are."

"Right, let's get this show on the road, shall we?" Jordan stood upright, turning away from the laptop to face us and repositioning his glasses on his nose.

"Let's do it," Tom said, right hand forming a fist in some kind of power salute.

"So, this evening we're just going to sit and watch a movie,"

Jordan started to explain. "All you need to do is to try and switch off from everything else around you and relax. Just enjoy the film."

I couldn't help myself. I reached across and patted Tom's hand as Jordan turned away to set up the film. Tom looked at me, his expression showing surprise at the touch, but also thankfulness. I wished I could wrap myself up in his arms and snuggle into his side to watch the film, instead of the pair of us sitting bolt upright in stackable chairs. Next time, I promised myself.

Jordan pressed a key on the laptop to start the film, and then sat himself down on the other side of Tom, bringing his rucksack with him and leaving it open by the side of his chair. We were ready.

The opening scenes began. A written narrative in monochrome inched its way up the screen eventually leading to a clip of Robert Kennedy announcing his candidacy and the reasons behind it. All was set against a backdrop of protests, bombing and riots, setting the tone of the film perfectly. Then the screen went dark and up came one word in stark contrast: *Bobby*.

I leaned back in my chair and made eye contact with Jordan behind Tom's head. It had been a risk putting on the film that covered the assassination of Bobby Kennedy, but it felt poignant, and what was life without a few risks? Tom stared straight ahead, already allowing himself to be pulled into the unfolding events. Not that the film was that much about the murder, anyway, but more about the lives of a group of different people on that fateful day. It had been slated by the critics, apparently, but I'd enjoyed it.

The three of us sat in silence, watching the film unfold in front of us. Tom seemed to be enjoying it, which was a result because if he'd nodded off, something that was entirely feasible given the state of him, everything would be ruined. I tried to lose myself in the story but was distracted by Jordan checking his watch every few minutes. He was undoubtedly keeping track of the running order of events and hoping to God that Seb would play his part by showing up on time.

Just as Kennedy started to make his acceptance speech on the screen, the door to the annexe creaked in protest at being opened by an interloper. Seb. Thank goodness. We'd run the risk of anyone being able to walk in off the street by leaving the front door unlocked.

"Hey guys," he stage-whispered. "Sorry I'm late."

"It's ok. Just take a seat," I told him.

Seb shuffled into the room, ducking down as he crossed in front of the TV, his jacket making a loud rustling as he placed it on the back of his chair in front of Tom and took his place. "Anyone got popcorn?" he asked, turning round to me, his usual dappy grin on his face.

I shot him a look of annoyance. The stupid idiot couldn't help a bit of ad-libbing to make his part bigger. Jordan looked panicked on the other side of our subject, but Tom seemed still immersed in the film, not appearing to let the intrusion get to him.

We all settled back and watched Bobby Kennedy finish off his speech, the crowds cheering for him as the film's backing track segued into 'The Sound of Silence' by Simon and Garfunkel. Every time I heard it now after what Leigh had told me, it gave me goosebumps, so the pathos to it was unbelievable. I hadn't shared that fact with Jordan, though. I liked my secrets. As far as he was concerned, we'd only used that song as a trigger because it had featured in the movie. I let him think that.

As the music played, the image on the screen flickered and was replaced by the monochromatic polka dot pattern that we'd chosen as our second trigger to put Tom into his trance state. I held my breath and watched Tom out of the corner of my eye as he slowly raised both hands to the sides of his head and pressed his index fingers to his temples. As he did so, I allowed myself to turn fully to face him and watched Jordan reach down into his rucksack, retrieve the gun and hold it out, open-palmed, in front of Tom. I prayed that Seb would just keep still and not do anything stupid.

Eyes wide open, and not even hesitating, Tom brought his hands back down from his temples and took the replica Colt from Jordan in complete silence. I could see Jordan's mouth hanging open on the other side of him, and I no doubt mirrored his expression of complete amazement. My hands felt clammy with sweat and I resisted the urge to wipe them against my jeans, not wanting to move a muscle in case it broke the spell. Instead, I watched as Tom slowly lifted the gun, both hands around the grip, finger poised over the trigger, eyes slowly focusing in on his target.

And then he blinked.

25

TOM

"What the fuck?" Tom's hands automatically fell apart, the gun spinning on his right index finger before falling with a clatter to the floor. As if shot with a bolt of electricity, Tom leapt up from his seat, sending it crashing to the floor behind him. He half climbed and half fell over the back of it to put some space between himself and the weapon that lay on the floor.

"Shit," he heard Jordan say from the right of him, and the guy whose head was only seconds ago being used as target practice turned to reveal a face that was slapped by shock.

"Tom, Tom, it's ok." Bethany rose on the other side of him, reaching out for his arm. "Try and stay calm."

"Are you fucking kidding me?" he shouted back at her. "I had a gun in my hands, pointed at someone's head!"

"Please Tom." Bethany tried again to placate him. "I know it's a bit weird, but it's all part of the experiment."

"Weird? This is fucking insane. You two are fucking insane." He backed further away holding his own hands up in surrender.

Jordan reached down for the gun that rested on the floor. "It's not real, Tom. Look." He held it out to Tom in the palm of his hand. "Seriously, look. It's plastic." He tapped it and Tom heard the clack of his nail. "It fires rubber bullets, too. Can I show you?"

Tom nodded, his breathing still coming fast and showing no signs of slowing.

Jordan carefully removed the magazine from the gun and popped out what looked like four bright green bullets with red tips. "Here, can I throw you one?" he asked.

Tom nodded again and caught one of the little cylinders, feeling what was undoubtedly rubber in his hands.

"Take the gun," Jordan offered, holding it out, the nozzle facing downwards.

Tom took it in his hands, amazed that he was holding lightweight plastic instead of what he had been convinced was solid, heavy metal. He turned it over and then passed it back to Jordan. "I don't understand. Why the hell would you give me a gun and make me think it was real?" Tom's hands went to his face, fingers rubbing at his eyes and pulling the skin taut.

"It's all part of our research, Tom. Please, why don't you sit back down?" Bethany had righted the chair again.

"If it's all the same to you, I'd rather stand." Tom started pacing up and down, three sets of eyes watching him, like visitors at a tiger enclosure in the zoo. He was fuming. "What research is this exactly?" he asked, drawing to a halt by the windows and opening one of the blinds so that he could look out into the car park. He could see a woman trying to juggle her shopping and a small toddler onto the back seat of her car and wished he was out there offering to help instead of being stuck in this room where the world seemed to have tilted on its axis. He could see the reflections of the other three stood behind him in worried silence, probably wondering exactly how to explain themselves to him. He turned. "Well?"

"Ok, let me try to explain." Jordan put the toy gun out of sight in his backpack, while Bethany still seemed rooted to the spot.

The new guy, who Tom hadn't even been introduced to, stood up and, looking uncertain, cleared his throat. "Hey, man. I think I'll leave you guys to it if it's ok?"

Jordan and Bethany didn't even register him as he collected his things and left without another word. Tom saw him hurrying out of the car park from the corner of his eye.

"Well?" Tom repeated.

Jordan exhaled deeply. "Basically, over the last few weeks, we've been using hypnotism and induced amnesia to see if you could be convinced to do something that was against your moral code."

"Go on." Tom leaned back against the wall, exhausted with the effort of standing up.

"The hypnotism has been going really well, and you've proved yourself to be a fantastic subject. Malleable and very open to suggestion. You're basically the ideal candidate for hypnotism."

Tom raised his eyebrows, suggesting Jordan should continue without pause.

"The induced amnesia means that you haven't been able to remember anything that happened whilst you were in a hypnotic state at our sessions. It's important so that your mind doesn't affect the experiment with its own beliefs."

"And so, what? You've been hypnotising me to do what? Shoot someone?"

Jordan looked across at Bethany and Tom followed his gaze. She looked back at Jordan and Tom could read that she didn't want to say anything that she didn't have to. He could see that she was silently pleading with Jordan, her arms straight and stiff at her sides, hands folded into small fists. Pleading for what, he couldn't tell.

"Aren't *you* going to say anything?" Tom turned his frustration in Bethany's direction.

"I…we…our research is based on whether a subject can be convinced to go against their conscious critical faculty to carry out an act that they wouldn't normally be capable of." Bethany's eyes were cast downwards.

"Look at me," demanded Tom, and she raised her eyes to look just to the side of his face. "Now, tell me in English."

"Well, based on the studies carried out back in—"

"Just fucking tell me," he shouted, aware of spittle shooting from his lips.

"We wanted to prove whether you could be hypnotised to carry out a crime."

"A crime?" Tom's eyes, tired though they were, were wide in disbelief. "Just say the fucking words."

Bethany's bottom lip quivered. "Murder."

As the admission fell from her lips in no more than a whisper, it was as though Tom's legs had lost their ability to stand on their own, and he slid down the wall onto his haunches, burying his face in his hands.

He wanted to cry. He wanted to scream. He wanted to lash out at these two idiotic kids who thought they had the right to play with his life under the pretence of helping him. He raised his head once again, which felt like it weighed a tonne, and looked at them both stood in front of him. Their heads hung down like two naughty school kids who'd been caught out doing something they shouldn't. Not even the decency to look me in the eye, he thought.

"What the absolute fuck does that have to do with helping me get over my sleep issues?"

"Tom, we never said that we could cure your sleep issues." Jordan had piped up again.

"Your advertisement clearly said that you would." With an effort, Tom pushed himself back up to standing.

"No. No, it didn't. We never promised that, Tom. It was only ever a possible positive outcome. I'm sorry if you thought otherwise."

Tom's mind felt as though it was spinning out of control inside a centrifuge, and he could feel his shutters that had been on their way to being opened wide with the suggestion of a miracle cure, come hurtling back down with incredible force.

"Tom, please come and sit down," Bethany pleaded. "We can talk about it. I can make you a cup of tea for the shock." She turned to head to the kitchen, and Tom's molten anger reached boiling point before it started to go cold. Ice cold.

"Fuck you, and fuck tea. I need a fucking drink."

26

BETHANY

I tried to grab hold of Tom's sleeve as he slammed his way out of the room, but caught nothing but air.

"Let him go," Jordan advised me. He'd stood back out of Tom's way as he crashed past. "Let him go and cool off."

But I couldn't. I couldn't stand to see the pain and confusion in his face as it made me hurt even more. He was my responsibility, now. I grabbed my phone and ran after him, out of the building, just in time to see him jump in his car and rev the engine. I made a move towards the vehicle, but I didn't stand a chance in getting to him before he floored the pedal and screeched out of the car park.

I wanted to call him more than anything, but I knew that it would be too soon. He'd already told me to fuck off once, and I couldn't bear to hear it again, even though I was sure that it was only said in anger.

Shaken, I stood underneath the awning of the building to avoid the spitting rain that had just started to fire its tiny bullets from the sky. I was cold and I'd left my coat inside, but I just needed to be alone for a moment out in the cool air, away from the suffocating comfort that Jordan would undoubtedly wrap around me the second I walked back inside.

Jesus, today had gone completely pear-shaped. There had always been the possibility that the experiment might not actually go to plan, but I really hadn't thought Tom would lose the plot like he did. I didn't quite know how to process the information properly.

I was due to turn up at Leigh's in under an hour for my usual session, but I wasn't sure that I was ready to be quizzed about today's events. I swiped my phone open and called up her number.

I prayed that her answerphone would pick up like it normally did when I rang. It wasn't a problem that she never actually answered the phone herself, as I knew she must be with other clients and would pick up her messages in between her appointments. Today, though, I'd obviously caught her during a break and it caught me off guard to hear her pick up.

"I can't come today," I told her. "I'm not feeling too good." The little white lie came easily.

"Oh, dear. Is everything ok?" she asked, obviously picking up on my upset. "Wasn't today the big finale of the experiment? Are you still going to be able to go ahead?"

I loved that she had remembered, that I wasn't just a number to her, another in a long line of patients. "Yeah, we've just finished. It didn't go too well." My voice cracked, thinking of the way that Tom had glared at me with such hatred.

"Oh no, I'm so sorry. Not the result that you'd hoped for, then?"

I sighed deeply, blowing my hair out of my eyes on the exhale. "No, not really. It looks like all we've done is to prove the case for the CIA. Apparently, you can't hypnotise someone to do something they shouldn't do if their moral code is too strong."

The phone went silent for a moment.

"Leigh? Are you still there?" I didn't really care if I'd lost her. I just wanted to stand out here in the rain and cry.

"Yes, yes. Still here. Are you sure you can't make it in? It might do you good."

God loves a trier, especially a salaried one, I thought meanly, immediately regretting it. She did seem like she wanted to help me. "Can we do tomorrow instead?" I asked. I needed to process everything first, deal with things in my own way before dissecting them with someone else.

"I really think it's important that we talk, Bethany," she pushed harder. "You don't sound like you're in a good place."

"I...no. I can't. I just need to go home."

Ending the call, I continued to stand outside, breathing in the smells of Spring and watching the leaves on the nearby hedgerow glistening from the rain, looking for all the world like they had a coat of varnish on them.

Tom had called me insane. He'd called me insane and told me to fuck off. And then he'd just left. Everything had been going so well beforehand, too. We'd started to go somewhere, and now...now I didn't have a clue what was going to happen. He was so angry with me that there was the possibility he could even go back to his wife, I supposed. I couldn't bear it. My mind flitted to my bedside table and the envelope nestled inside. I didn't want to hurt myself again, but I could feel the pressure starting to build inside me, itching underneath my skin. I was no better than a junkie who needed their next fix. I craved it.

"Hey, Bethany." It was Jordan, jolting me out of my dark thoughts. "You'll catch your death out here." He held out my coat and I took it gratefully, too tired for my usual scorn.

"Thanks." I threaded my arms through the sleeves, feeling my friend watching me closely.

"Have you been crying?" he asked.

I brushed against my cheeks with my fingertips, feeling the moisture there but berating Jordan anyway, telling him not to be so stupid. "It's just from the rain."

"I thought as much." He pushed his glasses up his nose, still looking at me without smiling. "Come on. I've packed everything up and we're going for a drink. I think we both need one."

TUCKED into a window nook in the pub round the corner from the library, and waiting for Jordan to get my second vodka, lime and lemonade, I started to feel a bit more like my normal self. Whatever that was.

It was early evening now and, outside, the sky was starting to lose its tenuous grip on daylight. People trudged up and down the High Street, shoulders hunched under umbrellas, probably on their way home after work. Not for the first time, I wished I could trade lives with one of them. I watched a man, arm protectively around his partner, holding an umbrella aloft in his other hand, making sure she was under cover. Her life looked good and I hoped she appreciated it. Made the most of it while it lasted.

I sighed and turned back to face the room as Jordan returned to our table with drinks and a bag of cheese and onion crisps. I hated cheese and onion.

"Thanks," I told him as he ripped the packet open, lying it flat on the table like a dissected lab rat.

"Well, it wasn't all bad today," he announced, grabbing some crisps and chewing on them too loudly. "At least we got a result, even if it wasn't the one we wanted."

"Really?" I raised an eyebrow and took a big gulp of my drink, wincing at the tartness of the lime and Jordan's ever-present positive attitude to life.

"Come on, Bethany." He swallowed. "I know you're upset about how Tom reacted, but there was always a risk that something like that could happen. It's the whole nature of research. You can't tell the subjects what you're trying to achieve, or you'll never achieve it." He took some more crisps and shoved them in his mouth, masticating like a cow.

"Yeah, I know. I'm just worried about him, I suppose. What if he does something stupid?"

"Like what?"

"I don't know, do I? He was so mad when he left, he could've had an accident or something."

Jordan stopped chewing and looked squarely at me. "Bethany, this isn't like you. Normally, you're the pragmatic one, telling me how it is. Why are you so worried?"

I couldn't tell him that the real reason I was worried was that Tom might now go running back to the arms of his bitch wife and would never want to see me again. Jesus, this is what love did to you, and it sucked. I should have learned my lesson after Daniel, but no, Tom had to come walking into my life with his injured soul and sad eyes. I didn't stand a chance. He needed me and, against my own better judgement, I'd fallen for him. "I don't know. What if we've messed him up?"

"We haven't messed him up. Don't be crazy." Jordan licked his finger, wiping it around the inside of the crisp packet to collect any tiny scraps that he'd missed, before putting it in his mouth and sucking. I hated him at that moment. Really and truly hated him.

"Don't call me crazy. I'm not fucking crazy." My tone was quiet, hoping to get the point across without anyone else nearby hearing us. "I've already been called insane today, and I'm not going to take it from you as well."

Jordan looked at me in surprise, taking his finger out of his mouth and wiping it on his shirt. "Hey, I didn't mean it. And Tom called us both insane, remember?"

I did, of course, but Tom had looked at me when he'd said it. It killed me to know he thought that about me, and it reminded me of

Daniel that time when he shouted at me in his garden, calling me a psycho, a nutter. His words had hurt me so much, I'd gone home and cut myself afterwards. I'd got a bit carried away that time though, and I'd woken up in hospital with my wrist bandaged and my mother and a policewoman at the side of the bed talking about me as if I wasn't there.

I couldn't help the way I felt, and it certainly didn't make me crazy. If anything, I thought that I was more empathetic than most people. I felt things more intensely, and their pain got all jumbled up with mine. I was just capable of loving some people too much, and that had to be a good thing.

"My round," I said, wanting to change the subject.

"But we haven't finished these ye—"

I knocked my drink back in one go and got up, my head spinning a little, but whether from the vodka or standing up too quickly I wasn't sure. "Speak for yourself. Do you want one or not?"

"Sure." Jordan shook his head in defeat. "Why not?"

When I returned to the table, fresh drinks in hand, Jordan had his phone pressed to his ear.

"Who's that?" I mouthed at him, and he put up a finger to pause me before speaking.

I put the glasses on the table, Jordan's pint sloshing over the top and soaking my hand. Damn it. I wiped it on my jeans before sitting down, my knee knocking the table and causing more lager to spill.

"Hi, erm Tom? It's Jordan here. I…we just wanted to see if you're ok. We're both really sorry about this afternoon."

I couldn't believe Jordan was ringing Tom without asking me first. Tom was my…what exactly was he? Not my boyfriend yet, but we *were* seeing each other. I could feel fury rising inside me at Jordan's imposition, but then reigned it in quickly. He didn't know that anything was going on between us yet.

"I hope you understand that in most research projects the

participants can't be made aware of what's going on, otherwise it would muck up the results." Jordan continued to dig a grave for us both. "And I know you hoped that it would help with your sleep problems, but I swear we never did promise that we could cure them, although we did try our best to alleviate them for you. Maybe some hypnotherapy would actually benefit you, though. In time… obviously. Anyway, give us a call when you can, as we really should have a bit of a de-brief. Ok. Um, bye, then."

Jordan finished the call and focused back on me. "So, what do you think? Was his conscious critical faculty too strong to be convinced to commit murder?"

"God, I don't know." I swirled my straw around in the glass. "I'd be surprised, bearing in mind how well he did in all the tests beforehand. I mean, he threw the cup of confetti in the acid test without hesitation, didn't he?"

"Maybe we should've used the other guy after all, the old bloke?"

I knew Jordan would bring that up at some point. Joseph had been his first choice, but I'd convinced him to use Tom instead. I couldn't even remember why now, but it had seemed like the right decision to make. It was almost like the choice had been made for me by a higher power that had brought us together. Not that I believed in God, as he'd never done me any favours.

"Well, it's too late now, isn't it," I pointed out. "Like you said, at least we've got some good results, even if they weren't the ones we were hoping for. Maybe the CIA never did hypnotise Bobby Kennedy's assassin, after all."

"Or maybe they did, but he had a weaker moral code of ethics," Jordan countered.

"Perhaps he was just a good liar."

"Maybe the CIA used actual hypnotists instead of a pair of useless uni students."

"Yeah, maybe…" I grinned.

We both sat quietly for a bit and it felt almost normal for a moment, whatever that was. It was almost like it was before this whole project started. But then Jordan had to go and ruin it, like always.

"What did Tom mean when he said he was sorry I couldn't make it yesterday?"

27

TOM

Tom had found a dingy old pub down the road from his housing estate. Not a place for families or young couples who wanted some nice pub food to go with their bottle of Sauvignon Blanc; unless you counted pork scratchings as good food and house white as good wine. No, this place was a proper old spit and sawdust watering hole, a place where nobody knew your name, and it was probably for the best.

Other than Tom, three old boys were seated on scuffed stools around the bar, making small talk with a bored barmaid whose dress made her resemble a plump Dalmatian. There were also two younger men in overalls engrossed in some incessant jangling game on a fruit machine against the far wall. The carpet reeked of stale beer, the walls were decorated a grimy yellow from many previous years of nicotine staining, and if you leaned on the bar, you ran the risk of your arm getting stuck to it. It was a dive, but it had alcohol and, Tom had discovered, a decent jukebox.

He'd piled some coins into it when he'd arrived and selected some heavy, angry music: Limp Bizkit, Slipknot, and Marilyn

Manson. The two lads at the fruit machine started nodding their heads in time to the music, and the old men at the bar turned down their hearing aids a little. You couldn't please everyone, Tom thought, and the music suited the way he felt.

Sitting at the table scrolling through his phone, Tom tried to find the original advertisement for the total shit show that he'd been a part of for the last few weeks, wanting desperately to be proved right.

Jordan hadn't lied, though. The promotion had never promised to cure anything. In hindsight, it was cleverly written, managing to dangle an elusive carrot while at the same time offering absolutely nothing. All he'd done was sign up to be a lab rat for whatever their research was. He'd literally signed up to be a murderer.

If someone else had been chosen as the subject, it probably wouldn't have been such a big deal to them. They would have just laughed it off, quite thrilled at the end outcome and not minding too much if their sleep issues weren't entirely cured. But it wasn't like that for him. This had been his last chance, his last hope to save his marriage. It was as if both he and Gemma had been so desperate that they'd read the advertisement in another language and then translated it to suit themselves, pinning absolutely everything on the outcome. Well, he'd done that. She'd given up halfway through and gone running off when things got too hard. Harder.

Eventually, his song choices came to a screeching halt and the automatic playlist kicked in on the jukebox with a random selection of music, which the old boys seemed to like better as they turned their hearing aids back up. Tom gazed in their direction, vaguely registering the barmaid wandering past with a few empties in hand. Gemma would have hated it in here. Shit, *he* hated it in here.

Tom closed his eyes and pictured his wife sitting on the other side of the table, pulling a silly face at him like she would do back when they used to laugh about things. He missed that about her. He missed everything about her.

He hadn't stood a chance when they'd met. He was always going to fall in love with her, and he knew it the first time their paths crossed. It sounded ridiculously sappy and if someone else had said it to him, he would have rolled his eyes and told them they were being a twat. But it was true. He'd met her and he was smitten. Case closed.

He'd only just started working at the hospital and it was pure luck that he'd been put on the same rota as her. They didn't even work in the same department as each other, even though they were both nurses. But as he'd sat at the nurse's station on his first day, waiting to be summoned into one of the consulting rooms, she'd walked past him with one of the doctors and caught Tom looking her up and down.

Instead of getting pissed off, embarrassed or big-headed, she'd pulled a silly face at him. Eyes crossed and her mouth wide in a smile, with her tongue poking out at him. She didn't even break stride as her companion continued to chat away, facing forwards and unaware of the gurning at his side.

And that was it. Tom had laughed his head off, which garnered some strange looks from the families in the waiting room, no doubt wondering if the male nurse sat laughing on his own should be a patient in the psychiatric department.

On his break, he'd managed to find her in the canteen where she was sat with a group of other nurses all looking tired, but putting the world to rights over their sugar-laden caffeine.

He'd got himself a drink and walked over to another table just within her eye line, his rubber soles squeaking on the polished floor as he passed. Now was the time to make an impression, like she'd done to him. He'd taken a seat facing her, and waited, hoping that she'd look in his direction.

Eventually, she'd looked up and locked her beautiful green eyes on him. Tom had his moment to win her over, and instead of raising his hand in a wave or smiling, he'd panicked, his brain going into lockdown, and he'd found himself pulling a face at her instead.

Fortunately for Tom, Gemma had laughed out loud before coming over to introduce herself.

"You're lucky," she'd told him. "My colleague Mandy thought you were having a stroke. I had to convince her not to rush over to check if you were ok."

They'd always laughed at that story. It was their private joke, and one that featured in their wedding speeches only a year later.

Tom chuckled at the bittersweetness of the memory and the men at the fruit machine looked over at him, probably wondering themselves if he was alright in the head.

"S'ok." Tom saluted them and they eyed each other before turning back to their game. Looking back at his drink Tom closed his eyes.

He'd loved everything about their wedding. Small and intimate with just a few family and friends to wish them well. The only bone of contention for weeks beforehand had been the song for the first dance. Gemma was desperate to use 'Make You Feel My Love,' which was her favourite Adele song, and Tom absolutely hated it. Well, not the song. He actually liked the song, but he just couldn't bear Adele. He couldn't even put his finger on why, but he just did.

For weeks, he'd tried to sway her with other contenders, but she wouldn't budge and eventually, because he loved her to distraction, he'd caved in.

On the evening of the wedding, once the meal was finished and the tables were pulled back to create some space, the first dance was announced. Tom had proudly led his new wife onto the floor. But instead of hearing the familiar piano intro followed by Adele singing the first line of the song, he'd heard a soft, rasping male voice intoning the same lyrics, rhythmically, beautifully, as though they'd been written for him alone to sing. The way it should be.

Tom had pulled back, looking at Gemma in surprise, and she'd smiled back up at him. "It's Bob Dylan. He wrote the song originally. I thought you might like it better."

"I love it," he'd told her, kissing her lips. "I love you."

"I love you, too." She'd rested her head on his shoulder and they had held each other, forgetting anyone else was there.

Now, already down by five shots of whiskey, Tom opened his eyes again and awkwardly pushed himself up. He stood, swaying as though manoeuvred by a light breeze in front of the pub's jukebox. He ran his finger down each list of songs, not trusting his eyes alone to be able to pick out the one he was looking for.

"Not bloody Adele," he muttered, flicking past the A's. "Here we go... The Doors, nope. Duran Duran, nope. Dylan. Yes."

He fumbled in his pocket for some change, feeding it into the juke box before making his selection and ordering his next drink, a double this time, just to save on the journey to the bar.

"What's this shit, mate?" one of the fruit machine lads asked Tom as he weaved his way back towards his table.

"This," Tom pointed at the nearest speaker, pausing for emphasis, "is not shit."

"If you say so, mate. Sounds like shit to me." The man sniffed, took a gulp from his pint and turned his back on Tom.

Even as he was doing it, Tom knew he was being an idiot, but he couldn't help himself. He threw his drink back and returned to the jukebox, colliding with a couple of tables on the way.

"Fucking piss head," he heard the bloke say to his mate.

Tom reached deep into his pocket, pulling out all his change and slamming it down on the table nearest the jukebox. He bent over and peered at the money, plucking out four pound coins and inserting them one by one into the machine. That would buy him twelve songs. What a bargain; he only wanted one.

"Any requests?" he shouted over to the fruit machine. "Nah, didn't think so."

As carefully as his whiskey-numbed fingertips could manage, he keyed in 'Make You Feel My Love' twelve times. Eleven times by Bob Dylan, and once by Adele just for good measure. He then turned, scooped his change back off the table and into his pocket before staggering back towards his seat.

"You fucking prick." The man jabbed his finger at Tom. "Who the fuck do you think you are?"

Tom stood his ground, brain too addled for a quick comeback, but more than happy to work off some of his aggression. "Come on, then," he taunted and felt the three old boys at the bar turn in unison to see what was going on. It'd probably be the highlight of their week to see a boxing match without having to pay for it on Sky.

"Oi!" came a shout from behind the bar. "Not in 'ere, you don't!"

Tom turned towards the barmaid, who was trying to squeeze her ample bottom through the hatch, and his opponent took the opportunity to give him a double-handed shove to the chest. Tom fell backwards, stumbling over his own feet, his backside landing on the grimy carpet. He was drunk enough not to feel it, but not sober enough to realise he should probably just get up and walk away.

Using a nearby barstool for balance, Tom pulled himself back up to standing, bent slightly in the middle, and launched himself at the other man.

"Don't just stand there," he heard the barmaid shout, he assumed to the other bloke in overalls, who was now stood, pint in hand, looking confused while Tom and the other man tussled.

On her instruction, the man put his drink down and grabbed his friend by the arm, trying to pull him away. "It's not worth it, mate," was his sage advice.

The next thing Tom knew, his arms were pinned behind him in what felt like some kind of martial arts grip. He struggled, twisting back and forth, eventually loosening his right arm, which he flung out, blindly, striking something soft.

"Oof!" A voice came from behind him, obviously the owner of whoever had him in an armlock. As it loosened further, he freed his other arm which allowed him to turn around.

The barmaid stood, glaring at him, one hand held up to her face. "I think you'd better leave."

28

BETHANY

I'd managed to divert Jordan's suspicions from the fact that I'd met up with Tom without him, but I knew at some point he'd come back to it. He had the memory of an elephant and the tenacity of a terrier. For now, though, he was content with my story that we'd met to go over some missing points on Tom's original application form; and bearing in mind I was the one who kept all the paperwork for our research, he couldn't disprove it. Not that it was any of his business anyway.

Against my better judgement, I'd agreed to come to Jordan's place with him when we left the pub. But, as he'd pointed out, it'd work out a lot cheaper to drink the large bottle of rum that his sister had got him for his birthday than to carry on shelling out what we were in the pub; and I still felt the need to drown my sorrows.

We'd stopped in the shared kitchen first to get a couple of glasses to drink from. I say kitchen, but it wasn't a place where any cooking should ever happen unless you had a very strong stomach. The table was littered with old takeaway cartons and crumbs crunched under foot on the dirty lino. The sink was piled with crockery and all that was left in the cupboard was a chipped mug and a plastic measuring beaker, so I'd gone with the mug, which I hoped was the more sanitary option. I still gave it a good rinse out beforehand though, just in case.

In stark contrast to the kitchen, Jordan's room was almost antiseptic. It was like a little oasis in a sea of mayhem. The walls looked freshly painted and his bed was made, his black duvet freshly smoothed out, with two cushions placed on top by his pillows. One, a cool black, white and grey union jack, alongside a contrasting mustard yellow one. His room was like a show home with nothing out of place.

"Do you actually live here?" I asked him as I appraised the pictures on his notice board. "It's all so…tidy."

He laughed and poured us two hefty rum and cokes, handing me the mug. "It's not that tidy. It's just that the rest of them here live like pigs!"

"Ha. You're not wrong."

It certainly made me feel better about my own shared house and, after a couple more large measures of rum, the edges of the whole crappy day had started to soften a bit, too. I hated to admit it, but it was nice just sitting here on a comfy bed next to my friend, our backs leaning against the wall, watching a load of rubbish on Netflix.

"Who'd have thought we'd be doing this together?" Jordan asked.

"What?"

"You know, watching Netflix snuggled up in bed." He laughed, the rum making him a bit flirtatious.

"Hardly!" I said, punching him on the arm.

"Ow." He rubbed the spot exaggeratedly. "I could do you for GBH, y'know."

"Hmm. Good luck."

We'd watched another few minutes before Jordan spoke up again. "Can I ask you something?"

"Sure, if you pour me another drink." I held out my mug and Jordan complied clumsily, the coke mixer splashing up its sides.

"How come you and Daniel split up?" he asked. "Was it just too difficult making it work long-distance?"

"Yeah." I started chewing my lip, missing the little ring that normally adorned it.

"You know, I used to wonder if you'd made him up."

"Oh my God! Jordan!" I was shocked. "Why the hell would I do that?"

"You know, to put people off. To put me off."

"No, he was definitely real. I loved him, but it just wasn't meant to be."

"How come?" The rum had made him brave, as he'd never questioned me about Daniel before.

I thought briefly about telling him some of the truth. It would be good to share it with someone, just to alleviate the burden a little bit, but I couldn't. The words morphed into a prevarication as they came out of my mouth. I just couldn't allow Jordan to see me as any less than the person that he wanted me to be. "He went off with someone else."

"Oh no, I'm sorry." Jordan shook his head, looking down into his beaker of rum. "I never should have asked." He looked back up at me again, eyes full of concern. "Are you ok?"

"I am now." My turn to look down into the depths of my drink to avoid eye contact. "It's been really hard." I felt Jordan's hand on my knee, the warmth from his palm permeating through the fabric of my jeans. It was exactly the comfort that I needed. It felt nice.

"How did you find out?" he asked.

"I caught them." The lie was out of my mouth before I even had time to think about what I was saying. "The last time I went home to see him, I saw them together, kissing. It broke my heart."

A tear fell from my eye, trickling down my cheek, although what had elicited it was the memory of seeing Daniel throwing the flowers I'd had delivered to him into the bin, before ushering his family in through the front door, glancing about worriedly as he closed it behind him.

"Damn." Jordan shook his head again. "What an arsehole. You deserve better than that."

"Thanks." I laid my hand on top of his and I could feel his eyes on me, studying my side profile.

"You know I like you, don't you?" he asked quietly.

I closed my eyes, accepting the inevitability of his comment. I'd known that if I'd come back here with Jordan and we both carried on drinking like we had been, at some point his feelings were going raise their persistent heads and start looking for affirmation.

I'd known it, but I'd come here anyway. Selfishly, I wanted the comfort. I needed it. Not permanently, like Jordan was so desperate for, but just the short-lived solace of being in close proximity to someone who cared about me. They were few and far between, after all.

"Yes, Jordan, I know." I turned to face him. "You know I've started seeing someone though, don't you?"

He nodded, taking his glasses off and cleaning them on the hem of his t-shirt. He looked so different without those smudged lenses covering his eyes all the time. "So why aren't you with him instead of me then?" he asked.

"I…we had an argument. It's all a bit complicated."

I didn't want to talk about the situation with Tom, as I wasn't even sure myself what was going on there anymore. It had all been so positive at lunch the other day, but after what had happened this afternoon, I just didn't know any more. He'd been so angry. I'd never imagined he could be like that and it almost made me change my mind about him. Almost. I took Jordan's glasses from him, wanting to change the subject.

"You look better without these," I told him and watched the smile spread across his face.

"You know I can't actually see you now." He crossed his eyes and held out his hands.

"Oops, sorry." I offered the frames back to him, which he took and placed on the small shelf at the top of the bed.

"I'm kidding," he said. "My eyes aren't *that* bad."

Jordan rubbed the little indentations on either side of his nose and I could sense he was building up to another question. I sipped at my drink and waited. I was pretty sure he was pouring me doubles, if not trebles, as the alcohol tasted so strong. I wasn't used to drinking rum, but it was nice, and maybe it was about time I embraced the university lifestyle a bit more.

"Do you want to talk about it?" he asked.

"What? Your eyesight?" I countered, trying to laugh off the deepening conversation.

Jordan rolled his eyes and turned down the volume on the programme we were ostensibly watching before tucking one leg under the other and facing me properly. "You can talk to me, you know. It's fine, it won't hurt my feelings."

I couldn't bear to look at his open face. It was just so…honest, and it demanded honesty in return. I found it uncomfortable. He didn't have a bad bone in him. The kind of guy who would let life kick the crap out of him before getting back up and asking for it to happen all over again. Why didn't I like men like Jordan? It would make life so much easier to have someone who liked me as much as I adored them for a change. Someone who would be content to just roll over and let me rub his tummy now and again. Like a dog.

"I guess I just always choose the wrong guys." I had to give him something.

"Well, yeah. That's obvious." He grinned.

"I just always seem to go for guys who end up treating me like dirt. I don't know why."

"I would never do that to you."

I smiled, knowing full well that it didn't reach my eyes. "Maybe you would, too, Jordan. You don't know. Perhaps it's something to do with me. They treat me like dirt, and then they leave me. Maybe I'm just not girlfriend material." I could feel my eyes welling up. Part of me thought it could be true.

"Don't say that." Jordan took my hand but I snatched it away again to wipe my eyes, turning away from him angrily, ashamed of myself for showing a real sign of weakness in front of him. "Come here." He pulled me towards him and I gave in, allowing my full body weight to rest on his shoulder. I couldn't remember the last time that anyone had held me in their arms and given me comfort. I supposed I had become too adept at pushing it away.

Jordan took the mug from my hands, putting it alongside the beaker and his glasses on the shelf before wrapping his other arm around me, too. It felt nice. Safe. And the unfamiliar feeling made me cry. I watched first one, then two of my tears splash onto his arm, and I felt his lips brush against my forehead.

"It's going to be ok," he whispered, and I closed my eyes, wishing that it were Tom holding me and comforting me instead. I couldn't help it.

Jordan's fingers stroked my hair and the rum warmed my belly, both lulling me into a more receptive state. What would it hurt to just give in and sleep with him? It's not like he wasn't attractive, after all, even if he wasn't right for me. Tom was clearly going to take some hard work and, for all I knew, he could be at home making up with his wife right now. I felt a stab of jealousy. What did it matter if I slept with someone else in the meantime, too?

I looked up at my friend and he gazed back at me, as though waiting for permission before taking a treat. Closing my eyes, I leaned into him and my lips met his, the softness of them surprising me a little before they parted, the kiss becoming deeper. It felt good and, just for this moment, it felt right. For one night, surely, we could both pretend that this was going to have the outcome that we both wanted.

My last shred of decency made me pull back.

"Jordan…"

"It's ok. I know I don't stand a chance of being in a relationship with you."

"It's not that, Jordan, I…"

I couldn't finish the sentence. He was right. I didn't want to be in a relationship with him, but I craved the intimacy. I thought briefly again of my packet of tiny silver blades tucked out of reach in my bedside table in my room and made my decision. I needed the release.

"Turn the light out," I told him.

29

TOM

Tom had made it back to his street but even though it was getting late and there was a fine rain coating the air, he couldn't bring himself to walk through the front door of his house. He stood, shifting his weight from foot to foot for a while, before turning and winding his way back to the off-licence that he'd passed a couple of streets back, where he chose a bottle of Bells Scotch from behind the counter.

The shop assistant had eyed him with suspicion as he handed the bottle over, holding out his hand for payment at the same time, probably expecting Tom to do a runner. As if he could run anywhere at the moment. It was all he could do to stand upright.

Tom snatched the bottle and left a small collection of scrunched notes and coins in the assistant's hand in return.

"Your change, sir?"

Tom let the door close behind him, unscrewing the lid of the bottle as he went, and mumbled, "Keep it."

As he made his way back to his street, Tom's anger swirled around him, like a crowd trying to incite a riot. Thoughts ran through his head about how badly he'd been duped. He felt stupid and hopeless and his mind cast about for a safe place to lay his blame.

Damn Gemma. It had all been her stupid idea in the first place. If she hadn't seen that advert, he'd never have known about it and they'd still just be muddling on like before. Unhappy, maybe, but by no means in this godawful situation.

He'd hoped she might have remembered that it was the final session today. Maybe managed to tear herself away from her amazing vocation and her new boyfriend to at least text him and ask how it went. That just showed how low down in her grand scheme of things he now was.

Maybe the whole thing was a set-up, anyway. Could Gemma have known all along that the study was a complete waste of time? Just an elaborate ploy created by her and Ash to get him out of the house so they could carry on together without having him in the way?

Back outside his house, Tom looked at the lighted windows, stark against the darkness. She was probably with him now, cosied up on the sofa or naked in bed. Gemma, not giving Tom a second thought, and Ash, probably relishing the fact that it had been so easy to slip into another man's shoes. The thought made Tom retch, and the taste of cheap scotch in his throat almost made him follow through, but he swallowed the bile back down. He breathed heavily through his mouth, and wiped his hand over his face, moist to the touch from the damp night air.

Instead of walking up his short garden path, Tom turned right and headed to the small park opposite, tripping over the curb as he went, his feet tangling into a knot beneath him as he landed with a bump. He'd managed to protect his bottle of Scotch, but his knuckles were raw where they'd scraped the asphalt as he fell. They stung viciously, no doubt adorned with bits of gravel that he'd have to pick out later.

It was the second time he'd been on his arse tonight and, while the first time in the pub had fired him up, this time, Tom just felt like crying. His hand hurt, as did his head, which he'd also managed to bash against the park railings; and the seat of his jeans was slowly soaking up the water from the puddle he'd landed in.

He pushed himself up on his hands and knees and used the railings to pull up to standing. Were they watching him? Were they in there right now? If he looked across at his house, would they be framed in the window of the lounge, laughing and pointing at him? He couldn't bear to turn until he was camouflaged among the foliage of the park.

Pushing past the wet leaves of bushes, causing a cascade of water to spray on his already wet jeans, he made it as far as the closest bench, near the play area and fell back against the damp wood. The rain had cleared a little, moved on by a cold breeze that stirred the swings, causing their mechanisms to squeak as they moved.

It was the only sound, other than the distant hum of traffic from the motorway, and Tom was relieved to be the sole occupant of the park that evening. Quite often, some of the young teenagers from the local estate would congregate on the roundabout, sharing a bottle of cider and a vape between them. Showing off in front of each other while keeping out of sight of their over-protective mothers. The weather had obviously kept them all at home in front of their X-Boxes tonight, though.

Life was so much simpler when you were a kid. You just didn't feel fear in the same way as adults did. You crossed the road without looking, you scaled the climbing frame without the worry of falling, and you hung out with the wrong kind of people in the park drinking cider, because mum and dad would always be there to bail you out if you got stuck.

Not so simple if you were the parent, though, eh? It was the job of the parents to feel the fear for their children. Bloody Gemma should be thanking him that they'd never had a child, instead of pushing him all the time. He was actually saving them from a lifetime of grief.

They'd never have to break their hearts when their child came home in tears after being bullied at school; they'd never be consumed with worry when their child didn't come home on time; they'd never be engulfed in fear if their child needed to go to hospital. They'd never be wracked with guilt if they failed their child in any way whatsoever. They'd never have any of that. They'd never have anyone else to worry about except each other.

But now, they didn't even have that.

Tom knew he was as pissed as a fart as his thoughts ran unrestrained, but he unscrewed the bottle and took a swig anyway. Less was most definitely not more this evening. Besides, he thought, looking at his bleeding hand, he needed a top-up for medicinal reasons.

30

BETHANY

The sex hadn't been too bad at all, really. Short-lived and lacking a bit of finesse, which was understandable bearing in mind how drunk we were and how much Jordan had been building up to it; but it had served its purpose, saving me from accumulating more bandages on my arms at least.

Jordan hadn't questioned why I'd wanted the lights turned off, either. I knew that he'd caught glimpses of the scars on my arms before, and he wasn't the kind of bloke who would force me into parading them in front of him, thankfully. It still hadn't stopped him from asking me questions afterwards, though. During that post-coital calm where lovers relax in each other's arms and ask those questions that can be answered when your vulnerable state dictates an element of truth should be told.

I hadn't meant to fall asleep next to him. I'd laid quite still for a while, tensely waiting for his breathing to slow so that I could manoeuvre myself out of the bed without him realising. The combination of today's events coupled with the rum and the unplanned sexual release, however, had knocked me out, even if it wasn't for very long.

Awake once more, I lay in the dark with my eyes wide open and my mind buzzing with uninvited activity. I'd only managed maybe an hour of fitful rest after we'd had sex and I was struggling to go back under. Each time a car passed by on the road outside, the noise of its tyres on the wet road would stir me, and the headlamps would briefly illuminate the Artex swirls on Jordan's ceiling through a small gap in the curtains. I tried counting them as though they were sheep, but it didn't help.

Jordan had wedged himself as close to the wall as possible to make space for me, but I was still clinging tightly to the very edge of his single bed each time his chest rose and fell. It annoyed me. Even though I knew I shouldn't feel that way, it made me want to slap him awake so I could tell him to be still.

I had no idea what time it was but it had to be pretty late, or early. I cast my eyes around for a clock but couldn't see one, so I rested my head back down on the pillow. Jordan's skin felt hot against my shoulder. I wasn't used to sharing a bed with anyone and his body heat alongside the weight of the duvet made me feel claustrophobic. His arm was draped over my belly, the pressure of it making me need to pee, so I rolled over onto my side, alleviating the weight a little bit.

My mind drifted to Tom, wondering what he was doing right now. I hoped to God that he was alright as he'd been so angry when he left, and anything could have happened to him. I reached out for my phone which was at the base of the bed and checked it for any messages from him. There weren't any. I wondered if Jordan would have any on his phone, but it was out of my reach on the desk.

There was one text message sitting in my Inbox from Leigh, which did make me pause for a moment, re-evaluating whether I should do what I was about to. I clicked on it, giving it a quick scan.

I'm worried about you, it read. *Please just give me a quick call when you can to let me know you're ok. It doesn't matter how late it is.*

It gave me a warm feeling to know that she cared enough about me to check in and see if I was ok after we'd spoken on the phone earlier. It was kind of her, and I was relieved that she wasn't cancelling on me for tomorrow as I knew that once the rum had worn off, I'd probably be best not left alone.

Holding my breath, I slid out from underneath the confines of the duvet and Jordan's arm, the chill of the room immediately nipping at my skin and giving me goosebumps. Behind me, Jordan let out a snore, and without my body filling the space beneath his arm, he rolled all the way over onto his front, cutting off re-entry, even though I didn't want to go back in, anyway.

I grabbed his phone and keyed in his password quickly, my heart racing a little. Jordan didn't realise I knew his password, but after what felt like a lifetime of sitting together in lectures, I knew it off by heart. It wasn't difficult to learn things about people when you watched them like I did. There were no new voicemail messages or texts from Tom or anyone else for that matter, so I switched it back off and replaced it on the desk, the new absence of light from the screen darkening the room once more.

I felt about the room for my clothes, using what little light there was which came from outside. I felt groggy from the rum, and more than once I had to lean on the edge of the desk and take a deep breath to stop my head from spinning. Once I'd located all my clothes, I dressed as quietly as possible, not wanting to wake up my friend and have him call me back into his embrace. I didn't need it anymore.

Using the torch from my phone, I cast it about Jordan's desk, shielding the light from falling in his direction with the palm of my other hand. I wasn't used to things being where they should be, but, eventually, I spotted a pot full of pens to one side. God, he was organised. I grabbed one and turned to a clean page in his notebook.

I'd never done this before, so I didn't know what to write. What do you say when you're doing a moonlight flit? I'd had a few men do it to me in the past using the excuse of an early golf game or having to catch the last train or just no excuse at all. There had never been a note, though. Normally, they just left.

I pressed the ballpoint to the paper and just wrote one word: *Sorry*. It would have to do.

Looking over at Jordan who was still fast asleep, I felt guilt wash over me. He was a good guy and he hadn't asked to like me the way he did, the same way that I hadn't asked to like Tom and, even though today had ended the way it had, I still felt like there was hope for me and Tom if I pursued it.

Yes, he'd been angry, but who wouldn't be after being deceived the way he'd been? He'd calm down eventually and realise that it wasn't my fault. I wasn't to blame for the way things had worked out. In fact, it was probably down to Jordan mucking it up somehow. He'd been the one who did all the hypnotism, after all. Idiot.

And now, he'd almost screwed it up for me again. Imagine if Tom found out that I'd slept with Jordan? That I'd technically cheated on him? He'd be furious. I knew I would be if I found out he'd gone back to his wife. It didn't bear thinking about. Him going back to her and leaving me. It would kill me. I couldn't stand to have someone else leaving me, trying to make it my fault. Trying to make out that I'd made them do it.

I collected the rest of my stuff together and, with my boots in my hands, I tiptoed over to the door, praying that its hinges wouldn't sound like an alarm as I opened it. They didn't. I gave Jordan another glance before I closed the door behind me with a click and I leaned against it to put my boots on. No regrets.

Once out in the chilly night air, I dashed off a tipsy fingered text to Leigh telling her that I was fine, and chucked my phone in my bag. It rang pretty much straight away, proving that she hadn't lied when she said it didn't matter how late it was. Swearing under my breath, I rooted around amongst the junk in my bag before the sound of 'Blinded by Your Grace' woke up everyone in the neighbourhood. Jesus, she was face timing me.

I answered and was rewarded by the image of my counsellor, unbelievably still dressed smartly at this time of night. Silk scarf draped casually over her shoulders, necklace in place, and Radley charm dangling at her wrist as she pushed her hair behind her ear. The familiarity made me feel a little better, and I couldn't help but wonder if she was wearing scruffy jogging bottoms and slippers on her lower half. I doubted it.

"Bethany," her voice sounded tinny through the phone. "Your text worried me."

"Wha? Why? Told you I was fine." I was conscious of my words slurring a little and gave myself a mental slap. The cold air seemed to have hit the remnants of all the booze in my system and her face registered understanding.

"Oh, right, you meant 'fine'. Your text said you were 'finished'."

"Did it? Shit. Bloody predictive text. Sorry." It would be funny if it wasn't so painfully close to the truth. "I'm fine. Honest. Just heading home. Big night out y'know."

Her face stared at me from the confines of my screen. I hoped to God she'd believe me and I wouldn't have to spend the next few minutes with her talking me down from the ledge.

"Are you sure, Bethany? I'm feeling a shift in your behaviour. It seems like there were lots of things that happened today. Lots of obstacles for you to negotiate, and some of them may feel wrong and some may feel right. We need to look at how they make you feel. Talk them through when you have a clearer head. Things will always work out at the end."

She wasn't making any sense to me. I put it down to the rum. "Wha?"

"Don't worry, Bethany. Let's end this now." She paused. "Things will feel so much better for you soon."

She was preaching to the converted. I didn't need it and I didn't have time for it as everything was clear in my head now. I wasn't going to let Tom leave me like everyone else had. I was going to make sure that he had no choice but to stay.

31

TOM

Tom woke with a start, immediately disorientated at his whereabouts, and not sure what the hell was going on or what had woken him up.

He was lying on his side on the park bench, freezing cold, with a bottle of scotch clutched in a tight embrace to his chest. He must have dozed off for a bit while he was sitting there. It wasn't the worst place he'd fallen asleep, but it was definitely up there with one of the most uncomfortable. He pushed himself back up to a sitting position, his joints aching from lying prone on the damp wood in the cold night air for so long.

Bleary-eyed, Tom looked at his watch and saw that it had just gone midnight. He must have been lying there for a good hour, at least. No wonder he felt so stiff and cold. He was just thankful that he was far back enough from the road that no one would have seen him lying there like a tramp.

"Jesus Christ," he swore at himself. "What the hell are you doing?"

He ran his tongue around the inside of his mouth and it tasted as though something had crawled inside and died in there. It was entirely possible, bearing in mind where he was. He hawked up some phlegm from the back of his throat and spat at the ground before giving his mouth a rinse with the scotch. He didn't spit a second time.

From the bushes over towards the road came a sudden screaming, which sounded as though animals were tearing each other limb from limb. At least he now knew what had woken him up. Could be foxes raiding the bins on the estate, but more likely to be the sodding neighbourhood cats shagging in one of the nearby gardens. Probably his cat, actually. Lucky bastard, getting his end away.

He pulled his coat tighter around himself, wishing he'd worn something a bit warmer. Not that he'd planned on taking a kip on a park bench when he'd left home that afternoon. Damn it. He still couldn't believe what had happened. His whole life seemed to have been tainted since he'd married Gemma, and this was just the latest in a long line of shit. In hindsight, this hadn't even been the worst day, by far. So what if those students had managed to hypnotise him to kill someone? He'd managed to kill someone before without even trying. What surprise was it really that he'd come to with a gun in his hands? Once a killer, always a killer, right?

He squeezed his eyes shut and opened them again, trying to blink away his muddled vision, and stared over at his own house across the road. The light was still on in the kitchen and as he stared at the illuminated rectangle, he saw a figure crossing from one side of the room to stand in front of the sink, silhouetted through the blind. He'd thought Gemma was still on nights, but he had no idea of her schedule anymore. Was she worried about him? Wondering where he was? Pacing the house and checking her watch until he walked through the door?

He checked his phone. She couldn't be that worried, as there were no messages other than the one from Jordan. Stupid twat. He could stick his apology up his arse. Maybe Gemma had just got home from work and was making a cup of tea before going to bed, creeping around the kitchen so as to avoid waking him and being forced into a conversation. Or maybe she'd just got home from seeing her boyfriend. Shit, he bet that was it. How could she do it to him? Tom took another swig of Scotch. He'd wait a bit longer, just until she went to bed, so their paths didn't have to cross and he didn't have to see the lies in her eyes when she told him she'd been at work.

"Go to bed." He spoke out loud, even though she wouldn't hear him. His words slurred and he could imagine the look of despair that his wife would give him if she could hear. "F'fuck's sake." His body had started to shiver uncontrollably and he just wanted to go home now.

He stared miserably as the figure eventually moved away from their position by the sink and the kitchen light was turned out, plunging his front garden into darkness. Finally.

Tom pushed himself up and forced his legs into a slow-motion stagger towards the edge of the park, not moving in the straightest line. As he got closer, he paused and squinted at his kitchen window. He could have sworn he'd seen some movement and the motion made him jump, loosening his fingers from their grip on the bottle. It fell, smashing on the ground and set off a chorus of barks from the neighbourhood dogs.

"Shit." Tom dropped to his knees, stupidly trying to gather together the shattered glass while trying to hide behind a bush to spare himself from any neighbours looking out to see what the commotion was.

As he peeked from behind his shield of foliage, he noticed the blind in his kitchen window being lifted and he paused, waiting to catch a glimpse of his wife from behind the glass. With the blind halfway up, a face morphed into view at the bottom of the window, but Tom couldn't see much but the shape, let alone whether there was any concern in the expression. He cursed himself for never having arranged to get those much-needed glasses. As quick as the face had appeared, it withdrew again, swallowed up in the shadows of the room, before the blind was pulled back down.

A shot of adrenaline fired into Tom's brain, instantly giving him the feeling of sobriety. It wasn't the fear of being caught, pissed, in the park by his wife that had caused it. It was the gut-wrenching realisation that, even without glasses, he didn't think it had been Gemma looking out of the window.

32

BETHANY

When I woke up, my first thought was that I didn't really want to wake up at all. I didn't exactly know why, but as awareness sent out its creeping feelers, I had a sense of dread that sat heavily on top of my whole body. Instead, I tried to force myself back to sleep, knowing that the second my consciousness clicked into gear, I was probably going to wish I was dead; but the sun coming through the window fell against my eyelids, lighting them up with a peachy glow and forcing me to acknowledge the day's presence. It was too late.

I groaned, the noise loud in my head as a memory of Jordan's ecstatic face loomed large in my mind. If that wasn't enough to remind me of what had happened last night, the dull ache between my legs confirmed it.

In fact, every inch of my body ached as though I'd run a marathon the night before. I had a dim memory of walking home in the middle of the night and throwing my uncomfortable boots into a bin on the street when they'd started pinching my toes. I bet my feet were filthy. I'd have to wash my bedcovers.

Oh God, what was I going to do about Jordan? Why the hell

had I gone home with him last night? Slept with him? He'd think he had a chance with me, now.

While most of the night before was only vaguely pieced together in my mind, I could clearly remember the adoration in his eyes and the gentleness of his caress. They spoke volumes without actual words.

Why did he have to be such a nice guy? I remembered crying once we'd had sex and was mortified at the memory. I'd tried to bury my face in the covers, swiping at my tears with his union jack cushion, while he'd held me in his arms asking me, "What's wrong?"

"Everything," I'd told him, seeing the hurt in his face. I had been drunk and emotional and the memory of my drama made me want to hide my face again.

"Oh." He'd pulled back from me, obviously taking my comment to heart when it wasn't even about him.

"Everyone leaves me," I'd said. "If you really knew me, you'd want to leave, too."

"You know that's not true."

My tears had continued, and then we'd lain in silence for a while. My eyes had just started to close when he'd spoken to me again. "Do you want to talk about it?"

I must have felt safe, or vulnerable, or drunk, or a mixture of all three, as I could remember a cascade of words vomiting from my lips while Jordan held me in his arms. While I didn't love him, and certainly wasn't in love with him, I remembered how amazing it felt to be wanted and cared for by someone else and I didn't want it to stop.

I wanted him to love me and worry about me. Well, not necessarily Jordan, but I wanted that feeling from someone. I craved it, and as long as I was getting that wonderful sympathy without question, I wanted to keep talking about my sad, sad story. I wanted his pity and for him to hold me in his arms and want to make it all better again.

The only problem now was that I couldn't remember what I'd told him. Everything was getting confused in my head between what I'd told Jordan and what I'd told Leigh in my sessions. It's not that I was a liar, but I just wanted to tell people what they wanted to hear. I wanted to put myself in a good light and fulfil their need to feel sorry for me. Or was it my need? I wasn't sure anymore, and the pounding in my head wasn't helping me find any clarity.

I licked my dry lips which were sore from kissing Jordan, I imagined, and shuddered, not from revulsion but from the fact that it meant I'd gone behind Tom's back. Tom, who I was in love with.

Tom.

Shit.

The experiment.

A whimper escaped my lips unbidden, highlighting the fact that I had a raging thirst. Opening my eyes just a crack, I reached out for the glass of water that sat at the side of my bed, praying that it wasn't a mirage, and knocked my small lamp onto the floor with a crash.

I pushed myself up on one elbow to take a drink, and the movement made my brain feel like it was rattling inside my skull. It hurt. Everything hurt.

I took a long drink, realising too late that the glass had straight vodka in it. I spat the liquid back out into the glass where my saliva swirled around in the clear liquid. Oh God, I must have carried on drinking when I got home. No wonder I felt so awful.

As I withdrew my hand, I noticed that my fingers were stained red. Not a bright crimson, the kind that you'd wear on your lips on a night out, but a dark red, deep in colour and crusted slightly around the sides of my nail beds where it had collected. If I didn't know better, I'd think it was blood.

But I did know better, didn't I? I was all too familiar with the sight of blood on my hands. My arms itched at the sight of it and I was disappointed in myself. How could I have come home and still fed my demons after my night with Jordan? That was the whole point of sleeping with him, to find release. I'd thought it had worked. But obviously not for long.

There was blood on my pillow, too. Not a lot, but enough to tell me I'd been busy when I got home. Fighting nausea, I sat and rolled up my sleeves, searching across the ridges of my arms for fresh cuts, but there weren't any.

I was worried now, and I threw back the duvet to check my legs. I hadn't often taken a blade to them, but they were my back up when my arms were too sore to cut. There was nothing other than the old familiar road maps.

I pulled my feet up towards me next, one by one, checking to see if maybe I'd trodden in glass as I'd stupidly walked home, drunk and shoeless. My soles were blackened with dirt, but they were fine. What the hell had I done?

I felt fear snatching at my skin with its long, pointed nails. Why couldn't I remember? What had I done? If only I could think straight without my head pounding. Everything in there was a confused jumble of half-memories, all so distraught that I could practically hear them clamouring for attention.

I needed to get up and start moving around. Try and piece together what had happened last night. Shakily, I got to my feet and made my way to the tiny sink in the far corner of the room. I had to wash my hands, first of all. Get this disgusting stuff off my fingers. I didn't want to accommodate the word 'blood', even though I knew that's what it was.

Sweat pricked my forehead at the discomfort of being upright and, as I made it to the sink, I rested my forearms on the cold pink porcelain, my head hanging heavy. I turned the cold tap fully on, allowing the water to cascade over my wrists, cooling the blood that fizzed and popped in my veins.

Taking the soap, I gave my hands a good scrub, making sure to get in and around the nail beds. That was better. I turned off the tap and used the lip of the sink to push myself upright, ready to survey the remnants of my makeup-smeared face in the mirror.

I expected the bloodshot eyes, I expected mascara down my cheeks, and I expected the pale skin holding it all together. What I didn't expect to see was all the dried blood staining my cheeks, the rivulets that ran, vampire-like down my chin, and the glint of silver in my lip.

"Oh my God! Oh my God! Oh my God!"

I gasped repeatedly, like a fish plucked from water, desperately trying to breathe in a new atmosphere. My eyes were transfixed to the mirror as though watching a scary film. It was too horrific to look away but too awful not to. My fingers flew to my mouth, and the searing pain in my lip sent them away, admonished, back to my sides.

Now that I'd seen it, the pain was blatant. How had I not realised earlier? This was bad. This was so beyond bad that I had no idea what to do. Cutting was one thing, when I was awake and aware of what I was doing. I knew that was shit. I felt the shame of it every day but did it anyway, like an obese person taping a picture of a skinny bitch in a bikini to the front of the fridge, then raiding it anyway. I hated it, but I'd accepted it.

This was new, this was scary shit. What had happened last night, for God's sake? I'd thought that sleeping with Jordan had eased my tension, my need for release, and it had. I could swear that it had. So, what the hell had I done? What had happened that was so bad that I'd come home and done this to myself?

What in God's name had made me brutally re-pierce my lip? And, even more worryingly, why couldn't I remember doing it?

33

TOM

The hot vomit rose in Tom's throat, and he only just made it to the toilet in time. After emptying what felt like the entire contents of his body, he sat, slumped on the cool tile floor, head resting against the rim of the toilet bowl and not even caring when the last time it had been cleaned was.

Sweat gathered on his forehead which banged and pulsed as though it was hosting a drum and bass party. He could have cried at the pain if there was enough moisture left inside his body to do so. His stomach roiled and the sour taste in his mouth made him retch once again, bringing up nothing but bile. His head screamed its agony at the effort.

He'd had hangovers before. Christ, he'd had shed loads of hangovers before. Approximately one a week for around fifteen years, ever since he'd discovered the delights of partying in his late teens. Obviously, there'd been a few more recently, but none quite of this magnitude. He felt like if he opened his eyes, he'd see his stomach lining and several organs floating in the toilet bowl. He retched again and burped.

"Go to your happy place," he instructed himself silently, before realising he didn't haven't one anymore.

Tom flushed the toilet and crawled on all fours over to the sink, eyes closed like a newborn puppy. He hoisted himself up and perched on the edge of the bath, opening one eye for a lopsided view of the room. It was all he could handle at the moment. The thought of too much stimulation to his brain was painful.

He saw that he was still wearing his grubby clothes from the night before, which would explain the smell, and when he carefully twisted his body, he noticed the pillow in the bathtub. Jesus, he'd obviously thought it was a good idea to sleep in there instead of in his bed. He'd probably come to the conclusion that it was a safe bet in case he threw up in the night. He'd been right.

Tom's one open eye had adjusted to the bright halogen lights now and he risked opening the second, slowly. He could almost feel the light beam filtering in through his pupil and travelling along his optic nerve to the brain.

He felt hot and cold at the same time, and the drilling in his head was intense. He'd have to take some painkillers to try and ease it off a bit. Painkillers, and then a shower before work. That's if he still had a job to go to, as he had no idea what time it was. Putting his hands on his knees Tom pushed himself upright. His back protested at the movement and the drilling in his head intensified. Ok, maybe just some painkillers and then sleep. Screw work. It's not like they'd miss him anyway.

He opened the medicine cabinet and caught sight of his hands. The left wasn't too bad, but the right was in an awful state. Bloody and cut to shreds. Jesus! What the hell had happened? It looked like he'd been in a fight and maybe one that hadn't ended too well. Although, it couldn't have been that bad or he'd have woken up in a police cell. He shook his head, trying to clear a path through the fog that swirled around his brain. He almost felt it rattle against the sides of his skull and it made him whimper in agony.

Everything was a complete blank from yesterday afternoon, onwards. He had a ghost-like memory of what had occurred at the library annexe, but he couldn't even be sure about that. It was too surreal, the memories melting around the edges like a clock in a Salvador Dali painting.

This must be what rock bottom felt like, then. That well-worn phrase bandied about in films about people who wind up in rehab. The first step is to admit you have a problem, blah, blah, blah. But it wasn't the alcohol that had been the problem, was it? The alcohol was the cure, his friend. It relaxed him, made things better. He looked at his bloodied hand again. When had it changed? When had it got out of control? He never used to wake up not knowing what he'd done. He never used to be an angry drunk either, but over the last few months, things had changed. It wasn't alcohol's fault though. He was just always angry.

Tom found some tablets and a bandage in the cabinet, then ran some water into the sink to soak his hands. He gently washed the worst of the blood off, surprised to see the actual damage to his skin wasn't that bad, mainly small cuts and grazes. He was obviously just a bleeder. It looked like his opponent might have been the one who came off worse.

Abandoning the bandage, Tom wrapped the hand towel around his hand and gulped back the tablets with some water from the tap. He was so thirsty that he could easily have gulped and gulped the faucet flow down, but he knew he'd just throw it straight back up again. A little would have to do, and it eased the desert floor of his mouth.

Venturing out into the hallway, he saw that the door to the master bedroom was firmly closed. He had no idea what shift pattern Gemma was on these days, but he assumed she'd either be sleeping off a night shift or already on her way into the hospital to start a new day. Hell, he didn't even know what time it was. Either way, the door was shut, and he knew his place.

He shuffled down the hall using the wall to hold himself upright, and on into the spare room where he pulled off his clothes, leaving them in a stinking pile in the corner by the door. The shower would have to wait. He needed to sleep before he could focus on anything. Before giving into it, he retrieved his phone from his jeans pocket and ran off a quick text to Sharon at work saying he was too ill to come in. Her reply pinged straight back at him as though she'd been waiting by her phone for someone, anyone, to get in touch.

Don't worry, Thomas. You rest up and we'll see you tomorrow.

Tom flicked the phone onto silent and crawled into bed. He gently lowered his head down onto the mattress, realising too late that he'd left his pillow in the bath. It was fine, it didn't matter in the grand scheme of things. There were bigger things to worry about right now, and he'd worry about them too, just as soon as he'd had a sleep. Everything would be clearer after a good sleep.

He closed his eyes.

34

BETHANY

I wasn't sure if it was my hangover, but Leigh's perfume was particularly cloying today. It clung to the air around her like a needy child, following her as she fidgeted around the room before settling opposite my position in my usual armchair.

"I'm so glad we could reschedule for this morning, Bethany." She removed her watch and placed it in its usual spot on the table. "It's not good to miss sessions if you can possibly help it."

"I couldn't help it. I was ill." I felt petulant, as though I'd been chastised. "I still am."

Leigh looked as beautiful as always, although not quite as groomed as usual. Her hair was tied back, and I noticed she hadn't bothered painting her nails, either. It was very unlike my counsellor to be anything less than perfect, but it was nice to see her looking more human. Maybe she'd had a heavy night too.

"Yes, I can see you still look a bit peaky. And your lip?" She gestured towards my face. "You decided to put the ring back in, I see. It looks rather sore."

I touched it with my tongue and grimaced, still tasting a little blood on the inside of my lip. I'd cleaned it up as best I could but there was only so much I could do without putting a plaster over the whole mess. It was still really painful, but it would be better in time. For now, though, it served as a reminder to myself to stay more in control of my actions.

I nodded my response and, not wanting to make eye contact, I turned, letting my eyes wander across the bookshelf. It looked like she'd had a bit of a clear out as there were quite a few gaps.

"Do you want to talk about it?" Leigh asked kindly and, not for the first time, I wished that she was just a nice person who cared about me instead of someone who was being paid to do so. I think that's what always stopped me from opening up too much. The fear that everything would go into a report, something to be shared with others. As if reading my mind, she leaned forward and patted my hand, the locket on her necklace twirling at the end of its chain. "Remember, what we talk about goes no further, Bethany."

I looked back at her with eyes that ran the risk of breaking their dams with unspilt tears. I wanted to believe her. I really wanted to. But what was the point? There would come a time when the money from my mother dried up, and then the sessions would come to an end, too, and I'd have spilt my guts all for nothing.

"I want to reassure you that I am here as *your* counsellor. Not your mother's. If you don't talk to me, I can't help you, and I want to help you."

I believed her. "I want to, I just…"

"You're in a safe place."

I thought of Jordan's embrace, then. Tucked into his arms, on his small, neat bed, inside his small, neat room. That had felt safe, briefly. "I don't know what happened last night," I spurted out, "but I think I might have done something really bad."

Leigh looked at me, urging me to continue with her eyes.

"It's just the experiment went wrong, and Tom stormed off, and then I got way too drunk with Jordan and we went back to his place. I feel terrible for leading him on when I'm in love with someone else. It's just a mess. One gigantic mess."

Leigh nodded. "Go on."

"I've been trying so hard to move on with my life, and yet there are obstacles that keep getting thrown in front of me. It's always the same. I get rid of one, and then there's another one. It's exhausting getting rid of them all the time."

"What are the obstacles, Bethany?"

"I don't know." I did, but I needed a moment to phrase things right before she caught me out. "Well, there was all that crap that happened back at home, wasn't there? I didn't do anything wrong, but I got the blame for it anyway. Now I'm here and there's Jordan and T-" I stopped just in time.

"Have you spoken to this new chap you're seeing?" Leigh asked.

"I…no. We've had a bit of a disagreement. See, another obstacle."

"I don't understand."

I stared back at her. "I told you he had a wife, didn't I?"

"Yes, of course. I can see how that would present itself as an obstacle."

"Not for long though, with any luck."

She appraised me. "You sound determined."

I liked that word. It was so much nicer than obsessive. I gave a weak smile and looked up at the tomography picture above her head, tracing the outline of the brain with my eyes. It looked like lots of small florets of cauliflower if you squinted, or if you were crying. My eyes were clouded with tears again after her compliment.

"Would you like a tissue?" Leigh asked, holding out the box.

I took one and scrunched it up in my hand, still too proud to dab at my eyes. If I kept looking upwards, I hoped they'd fall back into their tear ducts.

"So…" she paused, tucking her usual strand of hair behind her ear. "You mentioned that you can't remember everything that happened last night. Why is that?"

"I think I drank too much." I sniffed, my tears determined to make an appearance even if through a different orifice. "I can't remember much after I left Jordan's place. There's bits and pieces but nothing that makes much sense."

"Do you know if you were hurt in any way?" She looked concerned.

I couldn't help but laugh meanly, pointing at my lip. "Not unless you count this."

"Go on."

"I did it myself, last night." I sniffed again, holding the tissue to my nose. "But I can't remember doing it. I don't even know why I did it." The first tear trickled down my cheek and I just let it fall. There were going to be more.

"Carry on, Bethany."

"I'm just sick of hurting all the time. There's so much pain in me. In here." I pounded at my chest with my fist, the tissue still screwed up inside it. "It hurts…all…the…time."

Leigh looked at me. This was no doubt what she'd call a breakthrough. I couldn't stop.

"And the worst of it is that I don't know why. I don't know why I hurt so much, but the pressure just builds up and builds up until I think that I'm going to die from the pain and the only way to stop it is by—" I stopped, the words seizing on my tongue.

Leigh's eyes urged me on, but I'd swallowed them back down. "You can just show me if you can't say the words."

I was breathing heavily now, and tears and snot streamed unchecked down my face. I dropped the scrunched tissue on the table and slowly rolled up my sleeve, closing my eyes so that at least one of us was spared the sight.

The room fell briefly silent, although I could still feel the weight of her eyes on me as I pulled my sleeve back down. I concentrated on my breathing. In and out, in and out.

"You're very brave to show me that, Bethany." Leigh's voice through the darkness.

Brave *and* determined. Two words that had never been used to describe me before. I opened my eyes and looked at Leigh, carefully gathering the right words together before saying them out loud. "I think that's why I pierced my lip last night, to relieve the pressure, but I just don't know why. I thought I had it under control but obviously, something triggered it and I couldn't help myself." I swiped at my wet cheek, fingers accidentally brushing lightly over the lip ring. The fresh pain made more tears fall and Leigh passed me the box of tissues once more. This time, I took a bunch and dabbed them at my eyes.

God, I wished Leigh could come and sit next to me and just give me a hug. I knew that she couldn't as it would be breaking all sorts of patient/counsellor protocol, but it was a nice thought anyway.

"Do you think that you felt stressed after sleeping with Jordan?"

That brought me up short. "Did I tell you that?" I was doubting myself, feeling like I was losing the plot. God, everything was so confusing, and the hangover was just making it a thousand times worse. I was starting to rely on Leigh too much, telling her things that I wouldn't normally.

"Sorry." She looked awkward. "You said you led him on. I must have assumed. It was wrong of me."

Now I felt bad. "No, no. You're right. I did sleep with him. But it wasn't that. If anything, it helped."

Leigh put her head to one side. A question in the small movement.

"It stopped me from hurting myself after…after everything went wrong with the experiment." My eyes started welling up again.

"Is there anything else, Bethany? Why do you think you reacted the way you did when the experiment didn't go the way you'd hoped?"

I didn't want to tell her about Tom, the real reason that I wanted to plunge blades into my skin. Instead, I did what I always did, I skirted around the edges of the truth and embellished a tiny bit here and there, just enough to stop me sounding bad. And, like most people, she accepted what I'd told her.

I didn't want to talk about the experiment, either, really, although she was focusing on that now, and how the negative result had driven me towards sleeping with my friend. That was all in the past. Yes, it had been important to me. It was a big deal, but it was done. We'd not got the result that we'd hoped for, the exciting, mind-blowing Derren Brown special result, but it was still a result. Whatever. It was done and dusted and I didn't care about it anymore.

I also wasn't bothered about sleeping with Jordan. Not in the way I probably should be, anyway. It had served its purpose and it wouldn't be happening again.

What I was bothered about was what had happened after all that, after I'd left Jordan's house on a road to literally nowhere. No matter how much I jabbed at my arms or scratched at the memories, they were just out of reach. Elusive, like Tom. It was driving me crazy, and I didn't use that word lightly.

"Well, I think our time's up for today, Bethany." Leigh was picking her watch back up from the table, a gesture that always amazed me as it seemed to come so soon after walking in. "You've done really well."

I cast about, looking for somewhere to put my tear-soaked tissues and, not seeing anywhere to hand, I opened up my bag to put them inside. My phone sat on top and I couldn't resist pressing the button at the bottom to see my screensaver light up. I'd changed the old one recently for a photo of Tom. A still taken from some of the video footage from the experiment. I wasn't going to give up on him. Not yet.

Just above his image, a grey banner showed me that there were several notifications from Jordan, waiting to be read. He was at risk of getting obsessed with me. I sighed, knowing that I'd have to speak to him later, and zipped my bag shut.

"Right then," Leigh continued. "Did you want to stick to our normal slot next time? Or perhaps we can schedule something a little sooner, especially if you remember anything that you'd like to talk about?"

I fought the urge to fob her off. She cared about me and she was kind. I thought again how good it would be to have her in my life. Maybe once this was all over, we could be friends. It was definitely worth pursuing.

35

TOM

I t felt like Tom's body was finally trying to make things up to him for all the months of insomnia it had put him through. He'd woken up, but it was a struggle to keep his eyes open, and when he did, they still blurred in and out of focus.

His head still pounded, although not quite to the same extent as it had done earlier, thank God. He still couldn't remember much of anything after going into The Bull and Cock last night though, and the thought of drinking in that dive made him shudder. Whenever he'd walked past it, it had an aura of desperation about it. Cheap beer ensured that there was often a fight spilling onto the pavement outside. It was best to walk on the other side of the road, normally.

The clock on the nightstand told Tom that it was twelve thirty-five and his stomach rumbled in confirmation that it was hungry and he should be thinking about some lunch. Not surprising really as he couldn't remember the last time he'd eaten and the contents of his stomach had long ago been emptied into the toilet bowl. The thought of eating anything still made him feel sick, though.

What he needed more than anything was some water to quench his raging thirst. He gingerly made his way to the bathroom where he ran the faucet, scooping up handfuls of water into his parched mouth. He immediately felt nauseous and a wave of dizziness washed over him, causing him to rest on the toilet seat for a moment until the feeling passed. Everything felt so bright and slightly off-kilter as though he were still waking up from a dream, but for the first time in ages, he'd actually had a dreamless sleep. It was one thing to be thankful for, at least.

He sat still and breathed shallowly, elbows on his knees and his head hanging low. Eventually, the worst symptoms of his hangover started to retreat, leaving room for his mind to step in and start playing tricks. The more he started to think, the more he got an awful feeling in his gut that there was the possibility that he could have done something really stupid the night before. The cuts on his hands certainly looked as though he'd been in a fight, and his head…why wouldn't it stop pounding? He couldn't think straight.

He reached up to the source of the pain and felt a lump above his ear. Jesus, it hurt. Bloody fool. He'd probably passed out drunk in the street and been carted home in an ambulance. Another nail in the coffin for Gemma. God, he was sick and tired of being in this bright, white-tiled room. It was starting to feel like a cell.

Retrieving his pillow from the bath and tucking it under his arm, he left the room, looking right at the door to the master bedroom once again. It was still closed. The temptation to go in and just fall into the big double bed was almost overwhelming. Gemma was undoubtedly at work and she'd never know. It pissed him off that she'd staked the claim over the nice bedroom and the ensuite while he was stuck in the crappy single bed with the walk to and from the bathroom. He was wearing the carpet out in the hallway with all his trips there today.

He hovered outside the door weighing up his options. Just as he was about to reach for the doorknob, though, he caught a glimpse of Gemma's little blue Ford Fiesta through the landing window. It was parked up outside the house in its usual spot which meant that she must still be asleep in bed after a night shift. Shit, he'd nearly gone in and woken her.

Tom forced himself to walk straight past the spare room, flinging his grubby pillow onto the bed as he went. He had to hold onto the wall again as he made his way down the first few stairs. His legs felt like they belonged to a newborn deer and eventually, he just gave up and slid his way down on his backside.

The kitchen was still in its own twilight zone as the blind was firmly drawn, blocking out the world outside. It served to disguise the fact that the room was no longer cared for by any of the house's inhabitants. The bin was overflowing and used crockery was stacked up by the side of the sink. Tom picked up a mug and rinsed it out while he waited for the kettle to boil. He'd risk a black coffee and maybe a bit of toast to line his stomach if there was any bread.

He stood almost trance-like, staring at the clear sides of the kettle, watching the water as it started to bubble, reaching boiling point. It was comforting, losing himself in the familiarity of it, and he came to with a start as the cat flap clattered behind him. Baloo headed straight over to Tom's feet and stood, staring at him like a tiny psychopath just meowing over and over again.

"What the hell's wrong with you?" Tom eyeballed the cat, the noise hurting his ears.

Baloo continued with the racket and watched as Tom reached inside the fridge to get some cat food to try and shut him up. Holding his breath, he opened the tin, recoiling as the stench of it hit him full in the face. Without bothering to weigh it out, Tom dumped the contents into the cat's bowl and balanced the tin precariously on top of the rest of the rubbish.

"Go on," he said. "You can stop whinging now."

The cat turned tail and scampered up the stairs, leaving Tom standing alone once again, the smell of wet cat food deciding him against toast. He took his coffee and made his way to the lounge just as the home phone started ringing. Jesus, no one rang that number anymore other than salespeople and chancers, who, if you thought about it, were really the same thing.

He let the answerphone click in and heard the recorded message that he and Gemma had made when they'd first bought it.

"Hi, you've reached Gemma and Tom," his wife's perky voice. "We can't get to the phone right now, so leave a message and we'll call you right back." He remembered that she'd re-recorded the message about ten times before she was satisfied with the last one. The memory made him smile.

"Um hello. This is Susan Fludgate, from the hospital. Sorry to bother you, but I'm just concerned about Gemma." Tom paused in his tracks. "She hasn't turned up for work this morning and we haven't heard from her. I just wanted to check if she was ok as her mobile keeps going to answerphone. If someone could give me a call? Thanks."

That was unlike Gemma to not just turn up to work as she was one of life's more conscientious people. Maybe she'd just got her shifts mixed up. They always used to pin their shift patterns onto the fridge door for each other back when they used to care what the other one thought, and Tom wondered if Gemma had updated hers lately. He shuffled back to the kitchen and rifled through the last few rota slips, but the final one she'd pinned up was from weeks ago.

Maybe he should just go and check on her. The worst that could happen would be Gemma telling him to get out. On the other hand, if she *had* overslept or if she was ill and needed anything then surely, he'd be doing a good thing. He stood arguing the toss with himself for a few seconds in front of the fridge, then, decision made, he put his mug down on the counter and headed back to the stairs.

As he reached the landing, he found Baloo sitting outside the bedroom door, staring intently at it and doing his best to try and scratch the gloss paint off the wood. Tom tried to shoo him out of the way but Baloo stood his ground.

Tom knocked quietly on the bedroom door, using his left hand as his right was so badly cut up. He really should clean it properly and put a bandage on it. He told himself that as soon as he'd checked on Gemma, he'd have a shower and sort himself out, but the thought of all that activity just made him want to lie down again and sleep some more.

There was no answer from the other side of the door, so Tom knocked again, a little louder. The knocks were accompanied by Baloo who had started his incessant miaowing again.

"Gem?" he called. "Are you in there?"

There was still no response.

"Are you ok?" He knocked again.

Nothing.

"Um, ok. Gemma? I'm coming in, ok?"

Tom pushed open the door a crack, which allowed Baloo to slither past him and on into the darkened room beyond, miaowing as he went. That would certainly wake her up if nothing else did, Tom thought.

He opened the door wider, calling out softly as he did, so as not to make her jump. It was so dark in the room that he could only just make out the shape of Baloo jumping onto the bed. Those black-out curtains certainly did their job well. The bloody cat was still making a racket, so Tom doubted Gemma was even in bed at all, as he would have woken her up by now.

"Gemma, I'm going to turn the light on, ok?"

The sudden brightness in the room felt like it was piercing his head and Tom closed his eyes briefly, holding the heel of his hand to his forehead, massaging it a little before forcing his eyes back open.

"Jesus Christ, Baloo, would you just shut up...shit, Gemma!"

His wife lay on her back on the floor, one hand resting on the bedcovers, which were half pulled from the bed, eyes staring up at the ceiling. She was still, so very, very still.

Baloo had crawled his way onto her stomach and lay there, still miaowing over and over again, the only noise in the room.

"Gemma?" Tom edged closer, his eyes doubling up their focus to show him two images of his wife before he blinked one of them away. "Gem?"

If it wasn't for the situation they were living in, he would have expected her to jump up suddenly, full of laughter, shouting how she'd got him good. Pulling her silly face to make him laugh. But they weren't in that place anymore. They didn't play jokes or pull faces now. Gemma stayed still.

Tom moved closer, his heart pounding in his throat and his mind screaming in confusion. He couldn't take it all in. Was she awake? Was she unconscious? Was she breathing?

He knelt by her side and felt for a pulse in her wrist, registering the coolness of her skin. When it provided nothing, he gently lowered her arm and held his fingers to the artery in her throat. There was nothing. Not even the faintest pulse. Nothing.

Tom could feel all the blood in his body rushing around in a blind panic, his heart hammering fast enough to explode from his chest. Why wasn't she breathing? What was going on? She couldn't be…he couldn't say the word, even in his head.

The cat was still carrying on and Tom pushed him roughly from her stomach, gaining another scratch to his hand in the process. Tom's eyes blurred in and out of focus again as he noticed blood on the far side of Gemma's head. Jesus Christ.

"Gemma!" He heard his voice wailing as though it came from somewhere else. "Wake up! Please wake up!" All his medical training went out of his mind as he watched his hands grasping her shoulders through eyes blurred with tears. His already confused mind started to wax and wane with the unreality of everything.

He blinked the tears away and an image of his beautiful wife in his favourite dress floated in front of him just out of reach, a memory of kissing her neck; then his right hand grabbing the broken bottle in the darkness of the night before… Everything was off-kilter.

What was wrong with him? He'd slept the morning away, hungover and feeling sorry for himself while his wife had lain in here like this. He was nothing but a worthless piece of shit. If he'd come in earlier, he could have done something. Helped. Saved her. Stopped her suffering. He was to blame.

It had happened again. Someone had died on his watch. On his shift. He'd taken his eyes off the ball once more and someone else had died. There was no coming back from it this time, though. No excuses. No chance that he'd be found innocent, an unlucky victim of terrible circumstances. This time, he would have to take the guilt, adopt it like the child he refused to have, and make it his own.

It was time he held his hands up, wasn't it? Admitted that he was a violent drunk. An alcoholic who, while he had no memory, was obviously capable of atrocity. Tears and snot streamed down Tom's face and he took his mobile phone from the pocket of his dressing-gown, fumbling and dropping it once before managing to key in his password and dial 999 on the keypad.

"Emergency. Which service?" came the disembodied voice of the operator.

Tom took a breath and exhaled deeply. "Police, please. I think I've just killed my wife."

36

BETHANY

Seeing Jordan again hadn't been as bad as I'd thought it was going to be. Having been able to avoid him that morning while I had my session with Leigh had allowed me time and space to create a bit of distance between us and ease any embarrassment. Well, on my part, anyway. In my head, having sex with him had been like going to the doctor's when something's wrong and taking a pill to make it better. Nothing more complicated than that. I suspected Jordan might have felt a little differently, though, as he seemed to be struggling to look me in the eye today.

There was a short break in between classes, so we sat on a bench outside the lab. It gave me enough time to search through my bag for the assignment that was due in, and for him to deconstruct an orange as though he were searching for hidden treasure.

"You know you can eat the white bits, don't you?" I asked him.

"I can't stand them." He pulled a face and picked another bit of pith from a segment before putting it in his mouth and flicking the offending substance onto the ground. "I thought you'd decided to take that out?" He squinted at me, acknowledging my lip ring for the first time.

I shrugged, delving deeper into my bag, and pulled out some folded sheets of paper that looked familiar.

"Are we ok?" he asked, licking juice from his fingers.

God, we may as well be in a relationship for the amount of time one or the other of us asked that question. "Yes," I told him, slightly exasperated, "We're fine."

"Ok. Cool."

He went back to his orange and I unfolded the papers from my bag. It wasn't what I was looking for and I had a sneaking suspicion that I hadn't even done the assignment. Everything was so confusing lately.

As I shoved the papers back into my bag, I heard a shout from across the other side of the quadrangle and looked up to see Seb trotting over to us, waving a hand in greeting. "Hey, man, how's it going?" he asked one or both of us. In his vocabulary, you couldn't be sure if 'man' was singular or plural. "Have you guys heard what's happened?"

Bloody hell, if I was a feminist, I'd be really aggravated. Man. Guys. I sighed, feeling a little disdain sneaking into my eyes, but hopefully not enough to be obvious. Had Hayley got Botox? Been followed by some Insta-influencer?

Jordan finished chewing the last of his fruit and chucked its discarded outerwear into the bin next to us. "What?" he asked.

"That bloke. The guy who lost the plot at your experiment."

That got my attention. "What about him?" I shielded my eyes from the sun, which was poking out from the side of a cloud right behind where Seb stood.

"Oh my God. It's all over social media!"

"What is?" There hadn't been anything on there last night when I'd carried out my usual rituals of checking Facebook, Instagram and

Twitter. I was pretty thorough, so there's no way I could have missed anything.

"Oh my God. I can't believe you guys haven't seen it!"

"Seen what? For God's sake, Seb, just tell us." I whipped my phone out of my bag, taking care to cover it so that the others didn't see my screensaver.

"He's been done for murder."

My phone slipped through my fingers, clattering face-down onto the ground, and no doubt making yet another crack in its screen. I stared at Seb, who stood there, chest puffed out like a baby pigeon, obviously thrilled to be the one sharing this news. I couldn't form words. I couldn't even close my mouth, which I could feel hanging open.

"What the…? Are you joking me?" Jordan recovered quicker than I did. "Who? How? What happened? Who did he…is he supposed to have murdered?"

My brain jogged alongside his questions, listening to him and knowing what the answer was going to be already. Not needing confirmation, yet realising I was about to get it anyway.

"His wife, man. He killed his fucking wife!"

I heard Jordan audibly gasp beside me, and I turned to see him shaking his head like Shaggy in a Scooby-Doo cartoon. I half expected him to say "Zoinks!" Seb's head was going up and down like a nodding dog toy on the dashboard of a car. I'd always wondered if his whole surfer demeanour was an act and that underneath it all he was just embarrassed by the fact that he was a posh boy with a trust fund. Why the hell was I thinking about that now? It was all too surreal. My thoughts were all over the place. Why couldn't I speak?

"Oh my God!" Jordan had got his phone out and was rapidly typing something into the search bar, scrolling and scrolling, reading the tiny screen, and scrolling some more. His shoulders slumped.

"Hey, I gotta go, guys. Just thought I should tell ya."

"Hang on!" Jordan held up his hand and Seb paused. "You can't tell anyone about this."

"Are you kidding? It's all over the internet, man."

"He means you shouldn't tell anyone about us knowing him." I'd found my voice. "I mean, imagine if we were all implicated somehow." I could feel panic rising in my throat as I spoke. The truth of my words hit home to myself, as well as Seb and Jordan.

"What do you mean, implicated?" Seb looked as though he didn't actually know what the word meant and I wondered how the hell he'd ever got into uni in the first place.

"I just mean...Jesus, Seb, think about it. We were all involved in an experiment to see if we could hypnotise someone to commit murder."

"Yeah…but it didn't work…did it?"

37

TOM

Once Tom had rung 999, the police had turned up quickly, and he'd let them into the house without protest. They'd been decent to him, even letting him get dressed before escorting him to the station. They hadn't left him alone, though, and once the forensics team were finished with him an officer had accompanied him to the spare bedroom to keep an eye on him while he put on a pair of jeans and a sweatshirt.

At the end of the hallway, he'd seen the paramedics spilling out of the bedroom in a sea of green uniforms and he'd wanted to run down there and push them out of the way. What were they doing in his bedroom, his house, his life? He should be with Gemma looking after her, not a load of strangers. It wasn't right.

The police officer who'd escorted him upstairs had obviously seen the glint of desperation in his eye as Tom looked past him. He stood, blocking the hallway, giving Tom no option but to go back downstairs to the dining room where the rest of the officers were waiting patiently.

As he took a seat at the table, he could see the detective sergeant had clocked the hole in the dining room door that Tom had punched weeks ago, and he knew that it would be written up as evidence against him, understandably.

Tom knew without question that Gemma was dead. There, he'd said it. Not out loud because he wouldn't be able to bear it, but just quietly in his head. Even the paramedics hadn't said the word out loud as they'd stomped down the narrow staircase after tending to Gemma in the bedroom. They'd stood in the hallway, another day at the office, and shared muted conversation. Tom had heard snatched sentences about there being no cardiac activity and an absence of respirations and it killed him to know they were talking about his wife.

"Ok, Tom," said the sergeant. He had told Tom his name, but he'd forgotten it already. "We're going to take you to the station shortly, but I need to caution you first." Tom nodded, the weight of his head feeling like it could snap his neck in two. The sergeant continued. "You don't have to say anything unless you wish to do so, but it may harm your defence if you fail to mention when questioned something you later rely on in court. Anything you do say may be given in evidence."

He may as well have read a passage from the Bible or the song lyrics from a Bananarama song for all the sense it made to Tom. He was beyond caring, beyond thought. He just wanted to lie down again and sleep. And, if he was honest, he didn't care that much about waking up.

Allowing the officers to escort him to the waiting police car that was blatantly advertising itself at the curb, Tom could feel invisible eyes observing him from every window. Neighbourhood Watch was out in full force and he couldn't have cared less as he concentrated on putting one foot in front of the other.

The ride to the station was only a short one, but Tom's head had lolled uncontrollably to the side on the journey as he drifted in and out of wakefulness. Once stood in front of the custody sergeant at the station, he had to listen to the same spiel that he'd heard from the sergeant in his dining room. It didn't matter how many times they went over his rights, he wasn't listening.

"Do you want to let anyone know that you're here?" the custody sergeant enquired.

Tom shook his head. There was no one. Not now.

"Do you have a solicitor that you'd like us to call?"

Tom shook his head a second time. He couldn't remember the name of the solicitor who'd advised him previously and he wouldn't be able to afford her, anyway. It didn't matter. He'd get a duty solicitor. No doubt a trainee, lacking in experience but full of enthusiasm. Tom didn't care as he knew it was a hopeless case anyway. He'd already accepted his guilt.

The officers took him to a cell that smelled mainly of disinfectant with an underlying stench of despair. Tom knew that he was now adding to that smell with his despondency and confusion.

He'd been in this situation before, so he was familiar with the layout of this small room that he found himself in. Cells, it seemed, were not too unlike each other. They had similar set-ups and colours and a window that you couldn't open, just in case you wanted to jump from it.

Still feeling dizzy, Tom sat on the low shelf that masqueraded as a bed, and then twisted himself round to lie back along its length. The thin blue plastic mat underneath him may as well have not even been there for all the padding it gave, and he could feel his spine protesting.

Christ, how was it possible that he was here again? His life wasn't supposed to have been like this. He would have been happy doing a job he loved and then going home to the wife that he absolutely adored. Having a family. Having a life. But the option of family had been ripped away, alongside his beloved job. And now… now his wife was gone, too.

The only difference was that last time, while he'd been stupid and neglectful, he'd been cleared of all charges. Everything had pointed to the hospital being negligent and, to avoid a big court case, they'd done what was expected of them. They'd got rid of the problem. Tom had been the problem.

This time though, he'd really screwed up. He knew that much. It had all got out of control, shit piling on top of shit until he was buried under a mountain of it. He'd been living with a lack of sleep, self-loathing and an alcohol problem, and he'd turned all that hatred outwards towards his wife. The person he loved most in the world. The person who'd stuck with him when he'd wanted to leave himself behind. He hadn't even been able to bear seeing himself reflected in her eyes.

He couldn't understand what was wrong with him. At what point in his life had God decided to turn His back and let him fend for himself? Didn't He realise that Tom wasn't capable of looking after himself, let alone anyone else? Not that he believed in God, anyway. Maybe he should start. He'd heard that a lot of prisoners found God…either that or they started taking spice. Bearing in mind Tom's track record with analgesics, he was pretty certain of the route he'd wind up on.

Tom's mind struggled to make much sense of the day before, and it didn't help that he felt so woozy, so tired. He couldn't get his head around what had happened, but he knew it was his fault. He knew it like he knew his own name.

He'd been consumed with fury about Ash. Torn apart with jealousy and rage that she must be seeing someone behind his back. And what actual proof did he have? None. He was exhausted, scared and drunk most of the time and he'd accepted that he got angry sometimes, out of control, even. He knew that he could be an absolute bastard to live with, but he'd not realised until now that he was a monster.

Now he just had to wait. Tom rolled over onto his side, the thin mattress flattening underneath him. His head was still raging with a pain that wouldn't go away and he closed his eyes again, blotting out the harsh lights above him. He'd asked for some painkillers when he'd been escorted to his cell, but so far, none had arrived.

If only he could have a drink, a little something just to take the edge off. To ease the pounding in his head, straighten his thoughts out. He hated himself for even letting notions about having a drink take precedence over his wife, but he couldn't help it. He was desperate.

38

BETHANY

"Oh my God, oh my God, oh my God." Jordan was one step away from rocking back and forth like a crazy person.

Everyone else had cleared from the quadrangle now, heading off to their lectures at the four corners of the university. The thought of sitting through any more lectures didn't seem quite so important to me right now.

"What have we done, Bethany?" Jordan wailed. "Jesus, what have we done?"

My heart felt like it had done an emergency stop in the middle of a motorway. It sat there, stalled and motionless, while I tried to turn its key over and over until, eventually, it caught, the accelerator was floored, and it juddered back into motion.

I'd managed to extract a promise from Seb to keep his mouth shut until we worked out what to do. It didn't take much, to be honest. Jordan was my immediate problem now. He was slowly having a mental breakdown beside me, so I forced him to his feet and got him walking.

"Where are we going?" he whined. "Are we going to the police?"

"No, Jordan. Come on. We're just going for a walk. I need to think."

We went over to the sports fields and then through a small gap in the surrounding hedgerow to a wooded pathway beyond. Behind us, the large university buildings full of students working hard on their futures shrank back.

"We have to go to the police." Jordan spoke as soon as we were shrouded by the shadowy woodland. "We might've been the last people to see him before he did it."

"*If* he did it," I pointed out. "Let's be rational about this."

Now that my heart had restarted, it seemed to be beating twice as hard as usual. I wondered if this was how a cardiac patient felt after being defibrillated. It was a dreadful feeling, out of control, a tiny but forceful drum being beaten by a wind-up monkey.

"Oh my God, who else would have done it? It's obvious, isn't it? Shit, you saw how angry he was when he left us. He must have had other stuff going on that we didn't know about. What if it was the final straw? What if we tipped him over the edge?"

I turned to face him, putting my hands on his shoulders. He looked into my eyes, his own filled with fear. "Jordan, you have to calm down."

"I *am* calm," he hissed, his eyes saying otherwise. "Jesus Bethany!"

He walked away from me for a few paces and I could tell from the set of his shoulders that he was desperately trying to get his emotions under control. I waited for him, picking leaves from their branches and scattering them on the ground by my feet. A flower girl at a twisted wedding.

Eventually, he turned, eyes cast down, and retraced his steps towards me. "We didn't remove the hypnotism triggers," he whispered, shuffling his weight from foot to foot.

Of course. The time between Tom coming out of his trance and leaving us had been fraught, and there was no way we could have got anywhere near him to remove them. Since then, it hadn't even crossed my mind.

"Well, the likelihood of him going home and listening to 'The Sound of Silence' and staring at that specific pattern at the same time are pretty unlikely, don't you think?"

"I guess." Jordan looked sulky.

"Besides, the whole reason the experiment didn't work was because, when it came to the crunch, when he really thought he was about to kill someone, his critical conscious faculty wouldn't let him do it. He just doesn't have it in him, Jordan."

"He looked pretty angry to me. Maybe it's different…easier to kill someone you know?"

"There's no way he could have done it."

"Then we should go to the police…tell them that." Jordan opened his arms like a man pleading his case in court. "If he didn't do it, then he shouldn't be in prison, should he?"

"Oh, for God's sake, don't be so stupid!"

He looked hurt, like a little boy once more who'd had his teddy bear stolen. "What do you mean? Why's that stupid?"

I wasn't sure if he was going to cry or shout at me. I had to be careful here. So careful. There was no way in hell I was going to let Jordan go to the police and tell them everything that we'd been doing. No matter what I'd said to him about Tom not being able to commit the crime, I didn't want them knocking on my door, and that would be the very next place that the police turned to. The jealous girlfriend. The one who already had a record.

Of course, I didn't want Tom to be convicted of a crime that he hadn't done, but, by the same token, I didn't want to be accused of it, either. I had to think of myself no matter what the cost.

"Think about it, Jordan. Just think about it."

He pushed his glasses up his nose and stared back at me while my brain whirred, and spun and quickly knitted together an explanation that would steer him off his path of righteousness. It felt like a standoff, a challenge for me to come up with something feasible. It was ok, I was good at that.

"Who do you think they'll suspect if it isn't Tom?" I asked him.

"I have no idea." He leaned against a tree with one arm and shook his head. "Why don't you tell me, Bethany, as you seem to have all the answers."

"I'm just looking out for you, Jordan. For us."

"What does that mean?"

I walked over to him and tried to take his other hand. He let me hold it. "They'll blame us, Jordan. Actually, they'll probably blame you."

"What the hell are you talking about?" He snatched his hand away.

"Think about it. You're the one who did all the hypnotism. What if the police think you screwed it up? Planted some seed in his head that sent him crazy? You're the one who booked the library annexe. You bought the fake gun online, too. Even all the social media adverts are in your name."

Jordan looked as though he was currently on the worst ride of his life at Disney Land. His skin had paled, his breath was coming fast and shallow. It was starting to dawn on him that he could be in deep shit. "But this was your idea. The whole research experiment was your idea."

"Well, *we* know that, don't we, but no one else does. Even Seb thinks it was you. Remember when we were first talking about it in the canteen?"

"No." Jordan looked panicked.

"He overheard you saying what we were going to do, and that was when he came over. Come on, you must remember that?"

"No, I…but it was both of us."

"I know, I know." I reached out for his hand again and he let me take it. I held it and stroked his arm with my other hand. "Obviously, we're totally in this together. There's no way I'd leave you to take the blame for anything on your own, but you've got to admit, it doesn't look good."

Jordan stared up at the canopy of trees and I followed his gaze, noting the cool blueness of the sky just beyond their covering. He didn't know that my stomach was tied into a thousand knots with the web that I was silently knitting around him. It might be hurting him, but it was hurting me, too. Nevertheless, it was a small price to pay.

"Do you know what the worst thing is?" I said quietly. "It's all on video, too. All of the experiments with you hypnotising Tom."

"But you didn't want to be on film."

"I know. That's just me, though. I don't like watching myself on film, hearing myself recorded. You know what I mean."

"Yeah."

Poor Jordan. I felt awful doing this to him. Making him doubt his own reality. But it was the only way I was going to get him to back off from going to the police. I wouldn't call it bribery. After all, I wasn't a mean person. I wasn't trying to scare him for fun. I had to do this in the name of self-preservation, even if it meant losing someone else in my life. God, I was so unlucky. It looked like Jordan was going to end up leaving me, too.

39

TOM

Tom had managed to doze off for a bit in his cell, which he only realised when he opened his eyes to find a police officer standing over him, shaking his shoulder. All he wanted to do was roll over and close his eyes again to block out his new reality, but the uniformed officer was having none of it.

"Your solicitor's here to see you."

Tom levered himself up, groaning as his back protested, and allowed the officer to take him down the hall to a tiny box room. It had grey walls and a grey floor, and a single table with four plastic chairs set around it.

A young woman dressed in a navy power suit rose from her seat at the table and walked forwards, holding out her hand to him. Tom wondered if she'd chosen her outfit to give herself confidence or her clients.

"I'm Yasmeen Sharma from 'Hunter, Thompson & Wingrove,'" she informed him.

Tom grimaced at her and took her proffered hand, acutely aware that he hadn't had a shower for some time now. He must stink. Yasmeen seemed unaffected by him, however, and ushered him in to sit down on the near side of the table before she re-took her seat opposite him.

"I'll leave you to it," the officer told them as he stepped back out of the room, closing the door behind him and leaving Tom and his solicitor alone.

"Right then," she said, pulling a legal pad from her bag and positioning it on the table before crossing her legs. "Why don't you tell me what happened." She clicked the top of her biro and sat, poised, ready for action. The total opposite to Tom's slumped figure that just wanted to curl up into itself.

At least she didn't look like she was totally wet behind the ears, Tom thought. Sighing, he rubbed at his temples. His head was still aching and his memory struggled to retrace his steps that morning, let alone the day before. He squeezed his eyes shut as if making a concentrated effort was going to help and shook his head from side to side, which did nothing to aid his headache. "I'm pretty sure I killed my wife."

Yasmeen blinked, whether in surprise at his candidness or in a nervous response to being in a locked room with a murderer, he couldn't tell. She made a note on the yellow pad in front of her without looking down, keeping her eyes on him. "What makes you think that you killed her?" she asked.

"I don't know. I can't remember. But it has to be me. No one else would do it."

"And you *would* do it?"

"I loved her."

"And yet you think you killed her?"

Tom nodded, his head ending in its downward position, eyes gazing at his hands, wishing there was a glass of whiskey in them.

"Mr Newbold, you're telling me that you *think* you've killed your wife. Why are you not sure?"

"I can't remember doing it, but I know that I did. I was angry with her. Furious. And…drunk." He felt moisture on his cheek and

realised he must be crying. "I don't always handle my drink well."
His mind reminded him of the hole in the dining-room door, like
an exhibit in its very own court case. He shook it away, as he knew
the police would have flagged that up already.

"Have you ever been violent to her in the past?"

"No, I…I don't think so." Tom struggled to think clearly. "I
don't know."

There had been so many nights when he'd been angry with her,
so many nights when he'd succeeded in blotting out the reality of
the life they were living with alcohol, that he couldn't be sure
anymore. Had he ever hit her? Pushed her? He couldn't think
straight. Tom looked at his hands wondering if they had ever hurt
Gemma, if he had hurt her with more than his words.

"Ok, Mr Newbold, you've said you were drunk. Do you often
drink to the point of passing out? Losing your memory?"

Tears were rolling down Tom's cheeks now and he swiped at
them brutally, not wanting to touch his face with hands that might
have hurt his wife. God, he wanted a drink so badly, just to help
him think better, straighten up the jumble of images that were
presenting themselves to him. It was like looking into a box full of
jigsaw pieces, desperately searching for that one corner piece that
was going to be the start of putting the rest of them in order, seeing
the picture clearly in front of him.

He nodded. "I suppose over the last few months it's happened
more frequently. I guess I drink to try and forget things, to help me
sleep." He didn't want to admit it but his need for alcohol had long
overshadowed his need for his wife. Instead, Gemma had become
his nemesis, while alcohol had become his lover. The shame of it
made him want to die.

It was no wonder she had taken a lover of her own. Ash. That
faceless bastard who he'd never met, had wormed his way in while
Tom's back had been turned, while his attention had been swayed by
his obsession. His tears were coming thick and fast now, and his

legs, balanced only on his toes, were jiggling nervously up and down. It wasn't fair.

Why did Gemma have to go and look somewhere else? Why couldn't she have waited for him to sort himself out? He'd have done it…eventually. He just needed time. Time to get over the nightmares, time to get back on track. If only she'd given him a rest. Stopped pressurising him about having fucking babies. Christ, she practically drove him to drink with all that incessant nagging. No wonder he could've snapped. No wonder he could've pushed her off him, slapped her back from him, held her down until she shut the fuck up.

"Mr Newbold?" Yasmeen leaned forwards, crossing her arms over the top of her pad, staring at Tom intently. "Why don't you take a moment?" She handed him a bottle of water from her bag. He took it gratefully and gulped half of it down quickly, his brain imagining it to be full of vodka instead of mountain spring rubbish. Yasmeen continued to study him as he wiped the back of his hand across his mouth. "Better?" she asked.

"I don't feel great," Tom admitted, his vision blurring a little around the edges. He blinked it away and squinted at her. "My head…it's killing me."

"Ok, well, I'll try and keep it brief. We can come back to the events of the night in question shortly. Is there anything else that you can tell me that might affect things going forward?"

Tom had known this was coming, known he would have to talk about his past. He sniffed loudly and stared up at the barred window, taking strength from that fact that just on the other side of the glass was the rest of the world, which was carrying on its business as normal.

"I suppose I'd better tell you what happened at the hospital."

40

BETHANY

"You've reached Leigh Bateman. I'm afraid I can't take your call at the moment, but if you'd like to leave your number, I'll call you back."

Damn it. That was the seventh time I'd tried now, and it was still going to voicemail. I'd already left three messages, so I hung up and dialled the number straight back again.

"You've reached Leigh Bateman-" I stabbed at the red 'End Call' button on my phone and threw it across the room and onto my bed in frustration. It bounced and came to rest face down on my pillow. I was relieved as I couldn't bear to see Tom's face staring out at me. I would have to change the screen saver. Now more than ever.

I needed to speak to Leigh. I needed her to put my thoughts in some kind of order so that I could process the situation properly. It was ironic that I'd finally accepted I was free to talk to her with no comeback, and now that I wanted to, I couldn't get hold of her. I needed to feel the calmness and the warmth of her consultation room, to sit on the familiar sofa and be lulled into security, false or otherwise.

I'd managed to dissuade Jordan from doing anything rash, but I didn't know for how long. As scared as he was of being blamed for what had happened, I knew that his morals would soon rise to the surface again, clamouring for attention. Needing to see justice prevail. He couldn't help it. It was the way he was built. The same as I couldn't help the way I was. I pulled my sleeve up distractedly and scratched roughly at my arm, managing to rip the scab from one of my more recent cuts. I kept going, knowing it was the only thing that would rid me of the itch.

Why wasn't Leigh ringing me back? I looked at my watch and hoped that I might get a call just before the hour. It would be a good time for her. One out, one in. She might be able to squeeze me in, in the gap. Oh, how I needed to talk. I muttered to myself as I started pacing up and down the room. Five steps to the window, a turn, then five steps back again. Maybe if I started counting my steps then Leigh would call me back when I reached a hundred? It seemed like a good, round number.

I carried on walking, counting. At fifteen, I paused as I reached the sink and stared at my reflection in the mirror. My lip was swollen, my pupils were dilated, and wisps of hair had come free from the hair band holding it up in a ponytail. I looked a state. I shook my hair out and scraped it back up again, my lips still moving, calming myself with a running commentary of my actions. Then back to the pacing.

I still couldn't properly remember what had happened after leaving Jordan's place last night. All I knew was that whatever I'd experienced had affected me so deeply it had caused me to hurt myself in a way I'd never thought of before and then completely blank it from my mind. That was what freaked me out the most, the fact that I had no memory of it at all. I sobbed. I needed Leigh. I needed her to coax it out of me and diagnose me with trauma. I knew that if I could talk it through with her, it would all become clear. I glared at my phone and carried on pacing.

Twenty-six, twenty-seven.

Maybe my judgement was impaired. For all I knew, I could have Tom completely wrong. After all, I didn't know him that well, did I? He could be a wife-beater who'd gone too far, or maybe she'd pushed him to the limit and he'd lost control. I had a feeling that I'd gone to his house after leaving Jordan, just to check if he was ok. Had I witnessed him with his hands around her throat and blocked it out? I scratched again at my arm, opening the wound further with my nail.

Thirty-three, thirty-four.

No. No. No! That didn't happen. I may have only known Tom for a few weeks but I just knew he couldn't - wouldn't - do that to anyone, not when he was in his right mind. My judgement was good. I'd found a decent man this time. One that wouldn't leave me when the going got tough.

Thirty-nine, forty.

I got to the window and turned abruptly, not wanting to bring the outside, in.

Shit, what if Tom had done it through no fault of his own? I swallowed and picked up my pace.

Forty-five, forty-six.

What if Jordan was right? Could we have screwed up the experiment? Over-ridden some kind of latent desire in him to go home and kill his wife? I stopped again at the window, gazing up at the sky, a partial memory of what had happened scratching at my mind, a visual that my eyes might have captured then tossed out before it could be filed in my head. Stupid. So stupid. I'd remember something like that. I turned.

Fifty-one, fifty-two.

Surely, Jordan and I couldn't have turned Tom into a real-life killer outside of our experimental control. But what I'd said earlier to Jordan was more than half true. If the police did hear about the study, they'd be straight round to see us, laying blame. It would be just like the Bobby Kennedy theory, only we weren't the CIA. We were two university students who would be in deep shit.

Fifty-eight, fifty-nine. Where the hell was Leigh?

It probably wouldn't be Jordan that got into trouble. He was so squeaky clean it was unbelievable. But me? My past would come back and bite me on the backside, big time. Even though I'd only ever been ruled by love, there were plenty of people who would be more than happy to point the finger. Including my own mother, probably. And there were the police records to back them up.

Seventy-three, seventy-four.

I could lie to Jordan, I could even lie to my counsellor, but the one person I couldn't lie to was myself. I was scared. No, not scared. Terrified.

I didn't want to get into trouble again. I'd made a new life for myself here, of sorts. I'd made mistakes in the past but that was all they were - mistakes.

Seventy-nine, eighty.

I reached the window again and paused, resting my hands on the sill and finding a thin layer of dust beneath my fingers. I looked down to the street and saw a familiar face looking up at me. Jordan. Shit, his moral compass had kicked in quicker than I'd thought. Now what? He waved at me, a forlorn little gesture, and I opened the window.

"Can I come up?"

"I'll buzz you in," I told him. I still had twenty more steps to do but I could finish while he climbed the stairs. I carried on, speeding up yet again.

Eighty-six, eighty-seven.

I pulled my sleeves back down, thankful that I was wearing a dark-coloured jumper that would cover any blood stains.

Ninety-four, ninety-five. There was a knock at my door.

"Just a sec!"

Ninety-six, seven, eight, nine, a hundred.

My phone didn't ring.

I opened the door and Jordan burst through it. A man desperate for rescue. "I can't do this, Bethany. I can't just keep quiet. Whether we get in trouble or not, we need to go to the police."

"Jordan, it's not a good idea."

"I know you think that. But we have to do it, it's only right." His tall frame folded in on itself as he sat down on the edge of my bed without invitation. He always managed to annoy me with the stupidest things.

I was at a loss. I'd hoped my words earlier would have been enough to scare him away from thoughts of going to the police, but they obviously weren't. The only thing I could think of now was to try and seduce him, bribe him with the thing that he wanted the most. Me.

I knelt between his thighs, taking his face between my hands. His glasses were still a little opaque after coming in from the cold.

You know, that's one of the things that I love about you," I told him softly, burying my frustration.

My fingers traced around his hairline to his ears and lifted the arms of his glasses, placing them on the desk behind me. His deep brown eyes gazed at me, waiting to be told what. What was it that loved about him?

"You're such a good person," I told him, my fingertips going back to his face. I leaned my body towards him, and just as my lips were about to meet his, I was startled by the sound of a ringtone. My phone. It was ringing. Shit.

Jordan looked around behind him on the bed, spotting the phone on my pillow.

"It's ok, just leave it," I told him.

He lay back on one elbow, reaching over and grabbing it as it continued to garble its ringtone. "Here."

As he held it out to me, everything seemed to drop down a few gears into slow motion. The phone stopped ringing and as it did the screen lit up with a ping to tell me I had a missed call. The screensaver of Tom's face glowed briefly, just long enough for Jordan to notice and for his face to register confusion.

"What the hell?" He looked at me and I couldn't tell if he was confused, exasperated or angry. Probably all three.

I pushed myself away from him, sitting abruptly on my backside on the floor. "I can explain."

"Oh my God, Bethany, you'd better get on with it because I'm about to freak out." Jordan chucked the phone back on the bed as if it had burned his fingers.

I'd started crying. Hot tears on my cheeks. "I don't know where to start."

"From the beginning might be a good idea." He seemed unmoved by my display of emotion this time.

Even though I could no longer see it in his eyes, I hoped to God, Jordan still had some compassion for me. "Ok. Then I suppose I need to tell you about Daniel."

41

TOM

While Tom had struggled to remember the events of the past couple of days, he had no trouble whatsoever recalling what had happened to him before everything had started going wrong.

It was probably as clear as it was because he and Gemma had just been on the honeymoon of a lifetime to Thailand. The whole time they were there, Tom had to keep pinching himself to check that he wasn't dreaming. He hadn't been. He actually had been in paradise with the love of his life. They were young, they were happy, and he had even been looking forward to getting back to reality when they returned to England so they could start married life together. They were sickeningly in love and had flaunted it with abandon.

Their last day at the hotel had been spent on the beach, sipping Pina Coladas and soaking up the sun before heading back to cloudy England. If he concentrated really hard now, he could even feel the warmth of the sand creeping through his toes as he remembered standing on the shoreline taking photos of his beautiful new wife in the crystal-clear waters.

Everything had a warm glow to it. Gemma's sun-kissed shoulders and his rum-fuelled dreams. Life had been as near perfect as it was ever going to be. They had both been sad to leave that paradise behind them, but their future had lain ahead of them, and that had been something to look forward to.

The twelve-hour flight home was passed making plans for the future, working out where they would buy their first house, and arguing good-naturedly about what they were going to call their children.

When the air hostess had found out they were newlyweds, she'd congratulated them on their news and been kind enough to bring over a free bottle of Prosecco for them to continue their celebration with. They'd thanked her, eyes sparkling like the liquid in the little plastic champagne glasses as they'd toasted each other.

Finally back home in the late morning, Tom had insisted on carrying Gemma over the threshold of the apartment. She'd protested and wiggled about but squealed with delight as he'd hoisted her into his arms and edged sideways through the doorway with her, taking care not to knock her head.

She'd flung her arms around his neck and he'd kissed her deeply, her petite frame light in his arms, before lowering her feet gently back to the floor.

"Here we are then, Mrs Newbold," he'd said, pulling both their suitcases into the hallway after Gemma had scooped up the mountain of mail that had collected on the doormat. "Home sweet home."

The flat had had that un-lived-in smell that was always present in homes that had been left empty for a couple of weeks and could only be rejuvenated by unpacking, putting on the heating and making a cup of tea.

"Thank goodness." Gemma had collapsed into the first chair that she'd come across. "I'm exhausted. We've literally been awake now for…God, I can't even work it out. A long time. Fancy coming to bed, husband?"

Tom had indeed fancied going to bed with his new wife, but not necessarily to sleep. He'd let her get some rest, though.

"I'm going to stay up for a bit," he'd told her. "Try and fight the jet lag."

Gemma had kissed him lightly on the forehead before heading into the other room, and just as Tom had turned on his phone to check his messages, he'd heard the shower going on in the bathroom.

While he'd waited for his mobile to re-align itself with England, he'd made himself a coffee, then settled down in front of the lounge window to watch the clouds scudding across the sky as he'd listened to his messages.

There hadn't been many as most people had known not to disturb him on honeymoon, but there were a couple from the private hospital where he now worked asking him to call as soon as he could. He'd given them a quick ring.

"Hey, Tom. You *are* back. Brilliant. Did you have a good time?" Vicki, the Charge Nurse had asked him.

"It was amazing, Vic."

"That's great. I can't wait to hear all about it."

"I've got plenty of photos to bore you with," he'd told her.

She'd laughed. "I'm sure. Look, Tom, I'm really sorry to do this to you, but we're mega short-staffed. I don't suppose you can do a shift for me this evening, could you? You know I wouldn't ask, but…"

"Oh, Vicki, it's my first night back. I need sleep and I'm not supposed to be in until tomorrow night." Tom's heart had dropped.

"I know, Tom. I know. I'm sorry. I hate to ask but we really are desperate."

The shower had gone off in the bathroom and Tom had

imagined his new wife slipping into bed, her skin fresh and clean. He'd just wanted to get off the phone and be with her again.

He could get a few hours of sleep in, and then go and do his shift, he'd told himself. "Ok, fine. I'll come in."

Vicki had sighed with relief. "You're an absolute star, Tom. I owe you one."

"Yes, you do."

As Tom had begun his shift that evening, he was feeling tired already, which wasn't a good start.

He'd gone to bed after getting off the phone with Vicki, but thanks to Gemma's naked body lying next to him, he hadn't even tried to get to sleep for another hour. By then, jet lag had well and truly kicked in and he'd lain there, eyes wide open, staring at the ceiling, feeling as though he'd done a line of cocaine.

Finally at the hospital, when he needed to be at his most alert, he had struggled to keep his eyes open, which was sod's law. Only two hours into his shift and his body's circadian rhythm had been battling against him, causing his head to feel heavy and his mind sluggish.

It had been a quiet night on the paediatric ward, which would normally be a blessing, but that night, when he had been fighting the urge to sleep, it would have been useful to have something to focus on. He'd done his rounds, administering medications to those that needed it, but from then on all he had to do were routine checks throughout the night, making sure that all the children were ok. Unless there was an emergency, he'd known it was going to be a long night.

Tom had yawned and looked at his watch, noting that it had only just gone ten o'clock. That would be just after four in the morning in Thailand so it was no wonder he'd been struggling.

His only companion had been a young student nurse who'd accompanied him on the first round of ward checks, where all their eight patients had been sleeping soundly. He'd had nothing much else to give her to keep her occupied, so had suggested that she sort through the clean bedding in the storage room before taking her break. She'd accepted the task without question and headed off, promising to bring him a coffee when she came back.

Fighting the Sandman, Tom had pushed himself up from his seat at the nurses' station and wandered round the ward again. All had been peaceful so he'd headed back to the desk once more. Although he'd done it already, he'd forced himself to open up the day's records to have a quick recap. He'd known he wasn't firing on all cylinders so he'd wanted to remind himself whether any special considerations were needed for his charges. Better safe than sorry.

He'd rested his chin on top of his folded hands on the desk and started to read. Vicki had been on shift before him and as usual, she'd written just short of a novel about each patient. Her tiny handwriting in black biro packed onto the page in front of him, Tom had felt his eyes blur as he read, the words not making it very far into his awareness. He'd blinked his dehydrated eyes and then squeezed them shut for a moment. They'd felt gritty and dry and closing the lids was like a trip to a spa. He'd just wanted to keep them closed for a little longer. Just a little longer.

TOM HAD BEEN CRUDELY DRAGGED back into consciousness by the student nurse shaking him violently and hissing his name. Shit. He'd only closed his eyes to rest them, he hadn't meant to fall asleep. He'd noticed a damp spot on top of Vicki's written notes where he'd drooled in his sleep, and his neck had felt stiff from where he'd lain at an awkward angle.

"Shit. Sorry." He'd struggled to reach full responsiveness as his body fought to drag him back under. "So tired."

The student nurse had looked panicked as she stood back from him. "You have to come now. I think there's a problem."

The words had got Tom to his feet. "What do you mean? What problem? What's happened?"

"Come with me." She'd trotted off at speed, Tom trailing behind her. She'd taken him to the bedside of their youngest resident, who had lain very still within the confines of his cot. "I don't think he's breathing," she'd told him.

"Shit!" Tom had reached down into the cot and pulled the small boy into his arms, checking for signs of breath. He hadn't been able to feel anything against his cheek, and the infant's chest hadn't appeared to be moving. "Shit!" he'd repeated. "All his vitals were fine when we checked him, weren't they? What time is it now?"

The student had looked at her watch. "Eleven twenty."

Jesus. He'd been asleep for over an hour, missing his last round of checks.

"Actually, his breathing was a little fast when we checked him." She'd paused, looking uncertain. "It was probably nothing, though. You said it was fine."

Tom had felt his bowels loosening in fear, but had held himself in check. He could remember that the boy's breath had been a little fast and raspy, but it had seemed minor. He'd meant to check on him again in a few minutes but in his stupor, he'd forgotten.

Without wasting any time, Tom had sat down next to the cot and, holding the child firmly, had covered his nose and mouth with his own, giving five breaths. Nothing. He'd then given thirty chest compressions in the centre of the boy's chest with two fingers. Fast and firm. Nothing. Two more breaths.

"Should I call someone?" the student had asked.

"Do it," Tom had hissed, knowing full well that by the time the on-call doctor got there, it could be too late. He'd given thirty more compressions and still, there had been nothing. He'd blown again, twice, and withdrawn, ready to pump the boy's chest once more. Just as he'd started to apply the pressure, the child had gasped, his breath rattling, coughing, choking.

Tom had positioned the infant face down along his thigh, making sure that his head was lower in position than his bottom and had hit him firmly on his back five times with the heel of his hand. Still, the boy had struggled to take in air while Tom had worked on him, his breath becoming more and more faint. He had been fighting a losing battle. One that Tom would never forgive himself for his defeat.

"So, you see," Tom told his solicitor, "it was gross negligence, both on my part and the hospital. They had no choice but to get rid of me."

Yasmeen nodded, her biro scratching away at her legal pad as she wrote copious notes.

"I never served jail time, but they may as well have thrown me in prison because once word got out, I was branded a baby killer anyway. It's why we had to move. Life was unbearable for me, and I brought Gemma down with me. I practically killed her back then. Certainly, her spirit. I killed her spirit, and now I've killed her soul."

"I would strongly advise that you don't repeat that to the police in the interview." Yasmeen rested her arm on her pad and studied Tom. "And you still can't remember what happened the night the incident took place?"

"No, not properly. I just know in my heart what I did. I know how mad I was at her. I think she was having an affair, not that I can really blame her. I think maybe I came home and caught them, and then I think I might have lost my mind."

"Well, we aren't discounting that, yet."

Tom wasn't sure if Yasmeen was joking or not.

42

BETHANY

T he first time I kissed Daniel was at the Christmas do at my old university. When I thought about that moment, it still sent a shiver of longing through me.

I'd fancied him since I'd started that September, staring at him unabashed while he'd carried out his lectures. He must have known that I liked him, as I wasn't too subtle, but he did the right thing for the longest time, not wanting to break that teacher/student boundary. It was so frustrating as I knew he liked me too. I could read it in his eyes.

I wasn't even going to go to the Christmas party. I wasn't really one for big social gatherings and I didn't have a group of giggling girlfriends to go with, but when I'd heard that Daniel was going to be there, I'd thrown caution to the wind. I'd taken myself off to Top Shop to buy the perfect sparkly dress that would hopefully catch his eye.

Of course, he'd technically only been there as a chaperone rather than a guest. Someone of good character to keep an eye on all the alcohol-fuelled uni students who had been focused on having a good time at any cost. I'd known that most of them would either end up having regretful sex in the car park or throwing up in the toilets later.

Unlike them, I'd kept to the shadows along the walls of the room, and the only time I ever ventured onto the dance floor was to get to the bar.

"Who's your date tonight?" Daniel had asked me. It was about two hours into the evening and I'd all but given up on getting close to him. I'd finally found him at the corner of the bar nursing a gin and tonic.

"No date," I'd told him. "These idiots are all too immature."

"Ah, well that's us men for you," he'd said with a smile. "We all have a mental age of about twelve, at least until we're in our thirties." He'd taken a sip from his drink.

"How old are you then?" I'd asked him.

He'd looked hesitant to answer. "Thirty-eight. Way too old to be standing in a club talking to a very attractive young woman like you."

He'd been blatantly flirting with me. Restrained, yes, but flirting nonetheless. "I don't think you're too old," I'd told him with a smile. "I think that's the perfect age."

"Hmm, well I'm not too sure my wife would agree with you. She thinks I'm a boring old fart."

I couldn't understand what was wrong with her. He was so gorgeous, I'd have been worried about other women throwing themselves at him. Women like me. "Well, if you were my husband, I wouldn't let you out of my sight," I'd told him, leaning forward, ostensibly to adjust the strap on my shoe, but making sure I'd given him a glimpse of my cleavage. I'd noticed his eyes following the movement, drawn in despite himself.

We'd stood talking at the bar for most of the evening, uninterrupted by anyone else. No one had wanted to spend time with the quiet girl or the lecturer, so we were left to our own devices until one of the drunk 'it' girls had staggered over clutching a sprig of mistletoe. She'd waved it around as she'd worked her way along the bar, leaving a trail of kisses in her wake. She'd dangled the foliage over the top of our heads and all but screamed at us above the pulsing music to have a Christmas kiss.

"Ah, would you look at that," he'd said, leaning over and kissing me chastely on my cheek. "It's obviously written in the stars."

"So, that was our first kiss," I told Jordan, who sat listening to my story, so far unimpressed.

"I don't know what the hell that's got to do with anything," he replied.

I was still sitting on the floor, leaning against the desk behind me. "It was also our last kiss."

He looked nonplussed. "But he was your boyfriend. I thought you went to visit him every single weekend until you split up."

I rubbed at my arm underneath the sleeve of my jumper and took a deep breath. "It wasn't that simple," I whispered.

"What? So, you lied to me to get me off your back? Is that it?" He looked so hurt, especially without the screen of his glasses to shield his eyes. "Wow, that's sad, Bethany. You didn't have to lie about going to see him every weekend, you know? You could have just been honest."

"I didn't lie. Not exactly." I didn't know how to say the words, put them in the right order. I'd never expected to talk to Jordan about this. It should've been Leigh I was speaking to, if anyone.

Jordan spread his hands in exasperation. I had to do this. I had to get the words out as there were no more options. My head was buzzing and my stomach was knotted so tightly that I wasn't sure I would ever be able to undo it again. I took a deep breath in and exhaled. It was time.

"I did go to see him." I paused, steadying myself. "He just didn't always see me."

"I don't understand."

"Jordan, the whole reason that I came to this university is because Daniel took out a restraining order on me. He said that he didn't feel the same way about me. I'm not legally allowed within a hundred yards of him or his family."

Jordan's face looked as though I'd asked him to work out a really hard math's equation, and, one by one, a parade of emotions marched across his face. Shock, disbelief, horror, and fear. He stood up, and then sat back down again, his body and his mind not quite in sync with one another as he tried to process the information. "You stalked him?" He stared at me, and I had to drop my eyes from his gaze.

"That's what they called it." I was mortified, yet still indignant. This was the first time I'd even come close to acknowledging what I'd supposedly done.

"Jesus Christ. I…I don't know what to say."

"That word makes it sound worse than it is, though. I never did anything bad, Jordan, you have to believe me."

He looked at me, one eyebrow raised. "What exactly did you do?"

"It was just—"

"You know what? I don't actually want to know. If he got a restraining order against you, it's not going to be anything good is it?"

I hung my head, my thoughts full of the explicit photos I'd sent him, the texts. I was embarrassed by them now. If only he'd responded to some of them the way he should have done, instead of telling me to stop, then things would never have got so bad. No one likes being shrugged off as if they mean nothing, do they?

Yes, I'd hung around waiting for him after work. I just wanted to explain myself, for him to hear me out and see that maybe we could be together even if we had started on the wrong foot. If he'd given me a chance then I would never have had to follow him home, would I? I wasn't doing anything wrong, and no one would have been any the wiser if his stupid wife hadn't seen me. She made such a fuss, pulling their kids into the house and screaming at me to piss off. It hurt my feelings and she made me feel like a bad person. I'm not bad. I just make mistakes. I rubbed at my arm, the open cut beneath my sleeve throbbing, reminding me that I had unfinished business there.

"He called me a psycho, a nutter, but he just wouldn't listen to me. Wouldn't let me explain how I felt."

"Oh, Bethany."

"That's when I sent the flowers. I just figured if he thought I was crazy already, then why not really give him something to think about."

"The flowers?"

"I had them delivered while he was out. No card or anything."

"I don't understand."

"It was a wreath."

Jordan dropped his head, whistling through his teeth as it fell. "Jesus."

I hadn't been thinking, not properly. I was consumed with love and passion and hurt, and I hadn't been able to bear it. Just like now, I'd had to get rid of the pain, pass it on to someone else. Without thinking, I pulled up my sleeve and started scratching at my arm, blood smearing my arm.

"Shit, Bethany, stop it, you're hurting yourself."

Jordan had never seen me like this before. Out of control, my emotions and my arms bared for him to see. I didn't care anymore. I could see he was uncomfortable, torn between wanting to comfort me and wanting to section me. I wanted him to hold me in his arms again, like he'd done the other night. Make everything ok.

"I never did anything bad, Jordan. You have to believe me. I loved him, and I thought he felt the same way. I really did. I think it just freaked him out that I loved him so much. He wasn't ready for that kind of commitment."

"Bethany, he was married."

"That's not the point...he—"

"It *is* the point." Jordan's voice was raised now. "Shit, you're doing the same to Tom, aren't you? That photo on your screensaver, it's from one of the experiments, isn't it? He doesn't even know you took it."

"It's different this time."

"You need help, Bethany."

"No, Jordan. You don't understand." I untangled my legs and went over to sit beside him on the bed. He immediately got up, retrieved his glasses from my desk and started pacing the room, like I had done only minutes earlier.

"Why did you tell me all this now?" Jordan asked, pausing in front of me.

"I had to, don't you see? You wanted us to go to the police and tell them what happened with Tom, and I needed to explain why we can't do that."

"Because you've got previous?"

"They're going to think it was me," I admitted.

Jordan was at the window and he turned, leaning against the sill, the features of his face now hidden from me. "But you tried to blame me, Bethany. You told me that the police would think it was all my idea. Why would you do that?"

"I was scared. I knew I had to make you feel the same way to stop you going to them."

For a moment, we were both silent. Both caught up in our thoughts. Then Jordan rocked his head back, staring up at the ceiling, and let out a massive breath. "So, did you have anything to do with it?"

I was shocked. Shocked that my friend would ask me such a

thing. It was no surprise that my character would be in question, but it wasn't like him to think badly of anyone. "Of course not! I was with you that night."

"Not all of it. You left."

How could he be accusing me of this?

"Who's to say you didn't sleep with me to create an alibi and then head on over to Tom's house?"

"For God's sake, Jordan, how can you think that?"

"Did you go there?"

I didn't like the way this was going. "Please don't do this to me, Jordan." My fingers automatically made their way back to the ridges of my arm once again.

"Just answer me, Bethany. Did you go to Tom's when you left me?"

I gripped my wrist, desperate not to make things any worse, then looked towards Jordan's eyes, the glass in his frames glinting a little in the failing light of the day. "I think so."

My friend turned, his gaze edging towards the street, and I could see from his expression that I'd lost him.

I hadn't been able to stay in the room after that, and I grabbed my coat and bag and made a bolt for the door. For once, I was safe in the knowledge that Jordan wasn't going to follow me to see if I was ok. He knew now that I was the one he should be protecting others from. This was why I never told anyone the truth, because they couldn't handle it. Couldn't handle me.

I walked and walked with no clear route in mind, my trainers slapping the wet pavement. It was as much a surprise to me when I found myself on Tom's street, staring at his house where crime scene tape fluttered in the wind, trying to tear itself loose from the broken fence posts in the garden.

My memory fluttered alongside it and there it was again, almost like a glitch in the matrix. Tom, falling to his knees, dropping a bottle, it smashing. Him scrabbling around on the floor, drunk out of his mind. It was there for just a second and, as my mind reached to grab the image and pull it into focus, it was gone, like mist.

I turned on my heel and walked to the nearest bus stop, sitting alone on the metal bench. The sky had closed in while I'd been out and a fine rain misted the cool air. I shivered, and no matter how tightly I pulled my coat around me, I just couldn't warm up. It reminded me of that night.

Jesus, why could I only remember useless things? The weather and how cold I'd felt, throwing my uncomfortable boots into a bin. Shit, shit, shit. I pummelled my fists against the bench, the metal hurting my knuckles, but not enough. It was never enough.

As an old lady approached the bus stop, I made myself stop hitting the bench. Embarrassed at the sight of my reddened knuckles, I pulled my leather gloves from my pockets and put them on, covering my hands to avoid any awkward glances.

Why couldn't I remember? What the hell was wrong with me?

Had I gone to Tom's place and witnessed Gemma's murder through the window? Had it traumatised me so much that I'd then gone home and harmed myself? My gloved hand touched my lip as I remembered the blood on my face that morning. Had I blocked it from my mind to protect myself? Perhaps I was the one person that could help Tom plead his innocence.

Had I seen Gemma turning in surprise upon someone entering the kitchen through the side door, gasping in fear, her hands scrabbling behind her on the worktop desperately searching for a knife, scissors, anything to protect herself with? Coming up short.

Had I watched Gemma running up the stairs in an effort to get away, screaming, "Who the fuck are you?" before being hit hard around the head with a solid object. The crack, as it made contact, like a cricket bat against a ball, although maybe slightly duller.

Had I heard the screeching of a big ginger cat as it was thrown from its pillow across the bedroom, where it sat hissing?

And had I seen that same pillow lifted high above Gemma,

who'd lain prone on the wooden flooring before it was smashed down on her face? Held firm for several long minutes by hands hidden inside a pair of grey leather gloves.

Beautiful grey leather gloves. The same ones my mother had bought me for Christmas.

43

TOM

Whilst the law stated that remand prisoners were supposed to be treated as innocent until proven guilty, Tom had the feeling that it didn't quite pan out like that. He was just thankful that he had a cell to himself and he could keep his head down, for now.

On his solicitor's insistence, he'd been looked over by a medic who'd told him his short-term memory loss was possibly due to his heavy drinking. Tom had felt like saying, 'Yeah? No shit, Sherlock.' They'd followed up by saying they didn't know how much of his memory, if any, would return. To be honest, Tom would be happy if it never came back.

While he still had no memory of the night of Gemma's death, he knew in his heart that he'd caused it nonetheless and was prepared to say as much at his police interview. Yasmeen had prepped him, advising him that his best option was to say 'no comment' to any of the questions the police threw at him. Christ, he'd seen enough TV shows to already know that. He and Gemma used to sit on the sofa with a glass of wine in their hands watching blatantly guilty little gits saying 'no comment' over and over again. They'd always got away with it, too.

The interview had started off ok as the two plain-clothed detectives positioned themselves on the opposite side of the table to himself and his solicitor. They introduced themselves and went through all the formalities, but Tom could barely even remember his own name, let alone theirs.

"Do you often drink a lot?" they asked.

"No comment."

"Would you say you drank to excess?"

"No comment."

"Do you suffer from blackouts? Would you say you get angry when you drink? Was Gemma scared of you?"

"No comment, no comment, no comment."

"We've had witnesses come forward who say they saw you acting violently on a recent night out with your wife. Does that ring any bells?"

The waiters. The bloody waiters at the Italian restaurant. "No comment."

"Apparently, your wife appeared...scared of you."

Tom shook his head. It was true. He just didn't want to admit it.

"Is that a 'no', Mr Newbold?"

Yasmeen looked sharply at Tom.

"No comment."

"You were heard arguing about a third party. Someone called Ash."

Tom's eyebrows knitted themselves together in a frown.

"It was suggested that your wife might have been having an affair. Is that right?"

Tom's fists were clenched underneath the table. Christ Almighty. "No comment."

"You thought that your wife was sleeping with another man

behind your back and you couldn't take it could you, Mr Newbold? You got drunk and you got angry, didn't you?"

Tom squeezed his eyes closed, trying to blot out their words.

"In fact, you've already confessed to killing your wife, haven't you? When you rang 999 your words were…" the officer looked at his notepad, shuffling a few pages before facing Tom again. "I think I've killed my wife."

"Yes," he whispered.

"I'd like a moment with my client please," Yasmeen interjected before he could hold his arms out to be cuffed.

It was too late, though, and Tom was charged with murder. He didn't care. He wanted it, needed it. It was the right thing to do. He knew in the depths of his heart that he was to blame, and he loathed himself for it.

All those nights when he'd drunk himself into oblivion and been cruel to the person that he loved the most in the world. How had he let it get to this point? Why hadn't he listened when Gemma had begged him to get help?

He was a drunk. Worse than that, he was an angry, violent drunk who blacked out and did terrible things. Truth be told, he knew he'd lost the plot. It was time to stick his hands in the air and surrender. Prison was where he belonged now.

Back in his cell, Tom sighed out loud, uncurling himself on his metal bunk. He pulled his pathetic excuse for a pillow over his head, trying to blot out his tears so the other inmates wouldn't hear them. His beautiful wife was dead, and he didn't want to live anymore either.

44

BETHANY

I'd taken the gloves off as soon as I realised what I'd done, shoving them into my bag. I couldn't bear to have them on my hands, not now that I knew where they'd been.

I'd lost count of how many times I'd tried ringing Jordan while I still sat at the bus stop, watching buses come and go. Each time I called, the phone had just gone to voicemail, and each time, I'd just hung up and redialled, feeling more and more desperate to speak to him. It was ironic how the tables had turned in our relationship. Thankfully, my persistence paid off eventually.

"What the hell do you want, Bethany? I think we've said all we had to say, don't you?"

Jordan's words threw me. I was unused to this new, uncaring side to him. I supposed it was my fault. "Please, Jordan, don't hang up," I begged him, not liking the scared, whiney tone to my voice. "I need you."

"You don't need me. You need a therapist. I'm saying this as a friend, because—"

"I already have a therapist! I just never told you because I didn't want you to think I was mad."

"Well, you've done a pretty bad job, there."

"I didn't even call you about that. Please, Jordan. It's…"

"What? For God's sake, spit it out."

I swallowed down what could only be fear along with my words.

"Look, Bethany, if you aren't going to say anything then I'm just going to hang up. I can't be dealing with this."

"Wait! Please."

It was now or never. I briefly thought of throwing my phone in the bin and running, or maybe slashing up my wrists until there was no more blood left inside me. But I didn't have the energy to do either. I could lie. God knows I was well-practised. But, recently, the lies hadn't gotten me anywhere.

I cupped my mouth with one hand and spoke quietly into the phone, truthfully, and without pause. My voice shook alongside the rest of my body.

The line went quiet. Shit. What had I done? What the hell had I done?

"Where are you?" Jordan asked. "I'm coming to get you."

———

IF EVER I'D envisioned a white knight in shining armour, it certainly wouldn't have been in the shape of Jordan Haines.

He'd only taken about twenty minutes to reach me, but during that time, quite a few buses had pulled in and out of the bus stop. Each of them disgorging school children of various ages who stared at me warily as I paced up and down, counting out loud as I went. The numbers took my mind off the new reality that I found myself in.

Jordan rounded the corner at a jog and joined me under the awning of the shelter. I wished he'd hold open his arms for me to fall into, but guessed that would be too much to ask of him now. He made no offer of comfort, instead just removing his glasses and wiping the moisture from them on a tissue from his pocket before putting them back on and blinking at me.

"Why did you do it?" Jordan asked, sitting at a discreet distance at the other end of the bench, no doubt scared to get too close in case I stabbed him with something.

I'd expected him to tell me to go to the police. Of course, that's exactly what I should do, but something didn't feel right. I could freely admit that I was jealous of Tom's wife, hated her, even, but enough to kill her? That's what I couldn't get my head around. "I honestly don't know."

"Did you plan it?"

"No!"

"So, you just left me in the middle of the night and went over there and…" He couldn't finish.

"I can't even remember deciding to do it, Jordan. I swear to God, it's like one minute I was just going home, and the next I was at their house doing…that." I felt sick at the thought of it. The memory of it. I wished I hadn't remembered.

"Jesus Christ."

"I know you think I'm crazy, Jordan, and God knows you're probably right, but it feels almost like I was put there, you know?"

"I don't understand." He looked at me with eyes that wanted to believe what I told him, or so I hoped.

"I mean, it's all disjointed. I can't remember how I got there, but can remember grabbing a broken fence post and going into the house. I can see her face, I can remember…" I paused, feeling like I was going to hyperventilate.

"Go on." Jordan reached his hand out to me before pulling it back again abruptly as though scared of being stung.

I took my time, breathing deeply as another bus pulled in, three more children stepping from its warm confines into the grey afternoon. Once they'd meandered down the road, blatantly not rushing home to do homework, I continued.

"I think I hit her with the fence post."

"Jesus."

"That's not all." I took another deep breath, the exhaled air pluming in front of my lips. "I remember holding a cushion over her face so she couldn't breathe."

The tears came. They poured from my eyes and my chest heaved, trying to keep up with the great gulps of air that my lungs suddenly needed.

"It just feels so unreal, Jordan. I mean, I know it was me, but it's like it was a dream, you know? Kind of blurry around the edges. Did I imagine it? Do you think I could have wanted her out of the picture so much that I imagined the whole thing?" My hands were clasped as I held them out to my friend.

"We *had* been drinking," he offered. "Maybe it had some kind of adverse effect on you?"

"I wasn't that out of it! I mean, I know I'm not exactly innocent before you say so. I know I've done some really shitty things in the past, but nothing like this, you have to believe me."

"I just don't know what to say, Bethany." Jordan looked lost. "Have you spoken to your therapist about this? I mean, maybe they can help?"

"No, I can't." I was sobbing out of control. "I've been trying to reach her but she's not answering her phone. Maybe I've screwed up…said something that I shouldn't have done at my last session. Shit, I can't remember." Tendrils of cold fear slid around my heart, squeezing it. "She'd told me I could tell her anything, but maybe I told her too much and she's at the police station right now making a statement about me. Can she do that? Go to the police about a patient? Oh God, why can't I remember anything clearly?"

"Ok, Bethany, just…breathe." Jordan slid closer along the bench and I felt his warmth encompass my body as his inherent good nature finally gave in to holding me. "I'm sure that's not the case. You've only just remembered, right?"

I bobbed my head up and down, sobbing uncontrollably and tasting snot as it dripped onto my lips along with salty tears. Jordon rubbed my shoulder with his hand, letting me weep. Another bus pulled in and I didn't even care who saw me in this state.

"Well, then…maybe she's been ill, or, I don't know…dealing with some other patient." He paused, pulling back a little. "Look, why don't we go over there? Go and see her. Maybe she can help clear things up for you."

I sniffed and wiped my nose with my hands. Jordan reached into his pocket, pulling out the tissue he'd used on his glasses earlier. "That'd be good." I tried to smile and failed. "Are you sure you don't mind coming with me?"

"It's fine. Come on." He stood, pulling me up after him.

I SUPPOSE it was ironic that after sitting at a bus stop for so long, that we decided to walk to Leigh's building, but I couldn't bear the thought of other people seeing my face. The shadows of the grey afternoon were much more appealing a prospect to slip in and out of.

We arrived to see office workers spinning their way out of the revolving doors of the building, high on the fact that another working day had been completed. I envied them, just like I did nearly everyone that I met. Other people's lives always seemed to pan out better than mine. I sighed in the realisation that my self-pitying thoughts had started to even bore me.

Jordan and I entered the building and I led the way down the bland corridor that I'd become familiar with over the last few months. I couldn't wait to see Leigh, to step into the comforting warmth of her office and sit in my usual armchair.

I paused outside her door and looked at Jordan. "Should I just knock, do you think?"

He nodded.

"But what if she's with someone?"

"Well, then we wait."

I rapped my knuckles against the light wooden door and waited "Maybe we should go," I whispered. "I'd hate it if someone had barged in on me while I was in there."

"Just knock again," Jordan whispered back. "Worst case scenario, she'll say she can't see you."

I did as I was told and the door creaked open a couple of centimetres. I couldn't hear any voices coming from inside.

"Maybe she's just popped to the loo and forgotten to lock the door," Jordan suggested.

"Leigh?" I called. "Are you in there?"

Silence. I pushed open the door a little further.

"Leigh?"

Something didn't feel right. The lights weren't on and the room beyond was pretty gloomy in the late afternoon light. I strained to see through the gap in the door but the brightness from the hallway behind us stole whatever lay in the room from my eyes.

"I don't like this." I stepped back to the well-lit safety of the brown carpet runner in the hallway. "Maybe we should just go."

I looked at Jordan, wanting him to confirm what to do next and he reached past me, feeling around on the wall. Obviously finding a light switch, a warm glow lit up the room, I could see why things hadn't felt right. The whole room had been emptied. The walls had been stripped of Leigh's many certificates, there were no books on the shelves, no paperwork on the desk, and the horrible brain scan image had left nothing but a loose looking nail in the wall where it used to hang.

"What the f—?"

Jordan had followed me into the outskirts of the room and he now stood looking at me like the crazy person I clearly was. "Are you sure this is the right room?" he asked, his brow creasing as if he was doubting whether I'd made my therapist up, and, for a moment, I questioned myself.

"Yes!" My eyes darted around the cold, empty room. Familiar, yet not at all.

My friend walked over to the window, rested his palms on the sill and looked out, away from me.

As my tenuous grip on reality started to waver around the edges, a glint of metal caught my eye on the thin beige carpet where the armchairs used to be. I darted over and dropped to my knees, holding up the small silver Radley charm in my fingers like a prize.

And suddenly I knew. And while I didn't understand why, I knew deep inside that I'd been manipulated by someone much cleverer than me. Perhaps this was my comeuppance for my past. This was karma.

45

TOM
SIX MONTHS LATER

The visitors' hall in the prison was spartan and much bigger than Tom had anticipated. He was escorted to a table with seating for four, and was surprised to see that none of the furniture in the room appeared to be nailed to the floor, especially bearing in mind some of the explosive personalities he'd come across in there so far.

As he lowered himself into his chair, the woman seated across from him tucked a strand of hair behind her ear and gave him a thin smile.

"It's nice to meet you, Leigh." Tom held out his hand, which she ignored, so he sat on his hands, not knowing what else to do with them.

Only when the prison guard left them to stand at a discrete distance by the exit, did the woman speak. "You don't recognise me do you, Mr Newbold?"

There was something about her eyes that looked familiar but he couldn't quite place it. He shook his head. "No, sorry. Should I? I thought you were interested in helping me regain my memory. You're a hypnotherapist, right?"

"That's partially right, yes. I used to be a hypnotherapy counsellor before I had to take a long leave of absence."

"I don't understand. Your letter said you could help me. It's why I agreed to the visit."

"That's right. Just because I don't practice professionally anymore, doesn't mean I've forgotten any of my skills. Much the same as you probably haven't, isn't that right, Baby Killer?"

Tom felt his stomach drop to the floor. This wasn't the first time he'd had obsessives from his past trying to take the law upon themselves, and with the recent media coverage of his case, it had only been a matter of time before they'd started crawling out of the woodwork again. "Maybe you should leave." Tom pulled his hands out from underneath him, making a move to stand up and hoping the prison guard would see that something wasn't right.

"Sit down!" his visitor hissed, and something made Tom pause. "Do you want to know what happened to your wife or not?"

He lowered himself back in his chair. The eyes and the voice now, too, reminded Tom of someone. No one close to him, but someone he'd come across or seen on television, or in the papers maybe. His befuddled mind desperately opened and closed its filing cabinets, searching for the right memory, but it continued to elude him.

"That's better."

His guest started quietly humming a melody, one that Tom had become all too familiar with recently: 'The Sound of Silence'. As she hummed, she removed her grey and white spotted scarf from her neck, spreading it out and folding it into a square on the table between them. He couldn't help but notice how it matched her watch strap perfectly. Little hints of well-groomed coordination married together. The song and the monochrome pattern soothed him, lulled him into inertia.

"That's good, isn't it?" She stopped humming, and Tom found himself nodding compliantly. "Now you're calm and you can listen

to what I have to say without moving or speaking. I might even le
you remember some of it afterwards." The tight smile was on he
lips again, not quite reaching her eyes. "I've watched you for a long
time, Tom. It's been hilarious seeing you try to run away from you
past and start afresh. That was never going to happen, though
because I moved alongside you. It just goes to show that you shoul
always keep looking behind you if you're running away from
something."

Tom's mind swirled with questions, but none of them seeme
able to form on his lips. Each time he came close, the speech bubbl
popped and disintegrated.

"I kept close tabs on your wife on Facebook. Did you know she
was such a social media whore, Tom? I mean, my God, the numbe
of photos she shared of that bloody cat, stupid ginger thing, takin
pictures of it all over the house. On its bed, on the sofa, on you
bed. Disgusting…who lets a cat sleep on their pillow?"

Tom had never minded Gemma sharing what small pleasure
she had on social media, and he'd never thought it could be use
against her. How could they have both been so stupid?

"Do you know how easy it is to target someone on socia
media?" Leigh continued. "I mean, of course, it took me a while t
worm my way into her sad little online life but all I had to do wa
join the same groups that she belonged to, cat groups and sa
childless groups mainly…at least we had one thing in common,
suppose." She laughed without humour. "Sometimes, I even fel
sorry for her, you know? She never realised that she was messagin
someone who technically didn't exist. Of course, I set up my fak
profile carefully, a photo of a cat as my profile picture and limite
information about myself. She didn't have a clue who I really wa
just accepted Ash Hanks as who he portrayed himself to be."

Tom felt like he'd been trying to force a shape into the wron
hole for weeks on end and now someone had given him the corre
piece and it had slid in seamlessly. Ash. Fucking Ash, who'd create

so much jealousy in his mind, had never existed in the way he imagined. He should never have been jealous, he should have been vigilant.

"Ah, I can see those cogs turning." Leigh gloated. "Why didn't she realise I was female? All I needed was a little voice converter app on my phone. Clever, eh?" She laughed, smug in her intelligence. "Anyway, I certainly had to put the hours in to earn her trust, but once I had it, it was like taking candy from a baby. Stupid cow. She told me all about how her marriage was suffering due to her husband's 'issues'. It was exhausting listening to all her moaning. One less thing I have to do now."

She winked at him and Tom shuddered at the gesture.

"When I sent her the link for the experiment, I knew she was so desperate for help that she'd talk you into it."

Tom's heart dropped. Of course, the link had come from Ash. He wanted to reach across the table and slap this heartless creature in front of him, woman or not.

"You must be thinking what a big coincidence it was that a pair of uni students just happened to be doing a project on hypnotherapy at the right time though, eh?"

Her eyes flashed and Tom was struck again with that sense of distanced familiarity. He stayed silent and listened.

"These things take time, Tom, and very precise planning. It was about the same time that I started grooming Gemma that I set up my own completely illegal counselling practice. I was very picky with my clients, I can tell you. I say clients, but what I really mean is client. Singular. I had plenty of enquiries, plenty of poor, tortured souls to whom I had to offer introductory sessions before I found the right one. What I needed was someone with an unhealthy pattern of thinking, functioning and behaving. Someone that I could manipulate easily. Someone like Bethany."

Tom had been waiting for her to say the name, but he just hadn't realised how awful it was going to make him feel when he heard it. He'd always had a feeling that something wasn't quite right about her, but he'd been so soaked in his own issues that he'd shrugged off hers.

"When her mother got in touch and talked me through her history, I leapt at the chance. She paid me well, but I'd have done it for free. I mean, Bethany turned out to be perfect, and incredibly suggestible under hypnosis. After only a few sessions with me persuading her, she decided that she wanted to do a project on the Kennedy Assassination.

"I couldn't believe it had been that easy. She was so excited about that ridiculous project, not even knowing that *she* was the real experiment. Every time she came to see me, I'd put her under hypnosis using this." She fingered her necklace. "It worked like a charm and the stupid girl would open up like a book and give me all the information that I needed before I implanted what I wanted her to do next."

Tom rolled his eyes over to where the prison guard still stood against the far wall, chatting to a colleague and oblivious to the confession occurring in the middle of the room.

"I guided her into choosing you for the experiment by bombarding her subconsciously with your name. I hung a CT scan on the wall facing her, knowing that she'd want to discuss it and I could crowbar your name into waking conversations as well as those under hypnosis by repeating the word Tomography. Tom-ography. Good, eh? And a photo of Gemma's cat that I stole from Facebook and put on my desk in a frame. Tom Hardy, I told her his name was. I'm still quite proud of that one."

If Tom had been capable, his mouth would have been hanging open by this point, but he sat, unmoving, hands calmly in his lap, listening to the horror story continuing to unfold in front of him.

"You know, I even gave her the triggers to use on you for the experiment. Subconsciously, of course. I knew it was idealistic to hope that you would actually pass their childish project with flying colours and then go home and kill your wife, but I did have some semblance of hope. Crazy, I know!"

Leigh threw her head back, caught up in her own story.

"It didn't matter to me anyway." She straightened herself up again." I knew you wouldn't be able to hack it. You were too drunk to stand half the time, let alone kill someone. It just meant that there'd be slightly less poetic justice to my final retribution. You may have had a strong conscious critical faculty, but Bethany certainly didn't, and for that, I'm thankful. It was obvious from the beginning, which is why I chose her. I knew that with the right direction, the right triggers, if you couldn't hack it, she would go to your house and carry out the murder that you were too weak and too drunk to do."

Tom felt a rushing noise inside his head and sweat pricked coldly again the heat of his forehead. Bethany? Bethany had killed Gemma!

"I don't actually know if Bethany will remember anything. She may well do over time, but it doesn't really matter, does it?" Leigh shrugged. "Oh, look at your face. You're sweating. Please try to keep yourself in check, Tom, and don't feel too bad about her. There's always some collateral damage and some people are just born evil, so in the grand scheme of things she doesn't matter."

Tom swallowed, willing himself not to vomit.

"Did you know she was a stalker?" She waited as if he was capable of answering. "No, of course, you didn't. Well, she stalked some poor professor at her last university to within an inch of his life; sent wreaths to his door with his wife's name on and threatened his family constantly. She may not have carried out her threats, but only because the police stepped in in time."

Leigh's eyes bored into Tom's, her head tilting to one side.

"You really knew nothing of this, did you? Poor Baby Killer. That girl was lining you up as the next focus of her affections, even without any help from me. So, you see, it was only a matter of time before she hurt someone anyway. I just gave her a little nudge."

She sat back, watching Tom, her monologue coming to a standstill. Unable to do otherwise, Tom gazed back.

"Oh, good heavens!" Leigh sat bolt upright. "I haven't told you the best bit, have I? I mean, you must be wondering why I've gone to all this bother?"

Clearing her throat, she pushed her hair behind her ears with manicured fingers, giving Tom's memory another electric shock. He *had* seen her before. It was coming to him. That small gesture of hers had jolted the cogs in his brain, although the hair had been longer, blonde, and her nose, undoubtedly, had been a different shape. You could change your appearance, but not those little personality traits that made you unique.

"I can see your mind's almost there, isn't it?" She leaned in towards him, her locket swinging on its chain before she took it in her hands and reverently opened it up to reveal a photograph of a small child. "You killed my son, you fucking bastard. My beautiful baby boy. You slept while my child suffocated."

Tom's heartbeat almost drowned out her words as it struggled not to go into shock.

"That's right, Baby Killer. Recognise me now? I'm Ashleigh Benjamin, the woman you gave a life sentence to whilst you got away with fucking murder."

Tom swallowed, his breathing fast and shallow. It *was* her. He'd recognised those eyes from the papers, from the news reports. The eyes that held a universe of pain, now overshadowed by consuming obsession and instability.

"You took away the most precious thing in my life, so the only fair retribution was to take away the most precious thing from yours. Now you'll finally understand the pain of loss. You will serve the sentence that you always should have done."

Tom's eyes rolled in his head as Ashleigh closed the locket, pushed her chair back and shook out her scarf, tying it loosely around her neck.

"Well, I'd best be off." She excused herself as though leaving a reunion, which it was, of sorts. "Don't worry, you'll be able to move and speak again as soon as I've left the room."

Tom watched her steadfast steps as she made her way towards the door, the green exit sign shining brightly above it. She nodded to the prison guard, who looked across at Tom before opening the door for the departing visitor, and then she was gone.

Finally released, Tom's body did what he had fully expected, crashing spectacularly to the floor, causing other inmates and visitors to rise from their seats at the commotion. His mind whirled and fought against the urge to completely shut down while the guards tried to manoeuvre him into the recovery position.

Catcalls came from the other inmates, callous in their interpretation of events as Tom pushed himself up on his elbow. He had to get his words out before it was too late.

"I need to speak to someone," he managed. "I need to get out of here."

He grabbed hold of the guard's leg, who immediately pushed him off, causing Tom to fall back to the floor, his hand landing in something sticky.

"You don't understand." A tear fell, splashing onto the concrete beneath him, staining it darker. He looked back up at the guard. "I didn't do it. I'm innocent."

The guard's expressionless face broke rank and a grin spread wide across it. "That right?" he asked. "Well then, you're gonna feel right at home in here."

A NOTE TO THE READER

I really hope you enjoyed 'Hypnotic'. It was a long time in the making and started off as a small glimmer of an idea while watching one of Derren Brown's psychological experiments, before morphing into what it is now. It involved a lot of planning, and even then the characters would throw me a curveball occasionally by doing something that we hadn't agreed on. Not surprising, bearing in mind Bethany and Tom's unhelpful attitudes, I suppose.

Anyway, I got there in the end, and you obviously got to the end too as you're now reading this! I'd love it if you could take the time to leave me a review on Amazon or any other suitable forum. These are a huge help to authors.

You can find me on Facebook, Twitter and Instagram, as well as my website: sherryhostler.com. Sign up to my Readers' Club for news of my latest books and other treats here: sherryhostler.com/contact.

ACKNOWLEDGMENTS

Writing a book is one of the hardest things you can do, and if it wasn't for the following, it would have taken me a hell of a lot longer. So, here are a few acknowledgements:

First and foremost, I would really like to thank wine. Without it, I could never have written this book, and if you don't like the story, it wasn't my fault…it was the wine talking.

Secondly, I want to thank my hubby Jon for his unending support. He has put up with all the tears, the self-doubt, and drunken rants…and that was before I even started writing the book! In all seriousness, he is my rock and the person I always turn to for guidance, strength and love.

Thanks to Barkley, my bonkers German Shepherd. He is the biggest, fluffiest, most adorable twit that I know, and his constant nagging for me to take him out on walks has forced me to step away from the keyboard when I wanted to smash it to smithereens with a hammer. Everything is clearer after walking the dog.

Massive thanks to the lovely Jules Wake who has given me all sorts of professional writerly advice. If you haven't read her books they are fabulous, so look her up immediately.

Thanks to my wonderful editor and friend Claire Jenkins who is hilariously funny and loves a red pen, thank God.

I'd also like to say thank you to my proofreaders, Elaine, Andy and Sue. As writers, we are advised not to use friends to help out with this task as they are always too kind. Well, whoever gave that piece of advice hasn't met this lot. They were brutal and EXACTLY what I needed, although I am now wondering if they actually like me.

A big old thank you to all my friends, family and my writing group. I made the choice of telling them all that I was writing a book, and because they all kept asking me how it was going, it meant that I couldn't just give up. I regretted that from time to time, but it's paid off in the end.

Also, thanks to Heather for answering my nursing questions and Shula for all her legal advice. I now know the correct processes if/when I ever get arrested.

Last but not least, a big thank you to Derren Brown, yes, THE Derren Brown, as he inspired me to write this book, and I'm only slightly obsessed with him. The social media following kind of obsession as opposed to the night vision goggle type.

And now an apology. Adele. I'm sorry that Tom has no taste. I actually do like your music.

ABOUT THE AUTHOR

Sherry is the author of the psychological thriller 'Hypnotic'. Before this she spent many years 'living the dream' in various jobs which have given her plenty to write about.

Sherry enjoys a bit of 90s dance music and thinks she does her best writing (and dancing) after a few glasses of Rioja but this is possibly not the case. She loves her home in the rural southeast of England with her husband and dog, but often hankers for the sunny beaches of Australia where she used to live.

Her short fiction and non-fiction articles have been featured in 'Writers' Forum', 'Hertfordshire Life', 'Vale Life', 'Dogs Monthly' and various cake magazines.

Keep up with Sherry's book news on sherryhostler.com or connect on:

 facebook.com/SherryHostlerWriter

 twitter.com/SherryHostler

 instagram.com/adropofsherry

Printed in Great Britain
by Amazon